THOSE ACROSS *the* RIVER

Christopher Buehlman

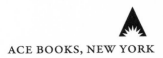

ACE BOOKS, NEW YORK

THE BERKLEY PUBLISHING GROUP
Published by the Penguin Group
Penguin Group (USA) Inc.
375 Hudson Street, New York, New York 10014, USA
Penguin Group (Canada), 90 Eglinton Avenue East, Suite 700, Toronto, Ontario M4P 2Y3, Canada
(a division of Pearson Penguin Canada Inc.)
Penguin Books Ltd., 80 Strand, London WC2R 0RL, England
Penguin Group Ireland, 25 St. Stephen's Green, Dublin 2, Ireland (a division of Penguin Books Ltd.)
Penguin Group (Australia), 250 Camberwell Road, Camberwell, Victoria 3124, Australia
(a division of Pearson Australia Group Pty. Ltd.)
Penguin Books India Pvt. Ltd., 11 Community Centre, Panchsheel Park, New Delhi—110 017, India
Penguin Group (NZ), 67 Apollo Drive, Rosedale, North Shore 0632, New Zealand
(a division of Pearson New Zealand Ltd.)
Penguin Books (South Africa) (Pty.) Ltd., 24 Sturdee Avenue, Rosebank, Johannesburg 2196,
South Africa

Penguin Books Ltd., Registered Offices: 80 Strand, London WC2R 0RL, England

This is an original publication of The Berkley Publishing Group.

This is a work of fiction. Names, characters, places, and incidents either are the product of the author's imagination or are used fictitiously, and any resemblance to actual persons, living or dead, business establishments, events, or locales is entirely coincidental. The publisher does not have any control over and does not assume any responsibility for author or third-party websites or their content.

FIRST EDITION: September 2011

Library of Congress Cataloging-in-Publication Data

Buehlman, Christopher.
 Those across the river / Christopher Buehlman.—1st ed.
 p. cm.
 ISBN 978-0-441-02067-6
 1. World War, 1914–1918—Veterans—Fiction. 2. Plantations—Georgia—Fiction. 3. Family secrets—Fiction. 4. Memory—Fiction. I. Title.
 PS3603.U3395T48 2011
 813'.6—dc22
 2011005232

PRINTED IN THE UNITED STATES OF AMERICA

10 9 8 7 6 5 4 3 2 1

For Christeen and Joseph Buehlman,
who gave me a home to dream in

ACKNOWLEDGMENTS

I wish first to remember Elaine Koster, a formidable and unforgettable woman who was my literary agent all too briefly. Elaine's assistant, Stephanie Lehmann, has my thanks for wading into the manuscript armed with an indifference for the horror genre and a keen eye for bullshit; she beat this novel until it had to die or get strong. Undying thanks also go to Ellen Twaddell, associate agent at the Elaine Koster Literary Agency, for fishing me out of the slush pile. Jenny Steiner Meisinger was with me through the first glimmer and the first draft, and Jennifer Rae Johnson (now Buehlman) saw it born in its current form. Danielle Dupont, an actual muse, never had any doubt; and those who know Karen already know where Dora got her eyes. I want to thank the readers who took the time to comment thoughtfully on this piece in its various forms: Ciara Carinci, Franc Auld, Michael J. E. Reilly, Chris Holcom and especially my sometime writing partner Allison Williams. Thanks to Alan Hutton and Kevin Daniels for their weapons expertise, and to Mouse, who helped me more credibly imagine what I have been lucky enough (thanks to men like him) never to have seen firsthand. Thanks to Brenda White Caballero for giving me, as the Spanish say, light. And thanks to Jack Bostick, a teacher who told his students scary stories.

THOSE ACROSS *the* RIVER

H E CAME OUT to see me in the cage because I belonged to him.
I was like a new racehorse he still found interesting enough to visit at night, when the others were asleep. He sat there cross-legged on the wet ground, unmindful of the light rain that was falling on him. It wasn't enough to extinguish his cigar, but it was enough to keep my ruined back waterlogged; enough to make me think my bones were made of cold pewter.

I had drifted in and out. He might have been there an hour before I noticed him.

"You're going to die out here," he said.

He didn't say it to frighten me.

He just said it.

"Yes," I said.

It occurred to me for the first time that they might eat me. Then I shook that thought away; if they meant to eat me, they wouldn't have let my flesh get this rotten. They wouldn't have left me with so little food. I wasn't good enough for them to eat.

"I'm not good enough for you to eat," I muttered into the rain, too tired to choose between thinking and speaking. You or I wouldn't have heard it. But their ears were very good.

"Maybe just your heart," he said, without irony or double meaning. It wasn't like speaking with a person. He was just a shadow against other shadows.

"Okay," I said.

Having my heart eaten sounded good and final. I wanted to lie down with the dead. I wanted to be numb and blind and without memory. But that's not what happened.

I kept my memory.

Especially the parts I didn't want.

CHAPTER ONE

THIS IS HOW it started.

Eudora and I pulled up the drive with the sound of gravel under the tires. When the house came into view she squealed.

"Is it ours, Frankie? Is it really all ours?"

"That's what the paperwork says."

"It's such a fine yellow. I think I'll call it the Canary House. Will you call it that with me, or will you feel silly?"

"The Canary House suits me fine."

She grinned and gave me a flash of her mismatched eyes; one lake-grey, one shallows-green. The most bewitching eyes I ever saw, or will ever see.

"Let's just sit here and look at it for a moment. We'll have some

gay times in that house, but we don't know what they are yet, so let's just hold on to that. The potential, I mean."

"Alright."

"Or, better yet, let's imagine all the things we want in that house. Can you imagine making love to me on the staircase? Within the hour?"

"Easily."

"Will you carry me across the threshold?"

"Let's save it for the wedding. And only if nobody's looking. We're already married, remember? At least as far as our neighbors are concerned."

"Neighbors. How soon will our neighbors be our friends, I wonder. Can you see us having friends over for dinner?"

"Yes."

"What about as old marrieds sitting on the porch? Holding hands with our closer hands and swatting flies with the free ones. Can you see that?"

"Not at all." I laughed.

"Well, perhaps I don't care to swat flies with you, either."

And then she kissed me so hungrily that we never made it to the staircase.

THE MOVERS CAME not at the hottest part of the day, but about an hour after that, when the heat had built up so that it stood under the eaves and porches and made the moisture in the ground steam underfoot. The truck, beaten-up and rusty, with a dent in

the front fender, pulled up just behind my own car. The moving truck's paint had once been white. That was why the blood stood out. Just a little of it, no more than a paintbrush would flick, but fresh.

That dent hadn't been there in Chicago.

The driver, an affable Negro with a broad frame and a wide, handsome face, saw what I was looking at as he cut the motor. Black smoke farted behind the truck. He stepped down from the cab. His smaller partner got down, too. Stuck close to him.

"We done hit a dog. He come quick from under a house. Crawled back under the house slow."

"Was the drive okay otherwise?"

"Oh, I done worse, yes I have. But the roads around here pretty rough."

I saw from his eyes that he saw Eudora come out of the house. Everybody looked at Eudora a beat longer than they should. Even before they noticed her eyes.

She came up beside me and offered the men coffee mugs full of water.

"There's no icebox or I would give it to you cold," she said.

They drank it down fast and thanked her.

She took their mugs and went back up to the house and the big man wiped sweat out of his eyes with the heel of his hand just to keep himself from watching her go. The little man was not so artful.

"Shall we get started?" I said, retiring my shirt and glasses.

"Oh no, Mr. Nichols. We paid for this. You jus show us where you want the boxes."

"Nonsense. Three will finish faster than two. And then we can eat."

THE MOVING-IN WAS hard, mostly because of the tight turn around the top of the stairs. My rolltop desk was the worst. I could have let the hired men do it, but I felt guilty. A man has to work for his extravagances. I mashed the Holy Ghost hellfire out of my fingers negotiating around that corner, though. Perhaps this was the required sacrifice for all the good writing I hoped to do. I caught the big Negro chewing on the inside of his cheek, trying not to laugh at the funny face I must have made when I hurt myself. I do make funny faces. Then he looked at my hand. It was the first time he noticed the missing finger. He looked away.

I went outside, shaking my hand, and found Dora lying across the hood of the Ford. She had poured herself deerishly across it, upside down, letting the hot metal sting her back through her thin dress. Her eyes were fixed where the sun hung forked in the trees. Her hat slid off her head, the hat with the dried rose on it, and now the light made the gold in her hair catch fire.

"You're going to pass out and fall right into the apples," I said.

"It's your own fault, Orville Francis Nichols. Had you not prohibited me from helping with the boxes, I would have something better to do with myself than lay here watching the world go by. You know, it goes by more interestingly upside down. That's a fact."

I walked over towards her.

"Besides, I am nearly one hundred and twenty-five pounds in weight, and if I follow your instructions not to lift anything heavy, I may not lift myself."

"I'll lift you."

"Not with those sweaty donkey-arms, if you please."

I lifted her anyway, braying like Nick Bottom, and she laughed and play-slapped at me.

"You handsome, dripping thing. You with your shirt off, trying to be a socialist."

I turned back towards the house.

"And your fine Italian shoes," she called after me. "Who's going to carry all your pointy shoes upstairs, Professor?"

I made muscles for her as I went in.

THE NEXT TIME I found her she was kneeling in the kitchen, using her thumbnail to slit the tape on a cardboard box. She pulled out a set of silverware from 1871, a wedding gift of her grandmother's. Benton Harbor money was in that silver, from her grandfather's vast Michigan orchards. All the pieces had engraved roses and the tines of the forks were so delicate they seemed to be made for children. She looked at herself in a teaspoon, upside down again. I melted away before she knew I was watching her. Good God, I was in love. Had been since I saw her in class all those years ago. The married girl who sat up front. The stubborn, funny one who was studying to be a teacher. The rich girl who didn't want Daddy's money if it came with rules.

I LEFT HER in the kitchen and, in the living room, nearly ran into the larger man who was cradling my cannon in his arms. It wasn't really a cannon, per se; rather a sort of oversized shotgun first used on the deck of an eighteenth-century ship, and then bastardized into a crude Confederate field piece in the States' War. They put grapeshot in it and sawed through men and horses at close range. A clever carpenter had even mounted it on a small wheeled carriage so a mule could pull it. I shot it off on the Fourth of July sometimes. I didn't mind loud noises so long as I was the one making them.

". . . war, Mr. Nichols?" was what I heard the driver say. As was my habit, I answered the question he seemed most likely to have asked. When your hearing goes, you'll learn that trick, too.

"Yes, I was," I said. "Infantry. Thirty-third."

"Oh no, sir, I asked was you *goin* to war with this here cannon. But I done served, too. They wouldn't let me near no gun, but they thought I'd make a good enough stevedore. Guess the only time I ever sat by and let someone else do the unloadin was the day I was born."

I laughed with him even though he'd probably said that a thousand times before. Stevedore. He was probably in Brest when I shipped in on the *Mount Vernon*, just another black face we all ignored on our way to glory while Uncle Sam made all the Sambos into pack mules. A rotten deal, I thought at the time.

"Where you want this? And that tub a powder?"

"In the study upstairs, please."

All the naughty masculine things went in the study. If it exploded, fired a projectile, had a sharp edge or contained more alcohol than wine, it went in the study. If it was made of wood or leather or was more than fifty years old without any sort of lace or floral design, it went in the study. Typewriter. Globe. Books. Binoculars. Drambuie. I was going to love that goddamn room.

OUR DINNER GUESTS weren't used to being invited to sit at white tables. At first they were reticent, especially the little man, but it was clear they were hungry. The big man—was his name John? James? I think it was James—ate two plates of corned beef and tinned beans and drank the last of our beer. I was glad to give it to someone who was so pleased with it. I ate the beans, but just bullied the beef around on my plate.

"Since when don't you like meat?" Dora said.

"I prefer the beans."

It wasn't worth telling her about, but I couldn't stomach corned beef since I had to choke back so many tins of that in France. "Old Charley" we called it; the same goddamn thing every day, and then whistles blowing and mud and mud and mud. Everything associated with that time had a pall over it, even seventeen years later.

After the men left—after their warm thank-you-ma'ams and good-luck-to-yas and their awkward backing out of the gravelly drive, bound again for Chicago—(Was I the slightest bit sad I was not going, too? Even before everything improbable and worse fell on us? Did my guts tickle just a little for my city on the

lake?)—Dora grabbed me above an elbow and hauled me up to christen the bed.

It was a squeaky old bastard of a four-poster, but there was no one to hear us. Our closest neighbors would have heard nothing short of a scream. Halfway through it she pushed me off her so she could open a window and let the trapped heat out of the room, but I took her where she knelt and dripped sweat on her back, and she panted out that window, *like a greyhound bitch* as the French say. And then she smoked a cigarette, blowing smoke into the leaves of the elm tree that grew just outside, unmindful that the sheet she wrapped around herself only covered one of her small, thick-nippled breasts.

CHAPTER TWO

I WENT FOR a walk. The tree shadows stretched long and finger-like on the dirt road that led into Whitbrow as the last light of the day spilled from the west. The few houses that lined the road were really little better than shacks, but even they looked worthy of portraiture with that amber glow washing over their pine-board and tin. Sometimes a dog would bark. Sometimes a face would appear and then recede behind the mosquito screen of a window. Once, a bony hand struck a match whose jab of flame then twinned itself on the wick of an oil lamp.

A barn owl sat on a branch pretty high up and turned its head to watch me. It noiselessly flew off into the deeper woods. Maybe I was so handsome it just had to tell somebody.

Even at twilight this place was hot. This wasn't my first time in

the South; Camp Logan in Texas had been hotter, but I had also been drilling in full kit and crawling and shooting on the range. On the other hand, I was nineteen, and that makes a difference. On this first day in Whitbrow I was thirty-six and starting to feel it. I had always been trim, but lately I had gotten just a little thicker around the waist. The sweat from my back was beginning to sop my shirt and trickled tentatively down the crack of my backside. *Look away, Dixieland.*

I was hungry.

I had little hope of finding anything open in this burg, but there was light coming from the general store. It sat just off the main square, up on blocks like the houses, asymmetrical in build— almost a trapezoid—and leprous with flaking white paint. A single kerosene lamp, wild with moths, backlit a sign that the failing light outside still allowed me to read: CLOSED. PLEASE CALL AGAIN! Sign or no sign, people were moving around in there. I put my face up to the greasy front window and saw some men bent over a checkers game, and another man hovering over them. He was missing an arm.

One of the checker players, a very fat man, noticed me and came to the door, the top corner of which struck a small, tattletale bell when opened.

"You must be Dottie McComb's kin," said the big man, who seemed to float like a zeppelin in his apron.

"That's right. Orville Francis Nichols, but Frank's just as good."

I gave the fat man my hand and knew when I saw him swallow it in his that he intended to give me one of those unfair, porter-

house steak squeezes around the fingers that doesn't allow a proper grip in return. I was right, but I made a point of not wincing.

"Paul," he said.

"A pleasure, sir. Are you all closed up, then?"

"Yeah, but it don't matter when the boys are over."

Two very old boys looked at him from mismatched chairs and nodded in acknowledgment. A younger, round, tough-looking fellow sat near the iron stove, which had sand around its base.

"Mind if I look around?"

"Suit yourself," he said, holding the door open for me while I brushed past his belly on the way in.

The shelves were mostly bare. Hard times here like everywhere else. Molasses. Lard. Rice. Eggs. Flour. A few cheeses. The tobacco shelf was well stocked, though, with Prince Albert and Red Man and bags of roll-your-own from local farms. A stack of straw hats on the counter leaned towards a jar teeming with pickles. Tongs sat in a green puddle on a plate.

On a shelf behind the register, a stuffed badger rearing up to do battle with an unseen foe neighbored with a serene-looking stuffed bobcat. Next to them, a stuffed dog had somehow been manipulated so it looked as if he were seated cross-legged on a stump, playing a small banjo. A deer's head stared above everything as if omnipotent. All had penciled-in price tags hanging from them.

"Sir, I don't see any wine here," I said.

"Don't see none cause I don't sell none. Like to, but cain't. You in a dry county."

One of the old boys said, "Been a dry county ever since that tent

revival come in nineteen and twelve, before the proheebishun. Snake handlin and all that. Paul remembers."

"Yeah, Paul. Why dint you git in there and grab you a rattler?"

"Too fat. They'd a caught on me."

"Not if you had enough Jesus in you."

"I ain't never had enough Jesus I wanted to grab no rattler."

"Say," the one-armed man said to me. "Ain't your wife that pretty new teacher takin Dottie's place over to the school?"

"You know damn well she is. You the one tole me," Paul said.

"Don't hurt none to ask. Just makin conversation."

The first old boy said, "You want wine, Mr. Teacher's Husband, you want to go on to the mill town in Caffery County. We in Morgan County here. All we drink is the blood of the Redeemer."

"Didn't the good book say the Lord turned water into wine?" I said.

"Yessir. Wedding at Cana. Round here we don't turn no water into wine. Just corn into shine."

The tough-looking man, who had been silent the whole time, looked up at Paul and said, "You gonna move a checker?"

ON THE WALK home I thought about how light the sack felt without a bottle of burgundy in it. Just pears, cheese, bread, eggs and coffee for the morning. No sugar. Dora would be sad about that with her sweet tooth, but not as sad as I would be without wine to help me sleep. I had a taste for it ever since I was a boy, when Father let John and me drink a glass each at the table. Mother had already

died by then trying to push out a dead daughter, and Father dove headfirst into a bottle. He had good taste in booze, though, and the money to acquire it; the hutch was always full of wines from France with their mysterious labels. The more alluring bottles, though, held strange liquor and cordials, amber colored and ruby and clear. These were forbidden. They were part of the grown-up world, along with pipe tobacco and mustache trimmers and the gun above the hall mirror that I couldn't reach without a chair. But Papa wasn't a mean drunk; just a sad, sleepy one. He didn't hit much.

The one time John got the fist instead of the belt was when he stole the hutch key and got into the Grand Marnier, adding water to even out the bottle. He was shit-faced by the time Papa got home from the Cicero racetrack with his friends in nice suits. They laughed their asses off, but my father didn't laugh. He just set about busting John a good one in the mouth, knocking him down. I didn't have any booze; I knew better. But because I was older I still got the belt for not putting a stop to it. Hard, too. We always got it worse when Father had guests. Like they had some running contest to see who was best at whipping his kid's ass. Come to think of it, that was the last time he ever hit me at all. This was a year before I went overseas, where I would one day recognize a bottle of Grand Marnier and drink it from the mouth of a plain-faced whore in the sixth arrondissement in Paris. I got no whipping that time, neither with belt nor solution of Mercury, but a buddy of mine in the next room was less lucky when we had to pull our britches down for short-arm inspection.

I looked up at the sky. Just enough cobalt blue lingered behind the western trees so you couldn't call it full dark.

"My Lord Jesus drinketh wine," I said aloud to nobody. "Quite a

lot of wine. He hath a port wine nose. He walketh drunkenly with me as I march home. *Left . . . Left . . . Left, right, left.* Keep up, Jesus."

THE LOCUSTS SANG hard as I walked up the path and into the Canary House. I knew by the darkness of the house that Dora would still be sleeping. I went upstairs as quietly as I could, but when I entered the bedroom she woke at the sound of a creaking floorboard and sat up, the curve of her shoulders and the crown of her head faintly outlined in the near absence of light. She gasped and swallowed before she said, "Frank."

I recognized the pause.

She had nearly said "Stephen."

That had been her husband, tenured professor and world-class stuffed shirt Stephen Chambers.

The first time I saw Eudora socially was at a U of M faculty luncheon where she and her spouse shared a table with a poet and two Japanese exchange students. That's where the pretending started, with a game of stolen glances while one of the girls tried, in wobbly English, to describe the intricacies of the tea ceremony.

That girl was plainly nursing an infatuation with the poet, a carefully coiffed but metrically disappointing former protégé of Robert Frost whose work was most enthusiastically received by nonnative English readers. Meanwhile, Professor Chambers trotted Dora before his colleagues like an expensive racehorse, too impressed with himself to see that she knew it. And hated it.

She was twenty, wearing a sweater the color of an Anjou pear.

I was still built like the St. Ignatius basketball center I had been fifteen years before.

We were in love before the salads came.

That had been four years ago.

The affair had lasted two.

Her first husband's name was finally dying.

As was mine, I suppose.

Dora was barren.

NEAR MIDNIGHT, DORA was sitting up in bed reading *Madame Bovary* by the light of three candles burning on the nightstand. The air was damp and still. The flames barely moved. I sat up with pillows bunched behind me, eating a pear with a knife. A small plate sat balanced on my belly, wobbling gently as I breathed.

"That's no good for your eyes," I said.

"You're the one who needs glasses."

I cut a slice of pear and lipped it off the knife. Dora allowed herself a sideways glance just in time to see a fat drop of juice miss the plate and fall into the sparse hair on my chest. She blinked and cut her eyes back to the book.

"It's better in French, you know," I said.

"I'm sure it is for those of us who speak French."

"Although some people find the content objectionable. Not the sort of thing that promotes marital fidelity."

"We'll have to take our chances," she said. "Are you going to let me read?"

"Of course, of course."

I took another bite of pear. She cut her eyes to watch me eat again. I swallowed, then said, "Have you gotten to the part where she poisons herself with arsenic and dies in agony?"

She closed the book.

"Orville Francis Nichols, you are a first-class son of a bitch."

"And how you've learned to swear. That book is eroding your morals."

"You have no idea," she said, taking the pear, knife and plate from me. She cut a moon-shaped sliver and set it on her inner thigh. I raised an eyebrow. She pointed at me with the knife, then pointed at the sliver. I bent to her and ate it.

"Slower, you fiend," she said, placing the next piece higher. I ate it. Slowly. She placed the next piece even higher. Then another. She had to move her nightgown to place the last one.

LATER, WHEN THE pear was gone and the book was on the floor, Eudora knelt over me, backlit by the candles. I was on my stomach. From the corner of my eye, she looked so powerful and beautiful in that posture that it occurred to me she might be a Sphinx.

"I like it that you let me touch your back now," she said, and I felt her finger lightly trace the scars. Then she kissed each one. Then my left ear. She lay down on top of me now and dug my left hand from under the pillow, kissing the nub where the pinky should have been. "I wish I could make it all better," she said.

"You do."

"You need a shave!" She giggled, rubbing her cheek on mine. "All these little white ones like grains of sugar make you look like old man Moses. Lucky for you, your hair's still brown. You look young and juicy when you shave."

Now she reared up over me, straddling my back.

How like a Sphinx in her nightgown.

"It is a man," I said.

"Excuse me?"

"A man goes on four legs in the morning, two legs in the afternoon and three in the evening."

"Ah, but you didn't wait for my question. Now I shall eat you by the gates of Thebes."

"I'm game."

"But I really do have a question."

"Okay."

"Are you happy? I know we're getting on well. We always get on well. But are you . . . *content*?"

"Alright, this sounds serious. Get off me so I can see you."

She flopped down beside me and I got my spectacles from the nightstand. One of the candles guttered behind her. I tried to see her eyes in the poor light.

"Yes," I said. "Unreservedly happy."

"It's just that we've been running ever since Ann Arbor. I feel like Adam and Eve, thrown out of the Garden of Eden, just barely making it. Sponging off your brother in Chicago. Now you come into this house and that's swell, really it is, and I have work . . . but something's wrong."

"Are you ashamed of me because I haven't been working?"

"Oh, no. Not at all. Everybody's got it tough now."

"Are you afraid I won't write?"

"Maybe I'm afraid that you will."

"What does that mean?"

"Your great-grandfather, the one who owned the plantation near here."

"Lucien Savoyard."

"Yes. I don't like him."

"He's dead."

"Not if you write a book about him."

"There are books about Napoleon, and he's still dead."

"But not completely. And I'm not sure a man who killed his own slaves for sport deserves that kind of resurrection. Even if he was a general."

"Brigadier general."

"I beg his pardon."

"Then don't think of it as a book about him. It is, of course, but it's also about the slaves who rose up against him."

"And killed him."

"Yes. As he deserved."

"With hammers and axes and homemade spears. It's all so brutal. Only men care about these things."

"I disagree. And it wasn't just the men who overthrew him, at least according to the Union soldiers who spoke to the slaves when it was all done. The women took up weapons the same as the men. All of them rushed the house."

"I would have, too, considering what he was doing. But then I wouldn't talk about it. Or read about anything like that. Violence

like that is private, don't you think? You don't like to talk about France."

"No."

"So what's the difference?"

"There's something to be learned here."

"And not France? Why don't you write about France?"

"I can't. Someone else will, later."

"I see. You'll write theirs and someone who's in diapers now will write yours."

"It sounds silly when you put it like that."

"Maybe not. Maybe I understand a little."

"Think about it . . . A Confederate military man who refuses to free his slaves and fights off a Union detachment, only to die at the hands of a blacksmith and half-starved field hands. I think the title will really make people want to read it."

"*The Last Plantation.*"

"Yes."

"It's good. You'll be the boy-king of States' War historians."

"Yes! By God, you get it!" I laughed.

"And get a fresh start at a new university. I know how much a book will help you with that. I'm just so sorry I spoiled everything for you."

"Dora."

"If you'd never met me, you'd still be in Ann Arbor."

"Lonely."

"But a professor."

"Cold."

"With nice coats and firewood."

"And some dull wife."

"Who could give you babies."

"I'm indifferent to babies, and they sense it. They cry at me in protest. This isn't helping."

"No, it's selfish. Poor whore-of-Babylon me."

"You're not from Babylon."

"I know you liked it better before. And I ruined it. I ruined your career."

"We don't need to talk about it, Dora-Dora. Tabula rasa, remember? Everything shiny and new. I lost one job and I took one licking. If you and I stay together, I paid cheap."

"I don't know if we're done paying," she said.

She closed her eyes and I imagined the film she was playing in her head.

BLACK AND WHITE. Jerky. A silent picture. Organist at the side. Stephen Chambers, professor of British literature, steps into the office of O. F. Nichols, professor of American history, a short walk from his own office in Angell Hall. He flings the door open. The adulteress, surprised, takes a step back from the desk of her lover. Stares at her husband. Does he know? Why else would he be here?

"STEPHEN . . ." in white letters on a black screen.

The husband, a shorter man than me, is breathing hard through his nostrils. Dora's mouth opens now.

White letters, black screen: "HE KNOWS."

Organ music. Stephen raises his pointed finger, his mouth a hole beneath his neat mustache.

"THIS IS HOW IT IS DONE IN THE HIGHER CIRCLES OF LEARNING."

I stand up. My height goads the smaller man, who leaps around the desk as if he were playing tennis.

"NO, STEPHEN!" from Dora.

The husband strikes the lover, knocks my glasses off, strikes me again and knocks me awkwardly to the floor. Keeps striking. The lover does not raise his hands. My hands. My tie hangs over one shoulder like a tongue. Dora speaks. Please remember the white letters on the black screen.

"STEPHEN . . . IT IS MY FAULT!"

The camera takes my perspective now, looking up at my attacker, teeth bared under the civilized mustache, wild eyes enhanced by eyeliner, too much powder on the face.

"I WILL KILL YOU!"

My nose breaks. I have time to wonder if I have lost a tooth. The adulteress rises up behind her husband now and begins to strike him hard with the heel of her pump, and this is funny. This is so funny I laugh hard with blood on my teeth. Again and again the cuckold's small fists flash. The shoe rises and falls. I laugh. Other professors appear at the door, assemble themselves into a totem pole of surprise; the one on top has his hands on his cheeks, his mouth a huge oval.

"STOP THEM!"

They pull the smaller man off. His hands are too badly broken

for him to unmake his fists. He looks at the camera, holding his ruined hands up as evidence.

"DO YOU SEE? DO YOU SEE WHAT YOU HAVE DONE?"

The organist turns to look, too.

"Eudora . . . Tabula rasa."

She opened her eyes.

Chapter Three

By and by I slept.

And, alas, I dreamed.

Not of the trench fight; that was the worst.

And not of Metzger's death, which was nearly as bad.

But I did dream of the trench.

Something about a gas attack, and I couldn't find my mask. But there was a dead guy half in the mud gripping his mask in his hands, and I couldn't get it loose. I was holding my breath and jerking at it, and pulling at his fingers, but they were like iron, even though his head was lolling. He was being stubborn. I was going to die. I woke up gasping.

But I hadn't yelled; Dora was still sleeping.

Morning?

Yes, morning.

It was dark, but the roosters were going at it.

Goddamn *roosters*.

How did I end up in Georgia?

I stuffed the pillow over my eyes and ears and just lay there for a long time, still mad at the dead guy who wouldn't let me have his mask.

WHEN I WOKE up the second time, I smelled bacon.

My stomach pulled me downstairs to investigate, and there was Eudora frying up breakfast; now that I was good and close I could hear the sizzle. I slipped my arms around her waist from behind while she slid three fried eggs onto a plate that already held bacon.

"Whose bacon is this?" I said.

"Roosevelt's bacon. What a question. And he stood up straight and chopped the wood for the stove, too."

"Thank you."

"Thank the president."

"Really, where did it come from?"

"Pigs, of course."

"You've been to town."

"What else was a girl supposed to do with her morning while her gentleman-friend slept? Moving all that furniture must have worn you out. It's nearly noon."

"I didn't see any bacon at the store."

"Neither did I. So I inquired. What a funny little town. Do you know, the butcher's shop is also the secondhand shop? Dresses and

the like, all in the back part of the building. You can get nylons and pork chops all in the same trip. And not just pork chops. Game, too. They really like to know who they're eating around here; mostly everything still had a head on it."

I remembered my dream from last night and stopped chewing for a moment. Movement caught my eye and I watched a spider make his way across the ceiling towards the top of a cabinet. Dora looked up, too.

"Are you going to kill that for me?"

"It eats the bugs."

"It is a bug."

"I'm feeling magnanimous."

"I'm not. I'm a fascist," she said, knocking the spider down with a broom and stepping on it.

"Maybe that fellow had a mother. Did you think about that?"

"He should have written more."

I chuckled.

"Speaking of writing, are you going to drop Johnny a note and let him know we're in safe?" she said.

She was fond of my little brother. So was I. So was everyone. I might have gotten the height in the family, but he was the charmer; and deadly with the ladies. Many nights Dora lay next to me in our narrow, borrowed bed, giggling because she said she could hear Johnny making some little bird coo upstairs. He was like the Prince of Chicago, bartending at the Drake.

"I'll write him a few lines today."

"He didn't want us to come here, Frankie."

"The bacon is really good."

"Did he?"

"Is there pepper?"

"On the counter."

I fetched the pepper.

"Did he?"

"No," I said.

And he wasn't the only one.

Dear Orville Francis,

My name is Dorothy Mccomb, older sister to your mother, Katherine, I doubt whether you have heard much of me owing to the troubles your mother had with our father who was ----- to her, and owing also to her desire to leave this town and never to return, and cannot say as I blame her and envied her for her strength in cutting herself loose from Whitbrow which is and shall always be bloodied, though they leave us be for now.

I would have left you alone, but i am sick with the cancer, it is in my stomach and the medicine stopped helping; but do not fear for me as I have made my peace and have not long to suffer, my husband and our two children, one drowned, one had his heart outside him, born dead, have gone before me,

Soon you will be contacted by my attorney mister Stowe. He will have you to Atlanta for a reading of my last will and testament which names you Orville

franknichols as the heir to my house and possessions
and some little money that I have saved back,your
brother john jacky/ will get the larger share of the
money, since the house is yours, which you MUST SELL

Although I know nothing of your character, i can only
assume that you are a good man if anything of my sister
passed to you & for that reason i ask you to sell this house
and to remain where you are, or in some other place. mis-
ter Stowe will see to the sale; although you must not
expect to have what a house of this qualitie might fetch in
another town I have it painted and fixed up so that it
might lure another, but not you frank NNichols frank
please do not make this your home you might think that a
man of your worldliness would go stale in such a place as
this frank but that is not what will happen, if you come,
there is bad blood here, and it is against you (YOu) for no
fault of your own & you will not have time to go stale in
whitbrow. this place will smell out I fear what is in you
and claim you,for its own, it, will, hug, your, bones, into,
the, woods, & you will wish you had never

Katherine in a precious letter to me said she called
you frankie

will you allow me frankie for a moment to imagine
you as any child i never had the fortune to know frankie
frankie by that sweet name.

your auntmy stomach hurts and i must stop
hopes to meet meet you in canaans land
dorothy mccomb

dottie

whom godofabraham soon fetches home

kiss you akiss where you stay wisely in the north

away from them.

That was the typed letter I got in February. It had this hand-written note paper-clipped to it:

Dear Mr. Nichols,

Please remember that at the conclusion of her days your aunt,
who insisted that I should send her letter without the benefit of
revision, was heavily dependent on opiates.

With condolences,

J. Stowe, Esq.

Had I received this missive in Ann Arbor when I was teaching and everything was ducky, I would have certainly taken my estranged aunt's advice and stayed away. An unusual thing happens, though, when a man has been long enough without work; he gets superstitious. After months of polite rejections from universities who already had a full history department (or claimed to; Dora's husband had pull at campuses from here to the Philippines) and further months scraping together a few bits between tutoring and day labor, I was ready to look for auguries in pigeon droppings. Dora was making out all right as a hostess at the Drake, and we had a roof over our heads thanks to Johnny, but what's that old saw? "Narrow is the stair and hard is the bread in another

man's house," especially when it's your little brother. I think that's Dante. Or Petrarch. One of those hoary old Guineas. Dora's ex would know.

Suffice it to say that the letter arrived in the mailbox with the force of prophecy; one more letter followed, in which a Mrs. Muncie informed me that my Eudora would be offered a job teaching at Whitbrow's school, as my aunt once had, provided "Mrs. Nichols" could supply a teaching certificate. She could, I explained, although under the name Chambers because of a "paperwork error."

I determined at once that we should go to Georgia, live rent-free in the warmth and fresh air, and get our feet under us again. Eudora was reticent. She would have preferred to do as my aunt had suggested, but she agreed that our other options were pretty skinny; we were both educators, but she was inexperienced and I was disgraced. Moreover, everyone in the Midwest who had a job was holding on to it with white knuckles. There were so many hard-up professors and teachers in Chicago that I couldn't get full-time work in anything better than a cannery (that lasted two weeks), and her teaching certificate wasn't worth a cup of coffee.

This way, she would have a job, we would have a home, and I would have a project that just might unlock a prosperous future for us both.

That is why and how, in the summer of 1935, we settled into our rural castle.

And, oh what a kingdom it overlooked.

Chapter Four

R IVER'S FAR AS I'm goin today," Lester said.

We had both hiked a good hour through the pine and red clay woods that aproned the town, but now we were up against a river with rock-shelf banks and lazy brown water that looked deep in the middle. A simple raft sat up on the rocks with a guide rope stretching across the river for pulling.

"Yer welcome to use the ferry so long as you cross back with it, too, and put it back up on them rocks. Nobody wants to go wadin this time a year for all the moccasins."

"Thanks," I said. "It's very nice of you to show me around."

I had met Lester the day before. It had seemed like good politics to get around to a few of the little stores bracketing the town square and introduce myself. Lester worked with his brother and a hired

boy at Gordeau's feed shop, which his father owned. The siblings were white-blond and lanky, and Lester was friendly as hell and curious about the wider world.

Lester had not only walked the several miles from town with me; he had even indulged me while I used my wife's camera to take a few photographs of a burned-down house we passed on the trail. I was so excited about the prospect of photographing the plantation, should I ever find it, that I had fashioned a little darkroom under the stairs so I wouldn't have to be bothered about sending film away.

The house wasn't much to look at, but I had to wonder if the Union soldiers on their way to force emancipation on the Savoyard Plantation had stopped there to get water for their horses; perhaps someone sympathetic to the rebels had stared stony-eyed at them from the porch of this ruin, now only partially visible through brush and kudzu.

Lester had told me a little bit about what lay beyond the river, but since most of his directions used flora for landmarks, I wondered how much I would really be able to remember.

Now we stared across the slowly running water.

"I don't mind stretchin my legs for old Dottie's kin. She was my teacher fore I stopped goin. Other kids thought she was funny in the head, but I figure she was just lonesome."

"And you think her grandfather's plantation house is back in there somewhere?"

"Yeah, but not nowhere close. Further than I been back, and I wouldn't guess there was nothin left of it anyhow. Them woods is deep and mean. Course, if they was two sticks standin together,

they'd be all yer'n now, seein as yer the only Savvy-yard. You play baseball?"

"Not lately."

"Shame. I know you're an older fella, but you still look fit's why I asked. Hell, my pop plays sometimes, an he's older'n God's baby shoes. We got games in the lot on Saturdays, dependin on the crops. If I shake my tail I can still make it back. You sure you don't wanna come?"

"What do you mean *mean*?"

"Pardon?"

"When you say the woods are mean?"

"Just stories poppas tell to scare their kids. Haint stories."

"Would you come with me if you didn't have a game?"

"No sir, not today."

"Tomorrow?"

"No sir, not tomorrow neither."

I DID GO back to town with Lester, and I did play baseball.

I took a long look at the woods before I caught up with Lester's retreating form, and for a moment I thought I might cross the river. It was funny how much thicker and darker the woods were just across that lazy body of water, as if a march by dogwoods and maples and live oak had been halted just at the banks and now the river was a frontier between them and their smaller, less robust cousins. But I'm skirting the real reason I didn't cross the river. I didn't go because the woods didn't want me in them. And I didn't want to go alone.

The baseball game was good. Lester invited me to play on the same team with his little brother, Saul, and their father, whom everybody just called Old Man. The brothers were impressive together, both with the same corn-silk hair and easy, fluid athleticism. Normans, I thought, still spreading their strong seed west. I recognized their dad as one of the old birds bent over the checkerboard at the general store that first night. He was checking me out good. Whomever the mayor was, this was Old Man Gordeau's town.

Turns out he was the mayor.

The captain of the other team was a carpenter named Charley Wade, and his best hitter was a curly, unattractive redhead named Pete. Those were all the names that stuck that first Saturday. Most of the rest were high school age, but I daresay most were not in school. Farm kids drop out.

I tipped one ball up so the catcher should have had it, and I even slowed to a jog when I saw how well-planted he was. Incredibly, he dropped it, and I hustled to first base, which was an old flour sack half-full of sand. I scored the first run when Lester plastered one out of the lot; it crested over the sparse trees between the lot and the town square, and thumped against the side of the hardware store. The man who owned it was the sheriff. He came out and threw it back. Good arm on him despite his potbelly.

I walked home happy with dust and clay on my shoes and my hand still reeking of the mitt I borrowed.

I would try the woods another day.

That evening I chopped wood in the backyard while Dora cooked. I still had to wear gloves, but my city-boy hands were getting a little tougher. Every third or fourth heft I had to swab my

head to keep the sweat out of my eyes, but I soon incorporated that into the rhythm. If I had known a good sea shanty I might have sung one.

My mind drifted to the Savoyard side of my family.

Had I really come from them?

It was as if they got weaker and more deranged with every generation. The one who fought with Napoleon sired the one who got rich in New Orleans. Who sired Lucien, my great-grandfather.

Heft, chop.

Heft, chop.

When his father died, Lucien came back from school overseas—though I have been unable to find out where—to inherit. No love lost. He didn't even come to New Orleans, just handled everything through an intermediary and bought the land in Georgia to ride the cotton boom. And speculate in slaves.

Then he fought for the Confederacy.

Just after the war, he wouldn't turn his slaves loose. The Federals tried to make him, but he got men from Whitbrow and Morgan to help him drive them off. The slaves revolted and murdered him, as well as his wife and overseers. And the dogs they used to chase them with. And the horses. They chopped them all up and put them in a common pit, and burned them. I imagine they would have sewn the earth with salt if it had occurred to them.

Heft, chop. Wipe.

Then Louis, my grandfather. Savoyard's bastard. What people around here call a no-account, the closest thing Whitbrow had to a town drunk. He lived off the money Lucien had given his mother to leave him alone, and when that was gone, and the town had

begun to talk about why his daughter Katherine had left at fifteen, he had the good taste to turn yellow and die of cirrhosis. He had no face in my mind's eye, as if a cloud of flies had gathered where his face should have been. Perhaps I just couldn't assign an identity to him knowing, or at least powerfully suspecting, what he had done to my mother. The faceless pedophile.

A cloud of flies, and flies for his eyes.

His other daughter, Dorothy, married well and prospered here in town. It was largely because of her reputation that I was not looked askance at, as I might have been had Louis been the last word on what a Savoyard was.

Heft, chop.

Heft, chop.

But to hell with that.

Heft, chop.

I was a Nichols.

Wipe.

I didn't have to look south to see why I liked booze.

"Honey?" Dora said, smiling at me from the doorframe, her hair matted to her head. "Are you talking to yourself again?"

"Heavens, yes."

"Well, finish your conversation and get washed up. There's a chicken here that's dying to meet you."

She slipped back inside and let the screen door hit.

I took one last look at the pile of wood I had chopped, then put my axe down and retrieved my glasses from the tree stump where I had lain them. It really was a beautiful summer evening.

The light was peach colored through the trees towards the west.

The crickets were singing hard.

I got out a cigarette and had just opened the hood of my lighter when a mosquito whined in my ear.

I put the cigarette away and went inside.

I wasn't used to them yet.

Chapter Five

"Dear Mister and Missus Nichols,'" Dora read aloud from a note in her hand. She was standing in the doorway to the bedroom where I had slept in yet again. "'Welcome to Whitbrow. I hope that you will attend the Social tonight so you can meet your neighbors who want to meet you. Signed, your neighbor, Ursula Noble.'"

"Who is she?" I said, sitting up and involuntarily making what I recognized as an old man noise as I did. I was sore from baseball.

"Not a Greek, but bearing gifts all the same," she said, setting a basket beside me. I blinked at it uncomprehendingly, then looked in it the way a little boy might examine a defunct wasp's nest. No

wasps, but two chicken eggs, a few horehound candies and a generous offering of wildflowers tied together with a blade of tall grass.

"She's the eldest daughter of the neighbors, a short walk up the road away from town. It's the only other house as nice as this one. Her dad owns the barbershop and that last filling station we passed just before we got off the highway. Ursie. Cute name. She fell all over herself introducing herself to me in town while you were being a Chicago Cub."

"Is she going to be one of yours?"

"Yes. She's fourteen. Doesn't write so badly, even if she leaves out the occasional silent g."

"Hmm," I said, trying to decide if this was going to be some drab church function.

"I want to go," Dora said.

"Really?"

"Sure. What else are we going to do?"

AROUND NOON WE walked down the road into the village of Whitbrow. It was another brilliant August day. The sun shone powerfully on the shops downtown, replicating itself in their windows (where there were windows) and on the windscreens and headlamps of the very few cars. The breeze blew like a draft from a steelworks. She swung my hand playfully while we took one lap around the town square, which consisted of an ancient pump well and a small garden of tea roses boxed by recently painted green

benches. The rest of the town was falling to hell, but those benches sure were smart.

Dora and I sat down and looked at each other, and then laughed at how sloppy with sweat we were. Her hair was pasted to her head at the temples and my shirt was darkening and clinging unbecomingly to my chest.

"They need shade here," she said, "a great big shade tree."

"Yes, but then people might actually sit on the benches, which would block the view of this fine English garden."

"Oh."

"Soda?"

"God, yes."

HARVEY'S DRUG EMPORIUM sat at the southeast corner off the square, next to the decrepit town hall. It was not until the door shut behind us that the counterman noticed us, so we got to enjoy the slice of opinion he was serving up to his passive customer, bending over the poor man with his arms extended like he expected to fly soon.

". . . And it's a good thing that once they got electric lines through here I put the machine in or I'd be boarded up same as the jeweler. Folks hit hard times, they go back to they grandmama's poultice, cain't be spendin on Vicks VapoRub, but I'll be a monkey's uncle if they don't find change for a cold soda when the weather turns . . . 'Scuze me, Mike. Afternoon! Hep you folks?"

I ordered two vanilla sodas.

"Say, you must be that pretty new teacher takin Dottie's place over at the school."

She allowed that she was, then quickly introduced me as her husband in the hopes that he might temper his unsubtle gaze. He did.

"So that makes you the nephew. Yeah, I guess I see that in the eyes. Pleased to meet you folks. I'm Harvey, but you probably guessed that already if you looked above the door afore you come in. This here's Mike. He's lazy."

The man at the counter, who I now noticed was missing his closer arm, nodded hard once and went back to spooning ice cream into his mouth. I remembered him now, standing over the checker game.

"You folks goin to the Social tonight?" Harvey asked.

"What time does it begin?" Dora said.

"Soon as the swineherds get back."

Swineherds? Did I hear that right?

"And what time is that?" I said.

"Looks like nobody's told you two about the Chase. Sort of a Whitbrow spectacle. They leave at two from the church and by the time they get home and cleaned up, it's right about eight."

"No, nobody's told us about this."

"Well, you might want to watch this one. There's talk that this might be the last one til times get better. Or til never."

Harvey set the sodas down in front of us.

"Do you know if Mr. Gordeau will be at the Social tonight?"

"Which Gordeau?"

"Lester."

"Well, I sure hope he's gonna be there. He's one a the swine-herds."

THE CHURCH, WHICH also served as schoolhouse for elementary and middle school students, sat beaming and white on a tract of well-kept land on the far side of the square. A crowd of forty or so had gathered to see the Chase begin, and Ursula Noble was one of these.

"There you are!" she shouted when she spotted Eudora, and she walked bouncily away from the gathering towing a two-year-old by one chicken-poxed arm. Ursula was a young-looking fourteen, still more girl than woman, wearing a faded floral print dress and boots that were too big on her. Her hair was so black it had bluish highlights. I thought of the Cherokee, how we dismantled their nation and shipped it west to die, but not before it pumped a gout of blood into the veins of the conquerors.

"I'm Ursie, the one that left the basket. And this is Sadie. Sadie, say hello."

Sadie looked at Eudora and me as if she were considering us for some post, but then became more interested in her finger and began biting the end of it. I noticed Sadie's eyes then. She was simple.

"So you're Ursula," Dora said.

"Ursie, ma'am. Ursula sounds like a bear."

"It is a bear."

"I know. You can call me that if you like, but I just sign that on

letters cause letters is formal. Mama calls me Ursula just afore Daddy gives me a whippin.'"

"And this is Mr. Nichols. Orville Francis Nichols when he's bad, which is pretty often. I thought I would bring him out to see the Chase."

"Well, come on then," Ursie said, taking Dora's hand with her free one. Dora took mine in turn, and Ursie led us all to the yard of the church in a sort of lopsided wedge. It was just at this moment that a smallish man in black stood up on the front step facing the crowd.

"That's Pastor Lyndon," Ursie said. "Don't let him see you slouch. You're not slouching now, but he says the Devil knows you ain't got the Spirit in you if he sees you hang-doggin around."

If good posture was the measure, Pastor Lyndon had Spirit all right. He held himself painfully erect like a proper little soldier for the Holy Host. As he prepared to speak, he brushed back a forelock that was just beginning to grey. He looked around at the congregation for a moment, giving them all time to stop talking to one another as his gaze lit on each of them. The gaze reminded the young ones he had married them and the old ones that he would speak over their caskets soon. It was a good trick. When they were ready to receive him, he spoke.

"Brethren and friends. We gather here as we do each month to give thanks to the Lord for His infinite bounty, and to show Him that we, as dutiful sons and daughters, know how to thank our Father. Even as it was of old that Jehovah commanded Abraham and his sons to make burnt offering to Him, so are we called, in our way, to keep covenant with Him, offering to Him the best fruits of our fields."

With that, Lester Gordeau approached one side of the steps, leading a massive, hairy-eared hog on a rope. Another young man led a slightly smaller sow to the other side of the pastor. I had to wonder if they were going to slaughter and burn the animals right there on the lawn of the church. Then of course husbands could bed their wives' handmaidens while widows lay with their brothers-in-law.

"Hold Sadie. I have to go do my part now," Ursie said, passing the toddler's small hand into mine. I felt a very unchristian distaste noticing how cool and wet it was. Eudora noticed this and laughed at me. Ursie trotted around to one side of the church to join other young girls who were readying something.

Pastor Lyndon went on.

"Let us remember this Sunday of the waxing moon that our food does not come to us of our own hand. No one of us can make the corn to stand high, nor the grain for our bread to flourish, nor can any man here call the chick forth from the egg until the good Lord shall say *Let it be so.* If any man before me can do these things, then let him take these pigs for his own and carve them shoulder and leg for his own plate. But if he cannot, then let him bow his head before the power of our Lord; let him take up flowers to throw before these blessed swine; and let him give thanks as a child gives thanks, humbly, and in the sure knowledge that, but for the kindness of his Father, he should have neither meat for his belly, nor door to bar against the beasts of the night."

Ursie came back into view with the other girls, and they tied wreaths of wildflowers, mostly daisies and black-eyed Susans, around the necks of the pigs.

"Now we know where she got the wildflowers," Dora whispered.

Pastor Lyndon spoke.

"Before we take these fine animals, let us remember that they have come from the pens of Miles Falmouth and his family, as is scheduled in the registry; and let us remember that Miles suffers a weakness of the back and hips that makes his work on the land very hard for him. And that his son is not yet at the fullness of his strength. Where we might lay down one coin to relieve a whole man's sacrifice in giving of his herd, let us lay down two for our brother Miles Falmouth. If you cannot give today, we will be passing the plate at regular service on Miles' behalf all month."

With this said, Lester and the other swineherd took up an earthenware dish and a heavy silver collection plate and passed them among those in the crowd, who began, with some reluctance, to search their pockets for coins. I put in a silver dollar for both of us. Dora gave me a look balking at the amount.

"It's worth it," I said. "You don't get a show like this every day. Pigs and flowers? Oh they're Jesus Christing it up, all right, but this looks more like some pagan-rooted festival from the south of France. And like the man said, this might be the end of it."

Pastor Lyndon spoke.

"Now let us send these beasts into the wilderness and give no more thought to their flesh, which belongeth now to the Lord, and which, though it might nourish the body of whichsoever of us should eat it, would surely damn his soul."

The swineherds took the ropes from the necks of the pigs and took up long branches twined in green ribbon, using these branches

now as crooks or goads. They herded the pigs across the square, taking care to keep them away from the tea roses, and then turned them left onto the small road that went past several dozen houses and then dwindled to become the path Lester and I had followed, the path the Federals took on their way to fight Savoyard, the path that led to the river.

The townsfolk followed them, singing hymns that neither Dora nor I had ever heard, stopping at the last house as the two pigs and two men headed into the woods. Only when they were out of view did the gathering begin to disband.

Ursie Noble, shining with sweat, discreetly fanned the top of her dress and then took her sister up in her arms, heading for home.

"See you tonight! At the Social!"

Sadie looked back over her shoulder at us for a long while.

Chapter Six

I N THE LAST minutes of daylight, Dora and I drove the Model A into town and parked it not far from where the main road had been closed off by tables. We kicked up a little dust as we went by, and people stared at us, but more because cars were such a rare species out here than because we put grit in the lemonade. Tables had also been set up on the patchy lawn in front of the courthouse, and, as the last of the sunlight bled away, I noticed an eclectic mix of lanterns hung from lines strung between trees. As soon as it was fully dark, musicians started in with fiddle, guitar and triangle. Teenagers and younger marrieds took to a wooden dancing platform I hadn't even noticed on the lawn and danced, but soon couples of all ages crowded on.

I watched the dancing long enough to see that they favored a

sort of two-step, then I pulled Eudora up and we danced until we were soaked. We made a good impression, and soon we were off the floor and talking with groups of our new neighbors, who were mostly interested in telling us about our other new neighbors.

I excused myself from one such group, wiping my brow with a handkerchief and dabbing ineffectually at my shirtfront. I walked past empty plates that had briefly held sandwiches and fried tomatoes, past a plate of grey-looking sausages with a quartet of flies buzzing around them, and then I wandered near a plate of salted fish. I inspected them to see if any one of them looked better than its fellows. None did. A small boy walked over, looking first at the fish and then up at me.

"No, you go ahead," I said. The boy took them all. A woman marched into view and glared at the boy until he replaced all but one.

"That one, too," she said. He put it back. Then she grabbed a hank of his hair and led him off into the darkness from which they had both emerged, saying "Ain't no Jesus here to make more of em. You better learn that sometimes people's jest bein polite. Don't you think that man was about to get him a fish afore he saw you lookin at em like a underfed dog?"

"No, Mama, he was makin a face."

"I don't care. You take more'n one a anything off a plate again an I'll . . ."

I turned away so my worst ear was towards them, cutting off the rest. When I turned, I found that a man had come up quite close to me.

"Looks like one little brave's getting summoned off to powwow," the man said, adding, "Have a drink, Mr. Nichols."

I recognized him; someone had pointed him out to me as the town's taxidermist.

He held out a glass of what looked like watered-down lemonade, and I took it. When it got near my face, however, the smell of grain alcohol rushed at me like something that had been too long in a cage. I drank gratefully, taking a good look now at the short, tough-looking man in front of me.

"My name's Cranmer, Martin Cranmer, taxidermist, but you already know that. I saw some of the old chickens pointing and whispering. Doubtless you've also learned about my cannibalism and ties to the communist party."

Young John Brown, I thought suddenly, struck less by the man's hooked nose than by the drilling grey eyes that hinted at some denomination of madness. A lush but forbidding dark beard mostly hid Cranmer's mouth and stood out in contrast to his suit, which was cream-colored, short at the wrists and crotch, and so ill-fitting generally that it might have been sent mail-order two sizes small and not returned out of indifference. It also looked innocent of professional attempts to clean it; stains on the sleeves were subtle but numerous, some of them likely dating back to Hoover.

"Thanks for the drink," I said, wiping my mouth with the heel of my hand. "Brother, you don't know how long it's been. Alright, only about ten days, but it feels like ten months."

"I have a still. It's a big secret I like to tell everybody."

Cranmer didn't have the drawl everybody else in town had. He actually said *I like*, not *Ah lahk*. What was that accent? Midwestern?

"Did you get some squirrel?" Martin asked, indicating a plate with several small, roasted carcasses on them.

"Not yet."

"Well, it might not look like much, but I peppered the little sons of bitches into a stupor, and it's a damn sight fresher than what the butcher brought. It would kill him to give away something he could sell. I think he's part Jew. Nothing against the Jews, except they like their money and they killed Jesus, but if they hadn't we wouldn't have anything to sing about on Sundays."

I laughed.

Martin continued.

"I wanted to say hello earlier but you and the young lady were having a fine old time dancing. I was sure the fiddle player would wear out before you two did. Of course, Sully only has one testicle, and it's natural to assume a fellow in that condition would have diminished stamina, although that's not necessarily true. Sully's still burning up that fiddle. They say he cut one off to stay out of the war. He should have done what I did and hid in the woods. Anyway, that's immaterial. All I meant to say is, it's good to see people really enjoy each other."

"Have you met my wife?" I said.

Did Cranmer raise his left eyebrow just a little?

"Later," he said. "It looks like she's occupied."

Eudora was standing with Ursie and her parents, moving her hands as she spoke. She sensed my gaze and smiled brightly at me without interrupting her speech.

"Quite a bond between you two," Martin said. "Shines, it really does. I like that."

"Are you a married man?"

"What do you think?"

"I think a wife wouldn't let you keep that beard."

"Good! An honest man. Me, too. Honesty's why I like hookers. Have to ride a fuck-all long way on my bicycle for that, though."

"I haven't done that since the war," I said.

"What, ride a bicycle?"

"That either."

Martin chuckled, then took a tin of cigarettes out of his coat pocket, lighting two of them and passing one to me as if it were sacred. He had rolled them himself, and the tobacco was so strong my throat would hurt all night from it.

"Thank God some new meat showed up in town. Not your lady. I mean you. I mean conversation. Quite honestly, you're the only reason I put on this ape suit and pedaled out here."

"I'm flattered."

"They say you're educated. A professor of history. Me, I'm self-educated. I like books. I like to talk about books. No offense, but most of the God-fearing folk around here have trouble reading a can of soup. I mean, they'll whip your biscuits in a game of checkers at the general store, and most of them can quote Genesis and Exodus alright, but chess is right out. The most political they ever got was when half of them wrote letters to Sears and Roebuck when they switched the catalog to glossy paper."

"Why did they care?"

"Because they had to go back to wiping their asses with corn."

I laughed.

"So does a self-educated man find satisfaction in the preservation of dead animals?"

"Satisfaction? Not exactly. But when I make a good mount I feel

like I beat God in a small way. As though the Almighty said, *Let thus and such critter be dead*, and I said, 'Fuck You, he can still play the banjo.' Are you a devout man, Mr. Nichols?"

"I can't say that I am."

"Excellent. We might be friends. But we won't hunt together."

"I don't hunt."

"I know."

"Excuse me?"

"You make a lot of noise and you don't see or hear too well. Don't be offended. You're a fine dancer. I dance like you hunt."

"You figured all this out tonight?"

"Not tonight. Yesterday. I was setting a trap near the Wheeler house, you know, the place that burned down. There's a rabbit warren nearby. Anyway, there you came with Lester, stepping on every twig and dried leaf you could find like the whole world was your friend, taking pictures with that little camera. Look close when you bring those pictures out; I'm probably in one of them."

Cranmer told me how to get to his cabin and left me with a standing invitation to play chess. He did not speak to anybody else, although he nodded at Lester Gordeau and made a troll face at a towheaded boy who stared at him too long. And then he clambered onto a bicycle and pedaled off into the night. I pictured Martin walking the bike through the rough terrain of the forest in his mismeasured suit, but the image did not make me laugh. No image of Martin Cranmer in the woods seemed improbable. He looked like he had been carved from the hardest tree in them.

CHAPTER SEVEN

Eudora didn't want me to go across the river on Wednesday.

"Those woods aren't friendly," she said. This as I laced up the hiking boots I had just oiled.

I played dumb.

"What are you talking about?"

"I don't know."

"Is it that pig business?"

"Partly, I suppose. It makes me wonder what else goes on around here."

"I understand they tie a nude virgin to the back of a bull to celebrate the equinox."

"Oh. Well, I needn't worry about that."

"Unless they ask you to be the bull. Stubborn thing."

That was a mistake.

"Who's stubborn, Orville Francis? No, I mean it. You're going no matter what I say or do. If I hung myself on the front porch, you'd just leave out the kitchen door."

"Now you're talking nonsense," I said. "We have no rope."

She just sighed at that.

"Would you feel better if I took a pistol?"

"Worse."

"May I take your little Brownie camera? I'll get a picture of the bogeyman for you."

"Fine. I don't care what happens to you anymore; you're too difficult. But have my camera home by dark."

I left soon after that, but her disapproval kept eating at me all the way up to the river.

Why?

Because she's right.

As I hiked along the path Lester had shown me, I mused about Dora and how she might be spending her day. If there had been anyone around to bet, I would have wagered my best pair of shoes that she was in the study nosing around in my affairs. Not that I minded. I had nothing to hide from her, and a woman who doesn't snoop after her man is either highly moral or doesn't care enough. Eudora Anne Chambers, née Morton, was not highly moral. Most probably she was leaning back in my leather chair with my photograph box open on her lap, sorting through pictures from before I met her. She did that a great deal. She was especially fond of pictures of my mother, whom she only knew through photographs.

My mother was uncommonly photogenic. Portraits from around the turn of the century usually made people come off stiff and doll-like because they had to hold their expression so long. Not so with Mother. She gave herself to the lens as if she knew she wouldn't last, and so entrusted it with a disproportionate share of her being. She stares back from photographs as though trapped alive in them. The most striking one shows her in Atlanta just before she came to Chicago with the touring company; she was playing the title role in a translation of Racine's *Phaedra*, looking very much the vengeful seductress with her high cheekbones and penetrating eyes. They were the eyes of a thirty-year-old. She was eighteen.

Piecing together things my father had said in front of me while booze loosened his tongue, I believe my maternal grandfather had taken liberties with her for quite some time. It was these liberties, I believe, which had provoked her to run away from Whitbrow to Atlanta at fifteen, where she found work first in vaudeville and then with a Shakespeare troupe. A discreet but inept medical procedure during her Atlanta years had likely been responsible for her later difficulty carrying children. In one photograph of her holding me in a lacy toddler's gown, her face bears an expression that most would take to be ecstatic distraction, but which I think may have been bewilderment.

There were a lot of pictures in that box that Eudora enjoyed mooning over. She liked my school pictures. In one of them, Dan Metzger, John Giangrande and I were posing on the basketball court at St. Ignatius. Dan was too husky for basketball and got dropped from the team shortly after, but in that photograph he looked as proud as he could be.

Dan was one of the friendliest and sweetest guys I ever knew. He was always half a head taller than the other kids and naturally built to carry weight, but he was soft. The meaner kids knew it and, when they could catch him alone, circled him like wolves around a bison. This never lasted too long before his friends came to help him and it turned into a proper tussle. If it was at school, Father Patterson would come out with two yardsticks taped together and scatter us. Following a general round of spankings (Father Patterson favored the backs of the thighs), it was even money whether his tormenters would get lectured for bullying, Dan would get lectured for not standing up for himself, or I would get lectured for my "flawed moral silhouette." For a Jesuit, Father Patterson was remarkably inconsistent; I think he believed Jesus was happy as long as everyone was beaten and anyone at all was rebuked.

When the war broke out, Dan and I signed up for the Illinois National Guard together, along with our mutual buddy from St. Ignatius, John Giangrande, whom the Poles, Irish and well-bred Anglo-Saxons of St. Ignatius had christened "Guinea-Granny" because of his name and the tiny, wire-framed glasses that were always slipping down his nose. We all had glasses, but his looked like an old lady's, and he was unmistakably Italian, so the name stuck for good. His friends respectfully dropped the "Guinea" part, but there was no shaking "Granny." He was two years older than us, but small and weak. He hung out with us gladly, having been socially rejected by his peers. Uncle Sam didn't reject him, though. When the army found out how good Granny was at chemistry, they yanked him out of the 33rd Prairie and shipped him off to the 1st Gas battalion at the Edgewood Arsenal in Maryland.

Dan and I stayed in the 33rd and went through training together stateside, both at Camp Grant and Camp Logan. He had barely made weight when we joined, but by the time he got done training he was skinnier than me. We were on that reeking ship together all the way to Brest. In short, we were inseparable from fourth grade until the shelling at Nine Elms trench on the Somme, which was in July of 1918.

We were so goddamned eager to go.

We were so stupid.

I MADE THE river around two.

Unfortunately, the raft or ferry I had seen with Lester was nowhere in sight; I had wandered off of the crossing point. I looked upriver and then downriver, but couldn't determine which was the right way to go.

Gordeau had said the river wasn't very deep, but looking at it didn't help; the surface just reflected the hazy brass sky above it while pieces of moss and sticks floated by. He had mentioned water moccasins, and I could see that the bunches of reeds and lichen-covered rocks on both banks would provide ample hiding places for such.

"To hell with it," I said to nobody.

I put the camera down, removed my shoes, tucked my socks in them and waded out to test the depth of the river. The bed was mostly soft underfoot, but the mud and clay were punctuated with rocks that proved slippery; I nearly fell twice before I got to the

middle and determined that it wasn't likely to get worse than hip-deep. I returned to the bank and, deciding it was too far for me to throw my shoes across, I tied the strings together and hung them around my neck. I carried the camera up over my head and crossed; about mid-river I got a case of the giggles when I imagined I was Saint Christopher holding the Holy Babe aloft.

What's your name, little fellow? My, but you are getting heavy. But I shall not drop you, for I am Holy.

Lester Gordeau's instructions had included a landmark called Madge-Eye Rock, which was as far as he had claimed to have ever gone in this direction.

"When you git bout a mile an a half pass the river, keepin to the trail, you'll come to a little spring called Madge-Eye Rock. Ain't too big, but the water out of it is cold and good drinkin, sept that taste like it come out of a skillet. S'pose to be bad luck to drink out of it, or not to drink out of it, I cain't recall. They's all kind a stories bout them woods pass the river."

"Magi," I said when I saw it, "as in Three Magi."

I had spent some time during my walk trying to puzzle out what a madge-eye could be, but now it was clear what the christener of the spring had seen; three separate but connected shelves of rock rose to chest level, each of them producing a small trickle of water that drained off into a sort of sink. Orange stains beneath the spigots and in the sink testified to large quantities of iron in the water, which I tasted when I cupped my hand beneath the central spigot and put it to my mouth.

Cold.

The source was deep.

I had tasted water from such a well, years before, in England, where I had convalesced after my injury in France. My dad had pulled strings so I got a good long leave overseas before I came home for decommissioning.

Everything in England was so tidy, though. America was the wild one now. The rock shelf wore a crown of ferns and moss, and, behind the spring, on the higher level, rocks jutting out from beneath the topsoil suggested a tail pointing deeper into the woods. It was pretty here.

I filled my canteen.

I pressed on another hundred yards. What I saw then did not precisely frighten me, but it made me uneasy. Pine trees had begun again to compete with their deciduous cousins, and two of them stood on opposite sides of the trail, like columns. Like some sort of gate.

They had both been gouged.

I mused that in colonial days the great pine forests of the South had been treasuries for resin, pitch, tar and turpentine, but that the British navy held American pitch in some contempt, for it was too hot and burned the ropes. I knew that sap was gathered by making slaves notch the trees on both sides and take from them until the trees died and could be burned to make tar.

These two pines did not bear the marks of agriculture; they had been savaged. Just at the level of a grown man's trouser pockets. No saw or axe had done this, but I was hard-pressed to say what had. I did not know if the gouges were intended to discourage further exploration, but looking at them gave me a curious feeling in my groin.

I kept going.

Soon after that I lost the trail and stumbled into a patch of nettles. They barbed the hell out of me, even through my pants, before I managed to peel myself free and continue on. I would have to stay more focused; I couldn't afford to lose time if I intended to find the battlefield, which Lester said his daddy told him was a half mile north of the trail two or three miles past Magi Rock, "in some young birch and dogwoods where they mix up with pine."

I felt embarrassed about losing the trail. Martin Cranmer was right about my woodsmanship; I was a Chicago boy through and through, awkward and top-heavy in the woods. What's more, it was no mean feat for me to even enter a forest after the Argonne. I had worked on that in Michigan, taking long walks alone in the woods near Ann Arbor, even if I had to get boozed up to do it; it wouldn't have done for a grown man to spend the rest of his life getting the tremors every time he was surrounded by trees, afraid the next snapped twig would be followed by the bark of a machine-gun nest opening up. By and by it had gotten better.

I thought about Cranmer crouching in the trees near the burnt-down house. Or was that a conceit on my part, imagining Martin *had* to crouch to avoid my notice? But then, Lester hadn't seen him, either. Dora had not seemed to like Cranmer very much. Had she gotten an extra earful of gossip about him when she was in town?

While I was musing on the war, Martin and Dora, I worked at removing a sticker that had gone deep into the heel of my hand. All I did was drive it deeper; I would have to dig for it later with whiskey and a pocketknife.

When I looked up, I saw that I had lost the trail again.

This time was worse because I had no idea how long it had been

since I went astray. I turned around 180 degrees and marched with my eyes fixed on the forest floor, hoping I would recognize the trail again when I crossed it. A distressing amount of time passed before I noticed a recession and turned right, praying it would start to look path-like. It did.

I stopped and crouched down on my heels for a moment to rest. I took a long, cool swig from my canteen, delighting in the taste of the iron. I thought back to my days in Glastonbury, England. Somerset County, where clotted cream on a scone was the culinary equivalent of a naked girl in a field of wildflowers.

I had worked several weeks for the gardener at the Chalice Well. Less for the money than for an excuse to linger around that odd little town. The spigot in the well had been made in the shape of a lion's head, and the water had been clean and cold and rusty, just like the water out of Magi Rock. There was a cat that used to nose my hand as I weeded or pruned, the cat the girl I was sleeping with called Bully because it bore the marks of so much fighting. My own wounds had still been fresh then, particularly those inside, but the waters of the well had helped to make me whole. I believe that. And I wasn't the only one who thought there was something to the stories about that place. I met other veterans there, too; the Chalice Well called the walking wounded to it. I had been twenty then, and I had liked to imagine the waters of the spring below running over the bones of Arthur and Guinevere, bringing their strength to those who needed it. Twenty years old and through with God—whose ears I believed had numbed with too much prayer, or deafened from the noise of shelling—I had asked that place to heal me, and it had.

Mostly.

This forest was a *place*, too, the way Glastonbury had been a *place*.

There was something powerful here, something beyond the reach of lightbulbs and combustion engines.

It was soon after I got going again that I began to feel watched. I stopped.

It was around five o'clock. The day's heat had reached its zenith and was easing off at last. The shadows had just begun to stretch. The feeling that I was being supervised was so intense it made the back of my neck feel warm.

I stopped and opened my mouth, which I often did to help my blighted hearing. I adjusted my glasses. I even tried to engage my nose. Nothing moved. I heard only the cruder noises; birdsong and the screeching of a squirrel warning its neighbors, whether about me or something else, I did not know. I smelled the stone-littered, black soil of the forest, how fecund it was. Trees in all their variety pushed sap, and summer flowers peddled their fragrances to the summer air; the drought that was parching half the state had not come to Whitbrow, as if the tops of these trees gouged the rain clouds and bled them out before they could save the farms over the county line.

I started walking again, minding the diminished undergrowth that comprised the trail, but keeping part of my awareness on the forest around me.

"Goddamnit, someone's out there," I mouthed. No one of my senses reported the presence; I simply knew I was not alone.

Could it be one of the pigs?

No. Pigs were not subtle. Pigs did not stalk.

I would have to turn around soon if I wanted to be home by dark, but I was not ready to turn around yet. Some part of me craved confrontation with whatever was out there.

Not far off to my right, crows called and took to their wings.

There it is; we have something.

"Salutations!" I called out.

Was it Cranmer? I didn't know the man well enough, after all, to know what sort of monkeyshines he was capable of.

"Martin?"

A tardy crow took off from the brush to join its fellows.

Crows don't spook easily.

"It is I, Nanook of the North, and I come in peace," I said.

That was when I saw him.

The boy stepped into view. A thin, pale mulatto just entering puberty. I knew this because the boy wasn't wearing pants. Just a dirty shirt that stopped at his navel.

"Hey there!" I said. "Are you alright?"

The boy said nothing. Just stood there with one hand on a tree, looking intently at me.

"Where are your pants, my friend?"

Silence.

"Fine, that's fine," I said, turning my gaze from the boy and continuing down the path. The boy kept his distance but kept pace with me. It was clear that he had not come forward because he had been discovered; it was simply time for me to see him.

The two of us walked for a moment silently, the other keeping about twenty yards off the trail.

I spoke.

"We can play this way if you like. You be the naked lad of the woods, and I will be the dressed man of the trail. Is it that you own no pants, or do you reject the idea of pants altogether? I can't say I blame you. It is a hot day. Perhaps, if I had any sense, I would remove my pants and cool off a little. The thing is, I know I would feel embarrassed. But look at you; you don't seem to feel embarrassed at all. I envy you that. Waving your pecker about in the breeze like a primal man, that's first-class."

No effect.

I stopped walking now, and so did the boy. I took a big, burlesque step to see if the one in the trees would mimic me, but the other stood still. Another clownish step, and a third, daring the apparition, but it did not move, not until I got fed up and started walking down the path again.

The boy caught up to me easily and regained his measure.

What in hell does he want?

I remembered a French *poilu* who called one light-skinned mulatto gravedigger *café au lait* during those bleak days of the Meuse offensive, how I had laughed with the other soldier just to have someone to laugh with. Besides, *café au lait* would be shoveling dirt over our blanched faces soon enough. *Café au lait.* It occurred to me to shout that at the boy who was stalking me now, and I felt disgusted with myself. How easily the paint of civilization peels off with a little bad weather.

"What do you want?" I said, walking. It was getting late. My guilt at the thought of using a racial slur gave way again to exasperation.

"Just say something!"

I tried to fight back my anger. What if the young man was a deaf-mute, or retarded? No. He had heard every word I said, and there was nothing dull about that gaze.

I was never going to make it back if I didn't turn around soon. I did not want to be out here in the dark, especially not with that boy. I didn't want the boy near me anymore.

"Get out of here!" I shouted. "What the hell are you looking at, anyway?"

I stopped, and the other did, too. Yes, here it came. I was losing my temper.

"Say, you don't mind if I take your picture for the wife? She won't believe me when I tell her I saw a real, live deranged person in the woods today."

I lifted the box of the camera to my face. Through the lens, I saw the boy stoop. I snapped the shutter just as the boy threw the stone.

"Jesus!" I said, and nearly dropped the Brownie. The stone had grazed my hand, not far from the knuckle of my ring finger. It would leave a welt.

"You son of a bitch!"

Another rock whizzed down, this one smaller, and I deflected it with the camera. Something cracked.

"I'm just about to slap you shitless!"

My free hand made a fist and I stepped towards the other, who backed up gracefully, not fleeing so much as keeping a precise distance between us. The boy put his arms out, hands open. His face, only too lucid, bore a hint of a smile, and the meaning was clear: *Yes, by all means chase me off the path, and when night comes I will show you other games besides the following and the rock-throwing.*

I stopped. The other took up a hurtful-looking flat stone. I backed up to the trail and the other kept distance with me. He threw. I sidestepped it, put the camera down and selected a rock of my own. I did not have the aim the boy had, however, and my missile whacked heavily into a tree that was closer to me than to him. The boy's fresh throw tumbled, another flat stone, and mercifully smacked my thigh broadside rather than digging in edge-first. It stung, though, and I yelped.

When I looked up, I noticed that the boy had the beginnings of an erection. I stared. Just when I decided that the stone-thrower was a lunatic, the boy did something that disturbed me more than anything thus far.

Though he had no trousers, he mimicked the gesture of a man reaching for something in his pocket. A watch. He opened the pretend pocket watch, looked at it and then looked up at the sky.

It will be dark soon.

The boy smiled fully then.

His teeth had been filed sharp.

CHAPTER EIGHT

No MORE STONES followed me out of the forest. I backed away
from the stone-thrower, who did not pursue me. I did not
have time to decide what I had seen; I could think about that later.
I simply backed away from it and it stood there, and, when I had
put some distance between us, I turned around and moved down
the trail at something less than a run but more than a walk.

I calmed down when I got to the river, although the sun had
westered so that it was nearly twilight. I would just make it home
if I kept my pace up and did not wander.

But I did not go straight home.

The frogs and crickets were singing in the darkening woods
when I got to Cranmer's cabin. It was only ten minutes from the
trail, past a series of little cairns he had left for moonshine buyers

to follow. I wanted very badly to talk to someone about the stone-thrower. This was not a confidence I would share with Eudora, and I would never be able to close my eyes if I had to take this quietly to bed with me.

I walked past the odds and ends of Cranmer's yard; an axe buried in a tree stump, a loose circle of stones describing a fire pit, an old boiler pitted with rust, a dry-rotten saddle and the still Martin had mentioned. It was a great mystery to me how anyone could make liquor out of such an improvised mess; a copper tub, a series of barrels, copper tubing everywhere. Mason jars lay around in disarray. Flies swarmed over a heap of innards and discarded skins set off from the main house.

The windows of Martin's cabin had makeshift bars across them, bars of scavenged iron through which nothing was getting in or out. As I approached the door I saw a peephole open in it, and then heard the sound of heavy bolts being drawn.

The door opened, and Martin Cranmer came outside, half shutting it behind him. His flannel work shirt was sopped with sweat, and the whole of Cranmer smelled like an old glove.

"What are you doing here?" he said, and when his mouth opened I smelled stale tobacco on top of everything else.

"Taking you up on your invitation."

"Invitation doesn't apply tonight. Go the hell home."

I said nothing.

"Don't just flap your gills at me, there's no time. Go home and stay there. And I mean run, don't walk. Shit."

"What goes on around here, Martin?"

Cranmer disappeared into his cabin and came out with his rickety bicycle. He took the camera from me, put the handlebars in my hands and said, "Bring it back tomorrow or the next day. Now, if I have to order you off my property one more time I'm going to stuff you and send you back to your wife with a glass asshole."

The door shut hard.

THE SKY TOOK on a chalky pink color and the moon rose fat and golden past the tree line as I pedaled home. My ass was sore from the hard ride, and the palms of my hands were skinned from a low-velocity spill I had taken about five minutes before. Dora was waiting on the porch, letting her feet dangle off the edge. She was opening and closing a parasol, one that had belonged to my mother when she used to stroll around downtown Chicago thirty-five years ago, so full of beauty it seemed the century would have to ask her permission to draw to a close.

I KNEW IT would come and it did.

I lay awake next to Eudora, who had already drifted into sleep still lying on her belly, the hand she had pleasured herself with supinated next to her hip. I had been unwilling to make love to her, unwilling also to discuss why, so she had done what she needed to get to sleep. I watched her back rise and fall with her breathing,

watched also a lock of hair that fluttered ever so delicately near where her lips bunched on the pillow. I loved that she never turned her face away from me in sleep, even when we fought. Not that this had been a fight; just a closing-off on my part and a gracious retreat on hers.

Oh, it was coming.

The dream.

When sleep finally admitted me to its parlor, it would show me something naughty.

I lay staring up now, listening to what must have been every dog in town baying at the rich moon shining china-white past the lace curtains. They admitted light generously; the room glowed. I tried lying motionless but became aware of the arm nearest Dora, and I began to alternate hooking it behind my head and crowding it into the space between our two bodies. I remembered the one-armed man at Harvey's Drug Emporium, and thought, *Well, I suppose there really is a bright side to everything.*

That damned baying.

Even with my fluid-filled, muffled ears I heard it.

The pigs are dying.

Yes, it was a very long time before I got to sleep.

The dream began with the steam machine that came to burn the lice out of our clothes just before the offensive started that September. I was part of a line of white-shouldered, white-haunched men standing in the rain, all of us holding our uniforms in our hands. In the dream the line was apocalyptically long. I noticed one louse crawling off my folded-up coat and onto my arm. The

dream-louse was slightly larger than the real ones, only slightly, and, like its corporeal cousins, off-white and translucent, holding the blood it had consumed in its cross-shaped guts so one could see the dark emblem within it. Like the German cross. Like the Germans had dropped them in cans to devil us.

The landscape had been so maimed by this new kind of warfare it was as if human architects of great genius had sat down to plan hell, since no two of them could agree on the design of heaven. Mud and craters. Rats and gas. Barbed wire and the walking dead. Even in the rain there always seemed to be a fire somewhere. The Book of Revelations read like fairy-tale poetry next to this harsh prose. The steaming of the clothes was just another bureaucratic flourish as far as any of us could see. All it took was sitting on a cot or brushing against another doughboy in the earthworks to re-infest a man, yet someone deemed it necessary. The same someone who was now blowing whistles, scattering the men from line.

An attack!

Every man in the trench, move, MOVE!

I was about to be maimed. I always knew that. I also knew that something was faintly wrong with the chronology; that we should be attacking the Germans, that I should have my clothes on, that my actual injury had happened in one of their trenches as we overcame their defenses. It was as if the nightmare-weavers wanted to show off their artistry by stripping me, making me face the attack again, completely unprepared, humiliated, cold.

I was the first one in, leaping down into the trench with no clothes on—*where are your pants, my friend?*—gripping a pistol in

one hand and a trench-knife in the other. My bare feet sunk nauseatingly into the puddles. For this dream, the artist had a simple palette, mostly grey and ochre. Milky brown water. White arms. Bright grey sky above. Dark grey helmets. The whites of German eyes. Oh, this would be intimate.

And these would be true Germans, scarred and skinny and full of fight, not the green conscripts from Alsace-Lorraine we had frightened off so easily at Bois de Forge weeks before.

The dream-trench was even more labyrinthine than the real one, unspooling itself in hairpin turns like the intestines of some cannibal giant, and I heard the Germans for a long time before I encountered them. My ears were good then, as were my dream-ears. I could hear their watches ticking, the sounds of their pipes and coins joggling in their coat pockets.

It was so slow.

The Germans came around the elbow of the trench at me in their blue-grey coats all grimed with mud. So slow. In life they had been surprised, but in this dream-trench they knew I was there, and I moved so slowly it seemed they waited for me to shoot them. I only had four shots before my pistol would jam, and I used these on the first two men. A thick brown mustache arched over the O of a mouth. A kicked fence of bad teeth. Oh, they watched me do it, and they watched me on their way down.

The pistol quit then.

I threw it at a third man, who ducked, unbalancing himself. I leapt as slowly as a cloud crossing a lake to close with this man, stabbing him so hard it numbed my thumb, stabbing him with his permission, his dimming eyes looking kindly into mine as if to say,

This is really alright, Mr. Nichols; I would rather fold up and sit in this brown water than to take one more step in the world, unfair as it is. No harm done, and I will see you again quite soon. The next time anything in waking life gets under your skin, in fact. Or perhaps just the next time I'm lonely. You see, nobody living remembers my face as well as you do.

The next German pointed his pistol directly at my face, then turned it and shot behind me, hitting another American boy instead, who shrieked womanishly, unforgettably. I never understood why I was spared then, or why I didn't cut the German as he ducked under my arm, as if we had a small, secret truce, agreeing to engage the men behind one another. I ran past him with a yell, ducking right to avoid the blade-edge of the next man's shovel, which missed me so nearly I could see individual dirt clots on its surface.

Then, as in the actual fight, I grabbed the shovel with my free hand and drove my knife for my enemy's middle. It caught the belt buckle at the wrong angle and torqued out of my hand, spinning into the muck beneath us. I grappled with the German, a boy my age with a simple white face and eyes rimmed red as if he had been fighting fever, bulling him up against the loose trench wall. I was stronger.

I pried the shovel out of the boy's grip and it fell, too, and then we fell, bracing our hands against each other's faces. My little finger slipped inside the boy's mouth and the boy bit down hard.

In the real event I had wrestled myself on top of the boy and held his face underwater while the rest of my company rushed past and over us to get at the other Germans, one of whom must have tossed the grenade, a potato-masher. The sound it made was the

clanging of St. Michael's sword on the brain-pan, so loud its noise was an absence of noise.

The war was over for me, and for several others caught nearby. The doctors said the only reason the shrapnel that entered my back didn't kill me was because it had to pass through other matter first. I never learned which of my dead friends comprised that other matter. Nor did I learn the fate of the boy beneath me. Had my body saved him from the grenade, or did the weight of it finish drowning him? I knew prisoners had been taken. I liked to imagine the boy was one of them. That he was released after the war. I liked to imagine the boy surviving to robust manhood; my favorite day-dream placed him on a farm in Bavaria, teaching a healthy blond son the game of locking middle fingers with an opponent and pulling to see whose grip was stronger.

The dream was different.

The boy and I sat up like children playing in the mud.

Where are your pants, my friend?

The boy clamped my wrist in an unbreakable grip and bit off the little finger at the knuckle, but he did not stop there.

He ate every finger I had.

Dora woke me, kneeling above me, shaking me.

"Darling, darling, Frankie, Orville Francis," she was saying.

I opened my eyes wide.

"GET OFF ME, STOP, STOP!! FUCK! Fuck. God. Oh God."

"You're alright, it's me, it's me, my love, you're fine."

We looked at each other, she kneeling above me in the moonlight, not crying as she used to when this happened.

How like a Sphinx in her nightgown.

A man. A man goes on four legs in the morning, two in the after-noon, and uses a cane at night.

"You're okay, Frankie. You're home."

She kissed my fingers.

I jerked my hand away.

CHAPTER NINE

THE MORNING LIGHT coming in through the lace curtains did much to restore my constitution. It was a grey light, threatening rain, and the wind was beginning to move in the boughs and under the eaves, but, as I watched Dora comb out her bob of blond hair in the mirror, I felt the unease slipping from me. It was a new day. There was nothing simpler or more healing. France and all its horrors had receded, taking that penny dreadful in the forest with it. Maybe I hadn't seen the boy at all. My exhaustion and the poor light had made my eyes play tricks on me. The bruises and welts weren't from stones, but from the little spill I took off Martin's bicycle. I nearly believed all this revisionism.

I looked at Dora in the mirror and her reflected eyes met mine, asking, *Is it alright now? Have you come back to me?* Then her gaze

shifted slightly off mine as she noticed the firmness I was developing under the sheet. *Yes, I suppose we are fine and well this morning.* A smile broadened across her face, taking its time. I got out of bed, holding the sheet before me like a torero's cape. She liked this game. She backed up, displaying the hairbrush before her in the *en garde* position, but I moved in on her quickly, wrapping the sheet around her head and shoulders. I threw her down on the bed while she squealed protestations that turned to softer noises when I set my mouth to the middle of her, her own mouth a damp indentation in the sheet.

At length, we breakfasted and took coffee. Dora cleaned up and put on a summer dress, as well as the hat with the dried rose, while I selected a tawny vest and my favorite sky-blue tie.

"I hope the old sawbones knows what he's doing. It would be a shame to bleed on this fine summer outfit," I said.

"Bleed all you want, as long as you pass," she said, adjusting a garter.

"Me? What about as long as *you* pass?"

"Oh, I'll do just fine."

"Of course. I forgot that you took one of these before."

"That was unkind, sir," she said, smiling, then reapplying lipstick. "I will remind you that one of us was rolling around Paris and London in the most undesirable company while the other was still drawing hopscotch squares on the sidewalk."

"Yes, and one of us put down her hopscotch chalk and marched straight for the altar."

"A frightful mistake. I insist on a civil ceremony this time."

"A pity you weren't a Catholic. You could have gotten it annulled. You could have said you showed up in your confirmation dress and this mean priest changed all the words around."

"My point, sir. You used that one before."

"No, I didn't! When?"

"On a whiskey roar at your brother's in May. The same evening in which you told everyone what a good teacher I would make because the perfection of my bottom would stun the class into silence when I turned my back to write on the blackboard."

"Forty-love," I conceded. "Now, if your face is sufficiently painted, I suggest we get that blood test before my syphilis finds my forwarding address."

WE TOOK THE measly and petty dirt roads that surrounded Whitbrow until they joined up with the highway that led to the mill town. Fat splats of rain hit the windshield about halfway there, but the sky withheld the deluge that farmers across six counties had been concocting strange prayers and even writing letters to the president to bring. One dispossessed family walking down the road was glad the rain had not come yet. The father carried a mattress on his back and looked only where he was going, but the wife and the older children watched our car pass them as if we might have the deed to their new house rolled up in the glove box.

By two o'clock the blood was sitting in vials at the clinic waiting to be sniffed for corruption. Eudora found a telephone and rang her

lawyer in Michigan, who confirmed that her divorce was settled and the papers would be in her hands within days, provided the post office did its job.

We decided to celebrate, so we went to a little family joint called the Victoria Café. Our roast beef, rich and fatty, would have tasted better without the image of the starving family marching down the road.

"I wonder if they have a soup kitchen here," she said.

"I suppose. Why?"

"I should like to work in it."

I said nothing, just looked at her and kept chewing.

She continued.

"I know it's not practical, or perhaps even possible, it's just that it's so damned dismal here, and it's hard to eat roast beef."

"You want to work in a soup kitchen so you'll feel better about eating roast beef?"

"Do you think things are worse here than in Whitbrow?"

"A mill town with two out of three mills boarded up is a hard place to scratch up a nickel. I suppose it is worse. At least in Whitbrow they can grow enough to eat. I mean, nobody there is starving, but they haven't got *things*."

"I know they haven't," she said. "Do you know that the teacher of the lower grades makes a present of a bar of soap to her best pupil every month, and the kids fight over it. A bar of soap."

She looked out the window at a freckled old man who stopped on the sidewalk to look up at the sky, which was still holding forth the prospect of rain. He held his hat to his head to keep a gust of wind from blowing it off.

"Lots of kids with bare feet, too," she said. "It seems they could buy an awful lot of shoes for the price of a healthy sow. Why do they do it, Frank? The Chase, they call it. Looks like they're chasing money they can't spare off into the wilderness. They must have just herds of wild pigs running around those woods."

Pigs, and something else besides.

Where are your pants, my friend?

"I don't know why they do it. Why do people build cathedrals, or flagellate themselves or throw salt over their shoulder? Maybe it makes the corn grow greener."

"So you approve?"

"I'm not saying I approve or disapprove. I'm just saying it's not our place to judge them."

"I don't like it," she said.

"So don't like it."

"So don't like it," she said, parroting me, stirring a piece of meat around in its gravy.

"Dora, we're here to have a gay time. In the big city. Let's not quarrel."

"Well," she said, her eyes shining with good humor, "what we're actually here for is to see if we're going to expire from a horrid social disease. But while we're in town, it wouldn't hurt for us to see the picture show. And try not to quarrel."

WE SAW A matinee, a pirate epic full of booming cannons that made me edgy. After the show we stopped for bottles of wine and

bourbon before we got in the car and headed home. She rested her head on my shoulder, but the air was heavy between us. I wanted to peek into that lovely head and know what she was thinking, even if it hurt me. Even if she was remembering a time before she knew me and thinking that was better.

Chapter Ten

Martin Cranmer sat across from me, absently brushing the wooden cheeks and mane of the knight he had captured. He had made that knight with his own hands, along with all the other pieces, the chessboard, the table it sat on, and the chairs beneath us. He had built his crude little house from scratch, from the hickory beams to the pine shingles. All of this was very humbling to a man like me who had trouble hanging a painting without mashing his thumb.

I could tell from the kingly way he jutted his chin up while waiting for my move that he felt good about the game; he had taken a pawn unanswered, then made me double up my pawns in another exchange. The knight he was so affectionately grooming had been hedged in and taken at the cost of two pawns. But the

time he had spent getting up on matériel was going to cost him; I had castled my king away safely in the corner, and now both rooks had found open pathways to the center of the board, pointing into Martin's splayed forces like a brace of cannon.

"Suddenly I don't feel so cocksure," Martin said, striking a match on the rough surface of his table and lighting a potent, home-rolled cigarette. He offered a second one to me, but I shook my head and pulled a civilized little Chesterfield from the cigarette holder in my trouser pocket. I could not remember having sat in a room so heavily impregnated with smoke, nor having met anyone so thickly cured with tobacco as this taxidermist.

I moved my queen, forking Martin's rook and the bishop Martin had left undefended in the earlier bloodletting. He moved the knight out to protect the rook from the queen's diagonal attack, so she slid laterally and captured the bishop.

"Oh, for Christ's sake," Martin said, standing up and gesturing with open hands as if to show a stuffed beaver on the bookshelf what a tale of woe was unfolding on the board. He paced for a moment and sat back down. His eyes remained nailed to the chessboard as he took another swallow from the jar of white lightning sitting on the corner of the table. It was not yet noon.

Martin did not speak again for the next series of moves, not until his king was checkmated, smothered behind its own pawns by rook and bishop. He stood up and paced again, looking at the beaver, then offered his hand to me.

"Fine playing. It's been a while since I've been beat, but that's not saying much around here."

"I thought I was in trouble at the start. You really came out swinging."

"Yeah, I came out swinging, but then I stepped on my filberts. Or you stepped on them. Anyway, they got stepped on. Fine playing. Now, if we talk about it anymore I'm going to get in a bad mood."

"Fine by me. What would you like to talk about?"

Martin sat down and leaned forward in his seat, pointing his hawkish nose at me. It looked like quite a weapon above that beard.

"How about what a man of your smarts plans to do out here in the middle of the wilderness. Other than sit around your new house all day in your skivvies waiting to get your first hemorrhoid."

"Too late."

He chuckled like a can full of gravel and then raised his jar of moonshine in a silent toast.

"They say you're going to write some book. That true?"

"Yes."

"What's the book about?"

"Brigadier General Lucien 'Luke' Savoyard, commander of the 18th Georgia Cavalry. Owner of the plantation that has been reclaimed by Megiddo Woods."

He scowled and tugged at his beard as if testing to see if it were real. Then he laughed and shook his head disbelievingly.

"What do you want to write about that fucker for?"

"Because he makes people react like you just did. And because he's my great-grandfather."

"I know. But if I were you, I wouldn't go telling people that."

"Why?"

"People have long memories around here."

"What I'm really interested in is how the slaves rose up and killed him after the Union troops failed to dislodge him."

"You don't know anything about it."

"It sounds like you might. I'd be grateful for whatever you could tell me."

"All I know is hearsay."

"That gives me someplace to start."

"Just rumors and gossip and bullshit. I won't insult your intelligence. But really, how did a reasonable fellow like you take an interest in a piece of . . . in a man like your great-granddaddy?"

"I love history. Maybe it's like your interest in taxidermy. God pronounces a critter dead and I say I can still make him play the banjo."

He laughed hard and his eyes shone with camaraderie. He filled my glass. I spoke again.

"Savoyard was always verboten. Forbidden fruit. My daddy's family was Illinois Yankee through and through. His father fought with Sherman. His grandfather was a banker who funded abolitionists. So he falls in love with this haunted young Southern belle and marries her. Now he learns her granddaddy was a Confederate cavalry officer, and worse: a slave speculator with an unparalleled reputation for cruelty."

"That's fair to say about Savoyard. Yep."

"Mother wasn't to talk about her family to me. And she didn't. But when I got to college, I started digging it up for myself. My father's secrecy about the Confederates on the other side of my

family tree is almost certainly responsible for my decision to be a history major. I wrote my thesis on minor engagements peripheral to Sherman's march, and touched on the action at the plantation then."

"'Peripheral to Sherman's march.' Christ, it's sweet to hear a man use big words that aren't Bible names. So you were in France?"

"I was."

"Did you lose anybody?"

"My best friend, Dan. We were getting shelled at a place called Nine Elms trench. The Krauts really had our number that day. They gave us two hours' worth. I had never been in anything like that before and I was starting to fall apart, what with all the noise and shaking and dirt raining everywhere. But especially from not knowing where the next one was going. Then it happened. One landed almost in our laps. The concussion blew Danny against the side of the trench so hard his pants came half off and a big loop of his guts came out his back door."

"Jesus. That'll fuck somebody up in a hurry."

"Yeah. He was done."

"I meant you."

"He just wanted his glasses on. I was so dazed I helped him try to find them, because that seemed like the most important thing. So we were both on all fours trying to pick up little sticks and hot pieces of shell, but my hands were shaking too badly, and there were no glasses anyway. He really thought everything would be okay if he could just find his goddamned glasses."

"What about your glasses?"

"What? Why?"

"Must have knocked your glasses off, too."

"I had spares. I always have spares."

"Prudent."

"I went to see his mother after the war."

"How did that go?"

"Like hell. She brought out a tray of coffee and cookies and was very polite, but every time she looked at me I felt her thinking that I should be in the ground instead of her baby. That I was tougher and could have protected him if I'd tried harder. Nobody ate the cookies. I thanked her for the coffee and left, because there was no way to make things okay. One of the hardest and truest things a grown-up learns is that sometimes it's not okay."

"I'm surprised all of that didn't cure your romantic streak."

"Well, I went to university after the war and got really absorbed in the States' War. That war seemed different. Like the way it should have been."

Martin laughed then, finishing off his moonshine and getting up to fetch another jar.

"You're not interested in the slave uprising at all. You like Savoyard. You *like* the fucker, think you shouldn't, then like him even more. Like some weak-kneed schoolgirl mooning at the town criminal."

"Maybe. Maybe I envy him for having gotten to ride a horse and fight with a saber and dally with the ladies. Childish things like that. But I can never condone his cruelty. His . . . perversity."

"You're disgusted with Savoyard the torturer but infatuated with Savoyard the cavalry officer."

"Yes."

"Seems like you got taught a lesson and wouldn't learn it."

"How so?"

"Most people who've been shot at don't want to hear about people getting shot at. Dressing it all up in different uniforms shouldn't make a difference."

"What do you know about it? You weren't in the AEF, were you? You said you hid in the woods."

"I didn't have to go to France to know France was a sack of shit. It's always a sack of shit. And I'm not blaming you for going."

"*Blaming* me?"

"But you ought to know better now. You ought to leave your general alone. Might not like what you find."

A tortured half minute ticked by.

"You're full of secrets, aren't you?"

His nostrils flared.

"Something else on your mind, Mr. Nichols?"

I think I flared my nostrils, too.

"Shit, just say it," he said.

"What went on the other night?"

"Goddamnit, I knew you were going to ask me that."

"Of course I was going to ask you that. It was very discouraging behavior from someone I was beginning to take a liking to."

"That's sweet."

"You didn't smell like booze. What gave?"

"Why don't you tell me a story, Mr. Nichols. You looked a little green around the gills. What was wrong with *you*?"

"I saw something I wanted to tell you about."

"So tell."

"Now I'm not so sure I saw it."

"That's probably better."

"What?"

"Some things it's better not to be sure about. Would you agree with that?"

"Perhaps," I said. "In general."

"Suppose I were to tell you that something which is outside of your realm of understanding goes on in those woods across the river. Suppose I get specific. You then have no choice but to think that I have boiled my brain. Now suppose I tell you that nothing unusual at all is going on in those woods. You will then remember the way I acted the other night and you will have no choice but to suppose that I have boiled my brain."

"If you dodged checkmates like you dodged questions, you'd be a match for Capablanca."

"I tell you in all seriousness that I have nothing to say that will satisfy you. If you saw something bad past the river, don't cross the river."

"Do you cross the river, Martin?"

"And if you don't like the way I acted on the night of the full moon, stay away from me then. And stay home. Think of those woods as a beautiful woman. Fine to play around with most of the month. But on certain days, go if you want, but don't wear your best shirt. That's all I have to say on the subject."

"Alright. Thank you for the game, but I should get back."

"That's fine, too."

I stood up and smoothed my clothes out, looking for my hat. I found it.

"Don't forget your camera," Martin said, smiling impenetrably. I picked that up, too.

My angry exit wasn't working out at all.

On my way out the door, I paused for a moment when another piece of Martin's handiwork caught my eye. It was a carved wooden diorama featuring a scale model of Miller's General Store, complete with tiny checkerboard and a shot glass for a pickle jar. All the regulars were stuffed mice. An overstuffed mouse in an apron was clearly Paul Miller. A strong-looking mouse in overalls represented a fellow named Buster Simms, whom I would get to know soon. There was a one-armed mouse, too.

"Don't bother looking," he said. "You're not in it. Not yet."

CHAPTER ELEVEN

In the week that followed, things went along just fine.

I was writing. I had introduced the character of Lucien Savoyard and then discussed his grandfather Michel, a Frenchman who had been a hussar in Napoleon's Grande Armée, survived the frozen march in Russia and one in Waterloo. Then I spent half a chapter on Lucien's father, Arnaud, a New Orleans tycoon who made a fortune investing in whaling ships, silk and slaves. These men didn't seem to have childhoods; the fathers had a tradition of shutting the boys up in faraway church schools until they were old enough to show up and inherit. The fathers drowned, or shot themselves in middle age.

The next thing was to introduce Lucien and discuss his decision to move the family's wealth and future to Georgia to take

advantage of the cotton boom. That would include a physical description of the house he would christen La Boudeuse—the Pouting House—and her Louisiana-style architecture.

Of course, what I needed to do quite soon was get into the woods and find the plantation. But not today.

Today I just had to get out of the cellar.

I had moved the dining room table and typewriter down the cellar stairs to get away from the punishing heat in the study, but now the smell of mildew had given me a headache. The greyish, overcast light coming through the cracked ground-level window compounded this. Also, now that I had lost momentum, I kept getting distracted looking at all the boxes of my aunt Dottie's old clothes and goods I had meant to free from their tangle of spider-webs and investigate. The spiders down here were legion.

I needed a break.

It occurred to me to take a walk to Miller's General Store and see about having a glass of sweet tea on the porch. I wasn't the only one that had occurred to; Saturday was a big day there. Several farmers had left their fields for these hours between noon and four to sit in the cool of the porch and play checkers, including a fortyish man named Miles Falmouth whose back had been grieving him "biblical," or "positively Ole Tessament." He was leaning sideways on his bench near the checkerboard, holding forth on the state of his health while waiting for Old Man Gordeau to move.

Gordeau was winning that game. He didn't lose many. Aside from being mayor of the town, he grew black-eyed peas and tomatoes, and kept horses, goats and pigs. His pride lay in his dogs, however. Part bloodhound, Gordeau's dogs had become a recognizable local breed, and he never failed to sell his litters to hunters even several towns away.

I stood behind one-armed Mike, whose attention fluttered between the drama on the checkerboard and the gospel music coming in warm and tinny from Paul's radio inside.

The other seat was filled by Buster Simms, whose wife, I later found out, was called "Mrs. Bust-her-seams" in less Christian circles; but never in front of Buster, whose hands looked big and strong enough to twist a horseshoe straight. Their children, while not attractive in the traditional sense, were a source of pride for the Simms family in that they outweighed any children born in Whitbrow since the Great War. Everything was round in Buster's life. In the summer he sold melons. Pumpkins in the fall.

Buster was the second-best checker player after the old man.

He leaned forward in a way that made his chair look delicate, eager to see what the old man's next move would be. Miles was opening his mouth to ask Paul to change the radio to try to catch a weather report or some feed prices, knowing beforehand that one-armed Mike would protest and lobby for another twenty minutes of gospel.

This was the tableau the large, bald black man froze when he walked past us on the porch and entered the general store, letting the screen door bang behind him so that its little bell rang. Paul Miller would later remember that flies came in with him.

Everyone looked inside to see what his business was.

Aside from the Chicago moving-men, I had not seen a colored in or near Whitbrow.

Jesus, he was big and strong-looking.

That was my first thought. My second was what a good subject for photography he would make; the structure of his face was handsome and symmetrical, and his broad shoulders and thin waist suggested an impressive athleticism. He would have to stand with new clothes, though; the ones he wore were none too clean.

He did not enter the store the way black men often entered white establishments. He did not look down, nor did he state his business by way of asking permission to approach: "Sir, I's comin to ask if you got any cornmeal and how much it coss." In fact, he did not speak at all at first. He just glided in with the light bouncing off the carefully shaved dome of his head, and he went to the goods he wanted as if he had stocked the shelves himself.

He bought salt, coffee and sugar. And a pickle.

"Anything else?" Paul asked, trying to sound neither hostile nor overly friendly.

I expected the man to shake his head, but he spoke. Everyone was looking at him, but he seemed to notice only Paul.

"No, sir. These shall be sufficient. If I think of anything else, I shall return for it."

What was that accent? Caribbean? West Indies?

And then he paid.

As he made his way out, he did something queer; he stopped, holding the door open, and sniffed the air on the porch. And then he looked at me. Not long enough to draw anyone's attention but mine.

He left then, letting the door bang good and hard as he went.

If the flies had in fact arrived with him, they decided to stay.

"How do you like that?" Miles said, once the man was out of earshot. "Nigger said *sufficient*. And Paul jes reached in an jerked him out a pickle like he was gonna get mad if he didn't get his pickle fast enough."

"His money's good," Paul said, coming to stand in the doorway, wiping his hands with a rag.

"Well, hell if I'd feed him, jes reach in and feed him. If you got to take his money, hand him over the tongs and let him get his own damn pickle."

Paul said, "Yeah, and if I'd a done that, you'd a said, 'I cain't believe you let that nigger touch your tongs.' Made me put out two pair a tongs. Ain't no pleasin you about a nigger. Like I said, his money's good as yours."

"Damn right his money's good," Gordeau said. "Less I miss my guess, that's the same one used to bring coins and jewels in to Harry fore he closed up. Old stuff, old watches and shit, God knows where from. I don't think he's been around since that year we got all them grasshoppers."

Buster Simms, who liked boxing and who had won some money at bare-knuckle fights in the mill town before love opened his huge fists, said he thought the man must be a visiting colored fighter.

"Nah," Miles said. "He's one of them sharecroppers working Dwight Newsome's land, up near Chalk Ridge. Either that or he's a squatter livin out in them woods pass the river."

"Ain't no Chalk Ridge nigger built like that," Old Man Gordeau

said. "They all got the pee-lagra. Look like scarecrows and cain't hardly lift their heads. Don't think he's no squatter neither."

"Wait, I know that ole boy," one-armed Mike said.

"Here it comes," said Paul.

"Yeah, he keeps roosters for a gang man outta Chicago. And they say he got him a white woman."

"With a white woman and everything. I love it," Buster said.

"Yeah. And he don't stay with her but in the winter cause he cain't be bothered with no wife come rooster season."

"Oh, Lord," Paul said.

"Frank here's born in Chicago," Gordeau said. "Did you know that, Mike? Could be he knows your gangster."

"I am the gangster," Frank said, "but they closed down my speakeasy so I had to make like a bird and fly south."

"When you gonna fight your roosters?" Mike said.

"Quiet as a church mouse all day, but once he gets started he don't shut up," said Paul.

"On second thought," I said, spying Dora across the town square, "I am the rooster. And if you gentlemen will excuse me, I see a French hen I have some business with."

I INTERCEPTED EUDORA as she crossed the town square. She was just about to reprove me for something, probably being away from my typewriter, but I kissed her so hard she forgot whatever it was. The sound of good-natured whistles from the porch of the general store cut us short, and we both giggled like kids.

We sat on the benches near the tea roses, and Dora told me about her day with the Nobles, how Arthur Noble showed her the pecan orchards he harvested to sell in the mill town and at his service station. She told me how Ursie bounced at her heels all day, manhandling her new kitten. She had wanted a cat for some time and, owing to a worsening mouse problem, Arthur had finally relaxed his opposition to the idea. Four days ago he had found a little grey kitten in a box with three dead siblings and brought the live one home. Having met Arthur briefly, I voiced my unworthy suspicion that he found four living cats but didn't want that many underfoot. Dora pinched me.

I was about to mention the Negro who came into the general store, but what was there to tell? A well-mannered colored man had come to the general store to buy salt, and when he left, the Southern gentlemen had mocked him and told stories about him.

At just that moment I saw him come out of Estel Blake's hardware shop with a spool of wire around his shoulder and the bag from the general store in his hand. He was chewing the last of his pickle. He crossed the square lawn diagonally, making right for us.

He was staring at Dora.

He stopped in front of us.

His nostrils widened as he took in our scent.

He kept staring at Dora.

Unbidden, the word *nigger* rose up in my head and almost pushed its way into my mouth. The barbarous impulse to spit that word at him and animalize him with it was so strong that tamping it down paralyzed me. For several long seconds all I could do was stare at him while he stared at Dora and she stared at the ground.

"I believe you are making the lady uncomfortable," I said, although neither of us was convinced by the undercurrent of menace I tried to inject. I was flatly no match for this powerfully built man.

He bowed cordially then.

"Beggin your pardon, marse," he said, and turned lithely away from us, walking off down the road that led east. Dora's nose wrinkled in distaste.

But she did watch him go.

I thought about him all the way home.

Was there an accent to his speech? It was faint.

He didn't sound like a Georgia black; that much was sure.

When I got home, I went back down to the musty, spidery cellar amongst the reeking boxes of my aunt's that might be full of trash or treasure. I sat in front of the typewriter for some time without hitting a key. I just stared at the dirty window without seeing it, thinking about the pregnant days before the States' War, the days when everyone knew what was coming, but not how hungry it was, how long it would stay.

Chapter Twelve

It was late August when I went to interview Bessie Wilcox at the Sunny Rest nursing home just outside the mill town. I hated the euphemistic names they hung on nursing homes, as if old folks were small children who didn't know what was in store for them. If I opened one I'd call it Yelling All Night Manor or Chafing Acres. Granted, I might not attract many tenants, but they would be realists.

Sunny Rest, while not as bad as some of the desperately over-crowded and perpetually uric facilities I had seen on Chicago's South Side, distinguished itself with a kind of hopeless torpor that had also spread to the staff, which on this hot afternoon consisted of a scarecrowish, twitchy white woman with her hair lacquered unbecomingly to her head and a pillow-bosomed colored lady who seemed half-asleep.

I asked them if I might speak to Mrs. Wilcox on the pretext that I was her nephew. They were accommodating enough.

I winked at Mrs. Wilcox, and she nodded from her bed and motioned Dora and me to sit down. The old folks waiting to die in these places would say the Devil was their nephew for the chance to talk to somebody new.

Her blue eyes blinked a lot behind her dirty glasses.

"You ain't my nephew. I got three livin. Two of em's in Atlanty and the last one's in the can. Tell me who you are, though."

"Frank Nichols. Dottie McComb was my aunt."

"Oh," she said. "You here for the money? Cuz I ain't got none. Or I wouldn't be here."

"No, ma'am."

"That's good. You're a good boy. I'd a never let Henry borrow that money if I'd knowed about the boll weevils; lost everything any damn way. Would you reach me some tea?"

She motioned towards a sweating, chipped pitcher on the nightstand and a cup with a blue flower on it.

Dora beat me to her feet and poured the cup full. Bessie took it, and got a lot of it on her chin and down her front when she drank. I saw Dora look around for a towel, but there wasn't one.

"Mrs. Wilcox, I'm actually here because I'm writing a book about the war, and I was hoping to ask you some questions."

"What's she for?" she said, indicating Dora.

"Taking notes."

"Huh."

"What do you remember about the States' War?"

"So you must be Katherine's."

"Yes, ma'am."

"Prettiest child I ever saw."

"Thank you."

"I was just a little girl durin that war. A little barefoot girl."

"Anything you remember would help."

"I wish my girls had been pretty like that, but Henry, he wasn't much to look at. After a pretty man breaks your heart, you're happy for a plain man. You gonna break this one's heart?"

"No, ma'am."

"No, I reckon not," she said, looking at Dora for the first time. "Reckon she's gonna break yours."

"Let's hope not," I said.

"Yep. She will. She got them crazy, two-daddy eyes on her."

Dora bowed her head and wrinkled her mouth, trying not to laugh.

"Mr. Gordeau said you were born in 1854. Is that right?"

"December. Almost a Christmas baby, but my mama prayed on it so I wouldn't be."

"Do you remember Lucien Savoyard? Did you ever meet him?"

"Mr. Savoyard? Everybody met him. He was a gentleman, like they don't make no more. He sat a good horse, all rich in his blue and silver waistcoat, prettiest cloth I ever saw. I remember askin my mama would the angels wear gowns made a that? It was silk. First time I ever saw silk. He let me touch it."

I looked over at Dora to make sure she was getting this. Her pencil flew.

"You look like your mama in the head. In your long, pretty head. But you got them soft eyes like she did. Like you'd let a lot of bad happen to you afore you'd stand up."

"I hope you're wrong."

"I ain't. So you're Katherine's?"

I nodded.

"Who's she?" she asked, pointing arthritic fingers at Dora.

"I'm his wife," she said. "Do you remember the Savoyard Plantation?"

"Course I do. Mama rode me by it on the mule once or twice, and I even got to go in one time. Just before the war. He threw a big Christmas party and opened his house up to all them from Whitbrow and Morgan wanted to come. He had put up these painted angels from France and all these glass icicles that caught the firelight. All the grown-ups were dancin. He danced once with my mama and that was fine, but when he danced with her again, Pappy made us go home. I didn't want to go. All them candles and ornaments and peppermint candies. The house nigger had oil on his face to make it shine. It was a magic night."

"Did they have a lot of slaves?" Dora said.

"Lord, yes. Always comin and goin. Always different ones."

"How did you feel about that?" said Dora.

"They was lucky. They was rich. We didn't have no slaves. My daddy was a pateroller afore he volunteered."

"Pateroller?" I said.

"Used to ride the roads lookin for coloreds without a pass from they master."

"I mean how did you feel about slavery?" Dora said.

I shot her a look, but she shot one back.

"Wasn't no way to feel about it, that's just how it was. That was slave days. Now, some of it was done right and some of it was done wrong."

"Who did it right?" Dora said. "I mean were there actually people who owned other people and did it right?"

"You make me tired," Mrs. Wilcox said. "I don't much like you."

"Shall I leave?"

"No, sugar, you just keep sittin there like the world owes you somethin. And reach me some more sweet tea."

Dora didn't move this time, so I did it. Mrs. Wilcox got more on the chin, so I got up and got a towel from the sleepy black woman. When I came back, Dora was walking towards me with pursed lips. She handed me the notebook and pencil.

"She called me a whore. I'll be in the car."

"Do you want us to leave?"

"No. She really is a splendid resource. But I might punch her if I stay."

I kissed her cheek and took the notebook. She strutted out of the Sunny Rest nursing home, giving me a warm look over her shoulder to let me know she was all right. A dazed-looking little bald man in a wheelchair waved a purplish claw at her in farewell, though she didn't see.

Mrs. Wilcox spoke for another half an hour after Dora left. She sang more songs to the faded glory of the Savoyards and what a

shame it was the Yankees won. She told me that when the slaves killed him, the pastor told his congregation to weep like the Israelites wept for Zion.

When she ran out of things to say, Mrs. Wilcox looked at me like she didn't know who I was, and called for the twitchy white woman, saying I wasn't her nephew and she wanted me thrown out. I played it cool, assuring the woman that I was, but that my aunt got confused sometimes. She nodded and went over to the old woman, who was thrashing her head back against her pillow.

It was time to go, and then some.

But I didn't make it out the door.

A very thin, very old man two beds away motioned me over. He had cancer on his face that was hard to look at, and huge spectacles that made his watery, yellowish eyes look like owl's eyes. He pulled my ear close to his face, but I turned my head so my better ear was closer.

"Don't you believe them horsefeathers about Savvy-yard," he said.

"No?" I said.

"No. He's in hell. And I'm goin soon."

"Why do you say that?"

"I ran his dogs on runaways afore I seen enough to quit. Then I'se fifteen. Old enough to join the militia. But the things I done. I helped take the skin off'n one nigger who ran away twice, and stretched his hide between two poles, like a jackrabbit, with his face still on it. Had a wheel to spin the niggers on till they lost they minds. But he didn't run dogs on his slaves when he hunted. He went out by himself. I saw him once, comin back naked. And they never came back. That place is haunted, young man."

"Thank you," I said.

"Do you like the banjo?" he said.

"Sure."

"Reach me my banjo an I'll play you a song. It's under the bed."

I looked under the bed, but there was no banjo. Just the feet of the twitchy white woman getting closer.

"I reckon this is your uncle?" she said, giving me the angry eye.

"Don't you fuss at him," the old man said. "This is my nephew. Now, get me my banjo, you witch. You evil witch. I want to play something pretty."

WHEN I GOT out to the car, I found that Eudora had put the top down. Her white legs were on display and her bare feet were on the dashboard. The smell of nail polish hit me. Her toenails were brick red and she had cotton between her toes.

"If I'm going to be a whore, I should look the part," she said. "Mind if I dry these out while you drive?"

I threw my head back and laughed.

Jesus Christ, I was in love.

CHAPTER THIRTEEN

IT WAS ON the first or second day of September that the vagrants came to town. Two men, one white and one black, accompanying a mannish woman who smoked a pipe and wore her hair up under a man's hat, established themselves on the benches in the middle of the town's square. The white man held a sign that read NEED WORK while the black man held his head down so the brim of his hat kept shade on his face and the woman smoked her pipe. The white man had a huge mustache that would have sat well on a cowboy's face. Nobody approached the town square for several hours, which was normal in the hot part of the day when the sun stooped and whipped the tea roses unmercifully, so around two o'clock they shuffled over to Harvey's Drug Emporium and ordered an ice cream.

That's where I was sitting, reading a collection of James Joyce, procrastinating again and glad to be out of the dank basement.

They were a penny short of the cost, so I slid one over to them.

Funny how specific the memory is; I still remember the sound of that penny going *ssshhhkkk* across the counter. They all nodded their heads and the white man thanked me. Harvey found it in his heart to scoop an extra half scoop on top since it was clear they meant to share it.

What struck me about the way they ate the ice cream was that they had a system; each took a level spoonful to be fair to the others, and their attack was almost choreographed. I suspected then that these were rail-riders, and that they had learned their table manners in those hobo camps I had heard about where men, women, blacks, whites, dogs and Chinamen all slept together and ate out of the same pot. I was fascinated.

"How are you makin it?" Harvey asked them.

"We makin it alright," the white man said. "Be makin it better with some work. We can all three of us chop cotton, split wood, fix a roof. You know somebody needs a hand?"

Harvey said, "No," then shook his head afterwards as if to emphasize the *no*, but more likely to shake the image of Miles Falmouth out of his head; Miles with his bad back and his oldest son just ten; the neighbors had been taking turns pitching in with the farm work. Miles, who had a little money now thanks to Pastor Lyndon's collection. Miles, who hated vagrants, but not nearly as much as he hated blacks.

"No, I don't know nobody," Harvey said, closing the matter.

That was all they had to offer in the way of conversation, except

for short, bland responses to Harvey's questions. He spoke to them about different things, like how hard it was to run a drugstore with the economy so bad, or how smart he had been to put in a soda machine, how that was all that saved him from getting boarded up like the jeweler, or he told them about his plans to buy a car when business picked up so he could get to the mill town without having to bum a ride off somebody, but after a while he saw that they were just looking at him so he gave up on talking altogether. It got quiet. Flies buzzed against the screen windows. The fan up in the corner made the only real noise, and the three of them knew that the quiet was going to get them kicked out soon. Harvey had removed the empty ice cream dish so they could not even look at that or hold it near them like a badge of their right to sit at the counter. None of them spoke until the white man said, "Mister, we just want to sit in your fan for a little while. It sure is plum hot out there."

"That's fine," Harvey said, and it was fine for a while until Harvey got thinking how no customers had come in the store and none were likely to with three rough-looking hobos taking up space, and one of them a darkie. Nobody passing on the street and looking in could think that they were going to smell very good up close, and the truth was they did not smell good. Harvey probably didn't want to be a bad Christian, but I imagine he got thinking how even in the desert Jesus and the others managed to wash their feet and anoint their heads with oil, having no money and no real work besides preaching. Harvey stood there at about three o'clock with a look on his face like he was practicing in his head how he was going to say something like, "Sitting in the fan is fine, to a point," or "Alright, I think if you ain't ordering it's time to move along," when

the black man noticed him thinking. He nudged the white man and the white man said, "Thank you," in his bland way and the three of them went out. The screen door banged behind them and Harvey was left with only myself and his fan for company.

My own soda glass had been empty the whole time.

Lester Gordeau later told me the vagrants went from business to business in Whitbrow asking if anyone needed help sweeping up that night, or if anyone had a leaky roof that needed fixing, but they found no succor. Lester was working at the feed shop that day, and he told them how to get to Pastor Lyndon's house, but then wondered if he had done the right thing. No telling with people like that. But then, what was a pastor for if you couldn't send poor and downtrodden folks to him for at least a few kind words?

The dinner had not gone well, according to Sheriff Estel Blake (he of the potbelly and the good baseball arm) when he later regaled us with the story at the general store.

Sheriff Blake had buckled on his belt and .32, pinned on his badge and closed up the hardware store to track the hoboes down. It wasn't hard. Estel found them sitting at dinner with the pastor, his daughter and his wife. It was a nice dinner, too, but it looked like the pastor had done without fried chicken so the strangers could have some.

The sheriff searched the woman's rope and canvas bag and found the stolen dress.

"What are we gonna do about this?" he said.

"Might these brethren not at least finish their plates?" the pastor said.

"If they do it quickly, I suppose."

So they gobbled down their food while the sheriff stood a little off from the table with his hat and the dress in one hand and the other hand not too far from his holster, which, he told Old Man Gordeau, he "discreetly unsnapped." They ate like dogs, Estel said, the woman breaking a thigh bone with her back teeth and using a splinter to scrape the marrow out. When they finished, he took them outside where the butcher was waiting on the porch. The sheriff handed the dress to the butcher and said, "Do you want to press charges, Hal?"

"What do you reckon, Estel?"

"Any harm done, Hal?" the sheriff said.

Hal might have looked at the pastor, or maybe at the three vagrants in their homemade shoes and worn-out clothes, before he said, "No, I don't reckon they's any harm done. Long as they git."

"Oh, they'll git alright. Maybe they'll even be good enough to say sorry, now that their bellies is full."

The white man said, "We sorry."

"What about you two? He sorry for all three of you?"

"We sorry, mister. Bad sorry," the black man said without looking up.

Now the sheriff looked at the woman, who did not speak or meet his gaze. The white man said, "She's Polish, from Poland. Don't speak no English."

"Shit," said the butcher, "she could a paid me in keelbossy if I'd a knowed that."

The sheriff laughed. He was glad not to have to drive to the jailhouse in Morgan, the small town half an hour in the opposite direction from the mill town. Besides, Estel was lower on the

pecking order than the full-time boys in Morgan and they never let him forget it. A real bunch of blowhards.

"Alright," the sheriff said loudly, just in case the woman really was Polish, "the man you took from says no harm's done, and I say the same. But there's goin to be harm done if you don't move on down the line, and I mean tonight."

The three of them started walking.

The pastor said, "These brethren were thinking of working for Miles Falmouth. Seeing as they are contrite and wish only for the means to have things honestly, I wonder would it do any harm to let them remain until we may speak to Brother Miles?"

They did not stop walking, but they slowed their pace to listen.

"Pastor, I know you're all washed in the Blood and I try to be, too. But I done my good turn tonight. I don't think you want these three to have the run of Miles' house, him as weak as he is, and them the kind of people they already proved they are."

"Sheriff, how would it sound if I let them to stay here the nights and work for Brother Miles by daylight?"

"I would say that you are a Godly man, but that my word is final. Miles is too sick to keep a watch on these, and him with just the young boy. And you know how he feels about the blacks."

"Alright, then. God bless you, Mr. Blake. I'm sure the Lord will remember the kindness you have already shown," the pastor said. And then he shouted, "And God bless you three. May you find the next doors open to you."

If they heard, they made no sign.

Chapter Fourteen

DORA AND I arrived early at the town hall on the night Whitbrow met to discuss the Chase of Pigs and whether to continue it. Even though school was starting in another few days and the roads needed attention and the bank in the mill town would no longer loan Whitbrow money, the question of the pigs was the only issue on the docket. The meeting was to start shortly before dark, but the sun was still round and orange just above the houses when we got there.

The place was packed.

A wave of human warmth hit us when I opened the door to the beat-up old building, and it was clear we were going to have to spend the night standing. The whole room fluttered with the movement of makeshift fans. I spotted Pastor Lyndon standing on the

far side of the room near his seated wife and daughter, looking unsure of what to do in a crowded room he was not in charge of.

God, the whole town had come.

It got worse.

By the time the meeting was officially begun, the doors had been stopped open so a growing crowd could listen in from the yard of the town hall. Some spread blankets. Those that brought chairs sat in these and smoked, and swatted at the mosquitoes that seemed intent on bleeding the whole town white.

"Lord-a-God," one woman near me said, "took them a while to know we wasn't in our homes, but they got our number now."

"In defense of the Chase of Pigs," Old Man Gordeau said as he opened the meeting in his capacity as mayor, "some would say we ought to keep it cause that's the way we always done. But times is harder now than they have been since I was a young man, and I don't rightly see the point in herdin good animals into the woods. Now, I didn't like it when them government sons a bitches came and bought up our piglets in '33 and killed em all. They cut babies out a sows and plugged the river up with dead ones. But I had to admit, that did raise the price of pork. The difference bein that they was doin it all over the country. We're the only idiots doin it now, and nobody's payin us a red cent." Some in the room started to clap, but Gordeau waved them down. "Pastor Lyndon here is goin to tell us God wants it, an he knows better than me what God wants, at least s'far as scripture goes. But I don't think God wants us to go hungry. And I don't think God wants us to turn animals that don't know how to fend for themselves out to die when they's

used to havin their corn give to them in a trough. That's all. And, Reverend, I'll start goin to church more."

The people in the hot hall were glad to laugh. This town liked its mayor, and those who wanted the Chase stopped felt their cause swell; as he sat back down, applause still rippled through the room.

Next up was Lester Gordeau, but as he took the podium Old Man Gordeau shouted, "Sit down, boy! Before I give you the wire end of the brush!" and got another spasm of laughter.

Lester did not laugh. His Adam's apple bobbed and he did not look up much as he spoke. He said, "I think we should keep the Chase because we always had it. It was ours as long as I can remember, and I don't think no other place had it even once. I mean, Morgan's always been a bigger town and they ain't got it. I know it costs and times is hard, but I'll keep givin what I can if others will. I mean, the mill town ain't even got it."

His father could not resist speaking out of turn again, and he said, "Know what they got in the mill town that we ain't got? Pork chops!"

The hall boomed with laughter and Lester sat down abashed.

A small but distinct sound of surprise rose from the gathering when Martin Cranmer was called to the podium. He came in from my left, pushing his way in from the yard, mumbling what looked like "Excuse me" through his beard, and then he stood and looked at the people for a long time before he spoke.

He was wearing the same tight, pale yellow suit he wore to the Social. His hard hands gripped the sides of the podium so the knuckles were white, but his face was calm. I was sure he was drunk in

that way that only career drinkers get; he seemed sober, but his eyes shone as if he had a secret and exclusive communion with the wellspring of all knowledge.

Martin said, "I know a lot of you don't like me and that's fine because I only like a few of you. I hunt things in the woods and I stuff them and I sell them. Some of you good Christians buy another product I sell in jars because I run it through twice for good measure, I charge the thump keg just right, and you know I don't cut it with embalming fluid like MacLeish did before you ran him out of town. Some of you trade me the yeast or corn or sugar I need, but other than that I don't need people. If you all disappeared tomorrow I would be as happy as the man in the moon."

"Get to the point," someone said from the back, not yelling, but loud enough to be heard.

"My point, without putting too fine a point on it, is that marching those pigs out into the woods is the most intelligent thing you people do. Every month I watch a couple of young men go by my house and to the river with the pigs. I watch the fellows take that little ferry off the rocks and load the animals on and pull them across the river and let them go. And sometimes, just sometimes, I hear squealing."

Now they were listening.

"Have any of you ever seen a pig running around loose in those woods?"

Nobody spoke.

"Lester, you fish that river. Have you ever seen one of those pigs?"

Lester shook his head in a gesture that was barely visible.

"So my point is that something, or someone, or something who

is someone is making a meal of those swine. And if you stop send-
ing them, do you think it is possible that your pig-eater, or pig-
eaters, might decide to come to town for supper?"

"You're eating those goddamn pigs!" Buster Simms shouted.
The people laughed.

"You are wrong," Martin said. "I do not eat the flesh of pigs,
and neither do I eat carrion, although I have been known to put
straw up its ass. I have become a Moslem. And if any of you holy
heathens would like to hear the true gospel of the prophet Moham-
med, I will be happy to testify while wearing the outfit that is tra-
ditional to the whirling dervish."

"Your time's up. Now git off the damn podium," Estel Blake
said.

Martin put his hands over his chest, performed a Moslem bow,
and then left, squeezing past frowning townsfolk. He stumbled and
nearly fell when he reached the door, then disappeared outside.

Paul, who was an aldermen as well as owner of the general store,
read from the sign-up sheet and saw that he was next to speak. He
pulled at where his tie pinched his neck and stood before the crowd,
saying, "I'm with Gordeau senior. Seems to me we been wastin a lot
a pig flesh. Two pigs a month don't sound like much, less it's your
turn to give em up. I know our folks took the pigs out startin in
olden days, but our folks also rode horses or mules and none of
them had the electric lights, which a few of our businesses have,
and our houses will soon. These are new times. Lot of you been
payin me on credit til times get better. Well, times ain't better.
Some of you ain't paid me in a year. Still, nobody owes me as much
as one healthy breed sow would fetch at market. The Good Book

says, 'Render under Caesar.' Seems to me a man ought to pay his worldly debts first. Thank you."

And so it continued into the night. Miles Falmouth stood for continuing the tithe of pigs, and his words carried weight since he was the last one to lose livestock. He also went off on a tirade about how squatters had been coming into town now and again, and how they were likely the ones eating the pigs since they had no professions and could not be trusted. Ursie Noble stood up and said that she liked plaiting flowers for the pigs, and that since she did not have much that was fun to do, she would hate to give it up.

Around ten o'clock Pastor Lyndon gave a long and rousing sermon using the story of Isaac and Abraham as a centerpiece, repeating the refrain, "If the Lord God desires it, it shall be done!" until he got even some of those from the other side riled up. Old Man Gordeau actually raised his hand before speaking out of turn this time, and said, "Forgive me Pastor, but I read the Good Book cover to cover and I don't remember no mention of leading pigs into the nettles with flowers around their neck."

Pastor Lyndon said, "And neither did you read about the town of Whitbrow. Yet you did read about sacrifice. Do you believe, Brother Gordeau, that sacrifice was meant only for the children of Israel? The Lord has made manifest His desire for the Chase of Pigs through tradition. We were not present when the Lord made creation, nor were we of an age to question when our grandfathers saw fit to lead the first pigs away. Will we call them fools that nursed us and nursed our mothers? Will we now walk over their graves to put meat on our plate? We should thank the Lord for letting the choice between Him and Mammon stand so clearly before us."

Anna Muncie, the teacher of the younger grades, had the unpleasant task of following Pastor Lyndon. She said, "I am just as right with Jesus as anyone here. Yet I think we are doing our children a disservice to raise them in the shadow of such an ignorant tradition as this. My late husband had been to Spain before we married, and he told me all about bullfights. That is also an ignorant tradition, although he allowed that he quite enjoyed them. Now, we have no control over what the Spanish do in Spain, but we have control over our own actions. I try to tell the kids about the marvels of the modern world and flight and medicine and all that, but then we stand around and let little girls decorate pigs we should be eating and shoo those pigs away for no good reason. Help me to help our kids not be savages. Thank you."

Old Man Gordeau called Eudora Nichols as the final speaker of the evening, noting that the meeting would reconvene the next night for others who wished to have their say before the aldermen voted.

She captivated them.

I watched her do it.

If the men wanted to hate her for being a woman or a Yankee, her beauty soothed them and her reason made them listen. If the women resented her beauty, then the kindness in her voice made them forgive her for it. The kindness told them that she would never try to turn their husbands, that she would never look down her nose at them if they were plain, nor envy them if they, too, were cleverly made.

She did not use any new arguments; the idea that the money saved from the Chase would help to ease at least a few of Whit-

brow's troubles had been addressed before. She did offer one new proposal, though.

"Why not fashion pigs out of straw or branches and decorate them? Perhaps the labor would be sacrifice enough. Ursula and the others could still weave flowers through them. And they could be carried out to the same place. I don't know. I'm not as religious as I perhaps should be. And I'm not from here, as you all know. But I care about what happens here, and I hope you'll agree with me that the money from the collections might do better buying clothes or paying bank notes for those who are struggling instead of reimbursing farmers for wasted animals."

She got considerable applause.

Gordeau called out, "I'm sorry I called you a carpetbagger!"

"Mr. Gordeau, when did you call me that?" she said.

"Not to your face, ma'am."

When she was done and she walked away from the podium, some looked back at me where I was beaming at her from my spot against the wall. Some looked at Pastor Lyndon to see if he was looking unfavorably upon her, but he was not.

When Paul called the end of the meeting and those of us who were inside went out and mingled with those who were outside, we all got treated to one more spectacle.

Martin Cranmer was on his bicycle. He rode around the town square fast like a little boy, and he howled. He did not howl loud enough for anyone to fuss at him about the noise, but he howled low so that when he circled near the town hall everyone heard plainly what he was doing. The ones nearest the road watched him as if he were a stuntman or an acrobat doing a trick, so he did a

trick. He put one foot on the seat and stood with the other foot held up high behind him, steering shakily and grinning at them through his beard.

"That man's three sheets to the wind," a woman said, and, as if he had been prompted, Martin hit a stone and fell, slowly and luxuriously, the way hard drinkers fall even in accidents involving machines.

Lester Gordeau's younger brother Saul ran to help the taxidermist up and the sheriff came over, too, and talked quietly to him so that he nodded his head and pedaled off gently.

"He's alright," Sheriff Blake said. "Nothing hurt but his liver. Let's all go home now."

And that was what they did, each to his own home.

And I believe none slept well that night, and none remembered any good dream.

THE ALDERMEN HELD their vote the next night, deciding six against three that no more pigs should be herded into the woods. This was the same margin by which the advocates of the Chase had won two years before when the same issue had come up following the slaughter of piglets for the Hog Reduction Program. The decision was read and entered into the minutes at 8:15. Lawton Butler, whose pigs were next on the registry and due for surrender in the coming weeks, reportedly got up out of his seat and raised his hands to the ceiling as if he were about to be baptized.

Eudora went to this meeting without me.

I had begged off so I could work, but what really happened was that I sat in front of the typewriter and nursed three glasses of Drambuie.

Dora said not many came at all.

ALL THE DRAMA and the most compelling speakers had gone the night before; besides which, it had been widely believed that the ceremony would not survive a second vote, so few were surprised when the decision was entered.

What did surprise the community was the death of Paul Miller, alderman and owner of the general store.

It surprised Paul, too.

The pain hit him while he was standing on a stepladder to stack flour on a high shelf. It shocked him so that he stepped off the ladder wrong and cracked his head, dropping a sack of flour, which burst all over him and the floor. This happened early in the morning two days after the vote.

Dr. McElroy, an old-time black-bag doctor who kept his office in the back of his house, was the only one who was not surprised.

He filled us in at the general store.

Why was I hanging around there? Why wasn't I at the typewriter? Because I had to go into those woods next, that's why.

Where are your pants, my friend?

"I told him his heart was not bad insofar as I heard no murmurs or irregular beats, but that his restin heart rate was high, and he didn't need an MD to tell him he was carryin too much. I told him

he had a clean bill of health so long as he'd promise to lay off the fat meat, cut his portions and start takin walks. He only heard what he wanted to hear. Like most of us, I reckon. Maggie Whaley found him all white with flour on his floor, an she came runnin for me. I told her he was dead when he hit the floor and she couldn't of done a thing; truth is, he was probably still tickin, but that's the kind a thing you say. Either way, he was all done when I listened to that big chest of his. No more prime rib for you, old man. It's a sorry damn shame is what it is."

Paul Miller was buried in a very large box. His funeral was well attended despite the rains that came on the tail end of a hurricane that had given hell to the Florida Keys. People strained to hear the pastor's words in the wind.

Some of those hunching under newspapers or shared coats owed him money. Of these, I'll bet some wondered if the list of debtors would be found by his wife, and struggled with whether or not to tell her. I was sorry that his big, generous face would no longer loom behind the pickle jar, and that he would be crushing no more hands with his aggressive handshakes. Many of the others were sorry, too, that his listless, rail-thin brother would likely take over the store, at least until he found out how much work it was.

The rain was heavy and warm and made small lakes on the potted road that led back from the churchyard. What we all felt that day, even those of us who were new in town, was that something had changed in Whitbrow, something had given way, and what would follow would not be to our liking.

CHAPTER FIFTEEN

EUDORA STARTED TEACHING school the Tuesday after Labor Day weekend, in the simple building on the outskirts of town that served as a high school. It had a tin roof, a potbellied stove, dirty windows and a sextet of rough-hewn tables with a few benches and mismatched chairs. The boys and girls shared pencils since ink for the pens had run out.

She saw right away that her biggest challenge was going to be keeping these grown-up-looking farmers' kids in school. She expected to lose a few temporarily, maybe permanently, during the corn harvest that would follow soon. A girl like Ursie would pose little risk; she was not needed at her father's businesses, nor in his peach or nut orchards where hired men worked the ladders. All she

had to do was mind her younger sibling and do light chores at night while her mama cooked.

Sarah Woodruff, on the other hand, wore her older brother's cast-off pants cinched around her waist with a leather strap, and her shoes had the backs cut off and the tops slit because she had long since outgrown them. Sarah was fifteen and fighting a losing battle with her parents to stay in school instead of helping them full-time with the farm. What good would numbers and letters do her when she was a wife? What could she want besides that? Her good looks had already caught Saul Gordeau's eye; more than his eye, his daddy seemed to think. This could have just been wishful thinking on the old man's part; the girl was more than just beautiful. She was positively *wholesome.* Pinup girl material, with her bright eyes and her chestnut hair and just that little bit of freckle.

Of course, Dora didn't care about that. She loved Sarah because Sarah paid attention. She understood. None of the boys could keep up with her at reading or math, but one of them was going to be her lord and master soon; if not Saul, then maybe the squarish boy who sat up front and talked about going in the army. One of them would take her by her pretty hair and drag her into his house to make her peel things and wash things and mend things under his mother's gaze. Eudora told me it would be her chief mission to keep that girl in school, whatever became of the rest of them.

One of the ways in which Dora hoped to keep the class together was by engaging them in conversation, reasoning that if they did enough talking to her and to one another they would develop a sense of belonging and they would fight harder to stay together.

So on the second day of school, Dora asked the class to talk about the pigs. She explained that since she was not from Whitbrow she needed to catch up on its stories. Did anyone know why people first started sending pigs out into the woods?

Sarah was the first to raise her hand.

"My daddy used to tell us scary stories about the woods east of town. Is that what you mean, Mrs. Nichols? Scary stories?"

"Yes, Sarah, any kind of story. Scary, nice. Anything you've heard."

Then several of them had raised their hands, but she nodded at Sarah.

"My daddy used to tell us how once upon a time there was a plantation out there, like when they used to keep slaves. He said that since the man who owned the plantation was so bad, God let the Devil come and take the man's soul away without waiting for Judgment Day. But now the Devil knows how to get out of Hell by a door he made back then, and when the moon gets full he comes up looking for a new soul to take away. And if you met up with him, it wouldn't matter if you were good or bad, he would just eat up your body and take your soul away with him. The Devil likes pigs, though, because they have feet like him. So when he finds a pig he takes that instead."

"Do you believe that?"

"It's just a story. But I know I don't like those woods and I'm not supposed to ever go out there."

Eudora called on Saul next.

"Well, my brother likes to fish that river out where it gets deeper, and he's took me with him before. But not across the river. He's

been, though. He says he ain't never seen nothin bad out there but snakes and ground-wasps. But he don't go much past the river, and he don't go at night. I don't neither. My daddy always held that sendin all them pigs was foolishness, but he did tell us some stories, too. To scare us, like, so we wouldn't go off wanderin at night. I guess all daddies do that and I'm like to do it, too."

"What did he tell you, Saul?"

"There's this death-dog out there," he said.

Other heads nodded.

"It's called a Look-a-roo. And if you see this dog, you's the next to die in town. They say it's black, all black, and as big as two dogs, and if you see it, not all the prayin in the world's gonna keep you from bein put in the ground real soon."

Saul started to sing then.

> *One-two, one-two,*
> *Don't look at me, Look-a-roo.*

Other voices joined in. They all knew this.

> *Three-four, three-four,*
> *Who'sat scratchin at my door?*
> *Five-six, five-six,*
> *Getcha while you pickin sticks.*
> *Seven-eight, seven-eight,*
> *Getcha if you stay out late.*
> *If I say nine-ten,*
> *I'll-never-get-back-home-again.*

"We used to sing that skippin rope," Saul said.

"Yeah," said another boy, "and whoever starts that last part 'nine-ten' gets a punch."

"We just go *awwww* at em," offered a girl.

The boy said, "Yeah, my daddy says Mr. Miller saw it on the way home from the store. Couple nights afore he died."

Eudora told me she was fed up with daddies and their ghosts, and I knew what she meant. Another way to keep the house in awe. It's good to hear the strong snore of a daddy in the next room when something might be lurking in the hedge, waiting to test your window.

The would-be army boy up front raised his hand.

"Way I heard it was a nigger gave hisself up to the Devil back in slave days so the Devil would come and eat up his master. Used a witch doctor and everything. But I guess that's like the other story," he said, and flashed a look behind him at Sarah.

But then Sarah raised her hand again, and what she said next was what made Dora fall sloppily in love with her.

"I think there are stray dogs out there. Or maybe there used to be. Sometimes when dogs go stray they make a pack like wolves and hunt and they're very dangerous. Might be someone got killed. Might be that's why they told stories about a death-dog or the Devil eating somebody. Might be they got scared and started sending pigs out across the river to keep what they thought was out there from coming to town."

A boy in the back said, "Yeah, but ain't nobody scared a no dogs. They'd a just laid poison or shot em. Don't make sense to give no pigs up for dogs."

"Alright, smarty-pants," Sarah said, "maybe it is the Devil. Why don't you go out and see?"

I MET DORA after school that day, the storytelling day, and walked her home. I pointed out the diurnal moon, which was more than half full, hiding like a shy spirit behind the branches of a maple tree. I got a kiss for this, a peck at first, but more after she checked to see that no kids were lingering nearby.

Then we walked on.

"Funny how they think the Devil would actually be interested in queer little Whitbrow," she said. Her hand slid up to feel the muscle in my arm. "But I'm glad you're here all the same. You won't let the Devil get me, will you, Frankie?"

"I'll spit in his eye and tie a knot in his tail."

"That's just capital. And when he wipes the spit out of his eye and shakes the knot out of his tail?"

"We run like hell, of course."

"Quite sane," she said, resting her head on my shoulder.

Our lovemaking was sweet and slow that night. It seemed she kissed my whole body as if it were a newly minted gift she could not keep long. And afterwards, when she thought I was sleeping, I caught her talking to the moon through the lace curtains. I couldn't hear her words, as low as they were, but I wasn't half bad at reading her lips.

"I don't need rescuing," she said. "I don't."

THE DAY MARTIN Cranmer got himself arrested, Dora and I were having a soda at Harvey's. I told her that Saul's story about the death-dog reminded me of Black Shuck.

"What's a 'Black Shuck'?" she asked.

I took another drink of soda. We had come to the drugstore to get out of the heat even though both of us knew the town was stunned and the mood was unpleasant in the wake of Paul Miller's death, and in the absence of a Social, which would have taken place that Sunday if anyone had the good will and energy to organize it. The town seemed lost without its heathen ritual. And without its affable grocer.

"Black Shuck was a sort of big, black hound that lurked in the barrows and fens in England. When I was in London, not long before I came home, I met some fellows in a pub. They had been soldiers, too, like everybody, part of that ghastly tank business in Amiens. They were from the East. Norwich or Norfolk, I can't recall. When the barman called 'Time, gentlemen,' one of them said, 'Let's go through Hyde Park and look for Black Shuck.'"

Dora smiled at my put-on accent.

"'He's a great fukkin black dog, big as a calf. Just watch out for his one red eye right in the middle of his forehead; if he looks at you, you're shyte. You're dead.'"

My profanity caused Harvey to look up from his barely audible radio and from his endless wiping of clean things, though his expression was so flat I wasn't sure at first if it was interest or reproach.

Then he turned up his radio and went back to wiping. Huey Long was getting buried in Baton Rouge and some reverend was speaking, calling him an unfinished symphony. Harvey was rapt.

"Anyway, we rolled out of the pub and went looking down dark alleys and under bridges and ended up passing out in Hyde Park. No Shuck. I always remembered that name. It sounds like a death-dog, doesn't it? It sounds like little Gordeau has a piece of that same story. Funny how legends travel."

"Nothing about this business sounds funny to me. The moon should be full tonight. Like it was that night you came home from the woods and had your dreams. What did you see out there, Frankie?"

"Nothing."

"Liar."

"Just the bogeyman."

"Now you're a smart aleck. You always get wise when something's bothering you. Can we just stay in tonight?"

"Sure. A night in with my best girl."

"Wife."

"Not soon enough," I said, brushing her bangs from her forehead.

I noticed that Harvey had left off wiping again because he was staring out the window into the town square where the merciless midday light illuminated a lone, squatting figure.

"Well, that man is a plum idiot if ever I saw one. What in hell does he think he's doing?"

"WHAT ARE YOU doing, Martin?" the big man said.

I had walked out so I could eavesdrop. I might have felt ashamed if I had been the only one.

The taxidermist looked up at Sheriff Blake, who had come out of the hardware store still buckling on the belt of his office, and who was now standing over him with the sun behind him. The big man looked more fatigued than angry, and he asked Martin again, "Now, just what are you doing?"

Martin placed upon his own head the garland of tea roses he had just crafted. He went from a squat to a sitting position, sitting Indian-style with a cigarette in his mouth.

"What I am doing," Martin said, "is fashioning myself a moon crown, since I am high on moonshine. I am tired of looking at these goddamned flowers and they are tired of being looked at, so I am putting them out of everyone's misery. If you like my headdress, I would be happy to make you one of your own. I am sure there are enough flowers even for your head, which is not small."

Estel hunkered down, removing his shadow from Martin Cranmer, and he said, "Now, how are we going to fix this?"

Martin said nothing.

"I'll tell you how. I'm going to trust you to take yourself home and tuck yourself in like a good boy to sleep off your drunk."

"That's not what's going to happen," Martin said slowly and jovially.

"And when you wake up, you're going to come back here and plant new flowers at your own expense."

Martin shook his head, grinning broadly so his yellowish teeth stood out against his beard. He stood up on legs that looked ready to buckle. The sheriff stood up, too.

"I have destroyed public property," Martin said.

"Yes," Estel said, "yes, you have. And if you don't make it right, maybe I'll come around to your house and destroy me some private property. Like some illegal property that turns mash into shine."

Martin, still smiling, noted that people, myself included, were standing under the awnings of the shops around the square now, and I believe it was mostly for our benefit that he undid his trousers and urinated on the remains of the rosebushes.

The sheriff waited for him to finish and button up. When he had, Estel said, "Now would you please wipe your damn hands on your shirt?"

Martin obliged, swaying gently.

"Thank you," the sheriff said, taking Martin's wrists and cuffing them behind his back.

"I really did not want to drive to Morgan today, you damn fool, I really did not. But you are under arrest for public drunkenness and indecency and maybe vandalism, too. We'll sort that out when you dry out. You get a couple days in the hole. Probably a fine I know you cain't pay. This is really a sorry business."

"You have no idea," Martin said, looking oddly sober for just that moment. "May I keep my garland?"

"Oh sure. You gonna pay for it, might as well enjoy it. Let's take a ride."

Some of those watching broke into applause when the sheriff led Cranmer away, but I did not join them. That's when Martin noticed me in the crowd.

He winked.

I'm nearly sure he winked.

CHAPTER SIXTEEN

WHEN NIGHT CAME down on Whitbrow it came down hard. It came down like an army that had been waiting for the chance to sack and plunder the roost of its ancient foe. Sherman had found Atlanta. Troy had fallen. Rome was upon Carthage and the moon was its general. Forgive me for invoking these images retroactively, knowing as I do what would happen that night on the eastern edge of town; but I have the impression that even then I knew.

Something.

The moon came up, and since it was filtered by dust it took a color between red and pink, like the tissue of a lung or some other tender organ stretched postmortem before a candle. In time it dried and yellowed and then went titanium white, hanging higher and higher, seeming to see everything beneath it.

I watched it rise from the front yard of the Canary House. I watched it for better than an hour, smoking cigarettes one after the other, which I had not realized I was doing until I left and saw all the dead butts at my feet.

When I went to bed I could not sleep with all the light in the room, no matter how many times I shifted my position. I wondered in how many beds one spouse tossed or feigned sleep while another slept hard, as Dora was sleeping, beautifully illuminated by but unmindful of the greedy moon outside our window.

I wondered if the good pastor was trying to quicken a child in the belly of his mousy little wife, and I chuckled at that. Then I remembered Paul Miller's widow, and wondered how she was making out sleeping on the edge of the valley her husband's mass had undoubtedly pressed into their mattress. That was a mean thought, and not funny after all. I let it turn to sand and blow out of my head. But my mind would not be quieted.

When I finally did start to sleep, I was startled out of it when I realized that Dora had jerked in the bed. She had been lying on her stomach, but now arched up, listening.

How like a Sphinx.

"What was that?" she said.

"I didn't hear anything."

"Far away," she said, and slept again quickly.

I knew she wouldn't remember.

I knew, also, that war dreams were coming.

I woke up choking, and the woman who would soon be my wife woke up, too, and stroked my head until I knew there was no gas in the room.

I HEARD THE news the next day at the general store.

Friday the thirteenth.

A hard-luck day, all right.

Buster Simms walked in purposefully and took his hat from his head.

"Y'all heard yet?"

"Heard what?" Charley Wade, the carpenter, said.

"Falmouth boy's killed. Somethin killed him."

"What d'ya mean, 'somethin'?"

"I don't know. That's what Old Man Gordeau said. He'll be here presently. Sheriff went out to look at what's left. Found him in the ruts of that old blowed-over locust tree not far from the Falmouths'."

I remembered that kid. Tyson. He had played baseball with me that first weekend on the lot near the town square; brown-haired and freckled. Polite. Jerky but a fast runner.

Ten years old.

His head was a little too big for his body.

The details came in all day, from different mouths.

Knowing what I know now, it's easy enough to put together.

Something was after his father's pigs.

He wanted to be a big boy, so he took his father's rifle and put on his father's slippers and went out to see what it was.

And he never came back.

Chapter Seventeen

It was upon the broad but soft shoulders of Sheriff Estel Blake that the weight of the next few days most squarely fell. Of course the family was to suffer immeasurably; but it was up to the sheriff to act. I believe he was a good man and that he tried faithfully to understand what was happening and to take prudent measures. In the end, however, he was no better prepared to protect his flock's flesh than Pastor Lyndon was to protect its soul. What they were facing was just too big, and too old.

And too goddamned rotten.

It was Saul Gordeau who summoned Estel out to the Falmouth farm. He rode up on horseback like all hell was behind him and yelled into the open door of the hardware store, "Sheriff! They need you out to the Falmouths'. Now! Quick! It's bad!"

I was on the porch beating one-armed Mike at checkers. I saw the sheriff walk out into the pale, overcast sunlight, blinking and cinching his belt under the roll of his belly. He had been napping. With some effort, he got on the horse behind Lester and they rode off, Estel's holstered gun awkwardly slapping his thigh as they went.

Mike said, "Dang," and closed his eyes hard, as if anticipating a blow. Then he got up and walked over to the hardware store, shutting the door Estel Blake had left open.

EARLIER THAT MORNING, Edna Falmouth had called her boy and three girls into the kitchen for breakfast but only the girls had come. Usually the smell of biscuits woke Tyson up without a summons. When he didn't answer a third call, and his bed proved to be empty, Edna went out the back door yelling his name. She came back in fast, and woke Miles from his sickbed.

He got his cane and went out to see, and when he saw he yelled at his wife to stay inside, and to keep the girls inside, too.

No matter what.

At first Miles hoped maybe it wasn't Tyson's. He hoped maybe Tyson had shot whatever made all those tracks. There wasn't a lot of it, but there was enough. Some on the posts of the hog pen. Some on the ground near the slippers.

But the slippers sunk him.

When people take their slippers off, they put them together.

This was one here and one there.

And the gun had all six rounds in it.

Something had knocked the boy out of his daddy's shoes.

Miles limped off where no father wants to go: in the direction he knew his son had been dragged.

WHEN ESTEL BLAKE came back, it was clear that the sight of the dead boy had kicked the wind out of him, maybe for good.

A locust tree had fallen over, probably in the storm last spring, and the fan of its roots overshadowed the depression in which the tree had stood anchored since before most people in town were born. It was in this depression that Estel Blake found the mortal remains of Tyson Falmouth.

Gordeau's dogs were on the way, but Miles was a good hunter, and by the time the sheriff caught up with him, he had followed the trail of blood and tracks and disturbed brush almost all the way to the locust tree. It had been a great mercy that Miles's back wouldn't let him walk the last hundred yards or so. Nobody should ever see that his boy was eaten.

But when?

And by what?

The tracks back at the Falmouth place, what was left of them after Miles and Edna walked all over them, had been animal tracks. Like wolf or dog, but bigger. And Estel was not sure, but he thought more than one of them had been around this tree making a meal of the boy. Whatever left those tracks could certainly have killed a ten-year-old without a fight, or maybe a thirty-year-old, for that matter.

Still, stray dogs, even very large ones, were more likely to be scavengers than killers. Maybe they found the boy already dead.

Miles Falmouth was sure it had been niggers.

Maybe one of the hobos he had heard passed through town.

Maybe that big nigger that had come to the general store.

Probably from the woods across the river.

ESTEL DRANK WITH me the next night, the night before the funeral. Neither one of us planned it. He came over to ask if Eudora and I had heard or seen anything new, and then the three of us fell to talking. We were glad for the company. The school had closed temporarily, and I was too disgusted with everything to write about anything. In other words, this boy's death had made us both useless. We had been sitting around the house reading, clearing our throats, not knowing where to sit or stand or when to move. I had played checkers in town until I saw black and red squares on the backs of my eyelids before I went to sleep.

Dora sensed that Estel and I wanted to talk man talk, and she left us on the porch, bringing out a bottle of bourbon for us to share. We shared it plenty. And Estel let loose.

"I CALLED THEM boys from Morgan, said we had a killin and I thought it might be someone holed up in the woods. I told em I think the boy surprised somebody while they was trying to get at

them hogs. Mr. Falmouth had them penned up real tight what with a lock and wire over the top of them and all. I told em how it looked from the tracks like an animal drug him, something like a big wolf, and Big Joe—he's the sheriff there—said they hadn't been no wolves around here since the States' War. Well, why don't you come see, I said. But maybe I do hold with Miles Falmouth, that some bad customer, some drifter, come up on him. He would a got a round off at an animal. Joe said the boy was scared so maybe he missed, an I said, no shit he was scared, *I* was scared. I'm gonna be reading the Good Book to get myself to sleep every night. Only I cain't pray. Not right. The words that keep comin ain't got nothing to do with Jesus, just *Why did I seek this post, Lord? I am heartfully sorry I sought this post. I water my couch with tears. My sore ran in the night and ceased not. Selah.* All that Book of Psalms stuff. I don't even know what *Selah* means."

He took another drink of bourbon like it was weak tea.

"You know the worst thing, Mr. Nichols?"

"Frank."

"I said I wanted whoever killed that boy in the ground. I didn't want no trial, no lockup. Just wanted it done, in such a way that nobody had to talk about this no more. That's what I said to Joe. And he took me at my word. And I think something real bad happened. But I wasn't there when it did."

I REMEMBERED SEEING the boys from Morgan arrive.

I was at the store, at my usual post at the far end of the porch.

There were lots of men there. The women had gone to the Falmouth place and offered to watch the girl children or do the cooking or slop the hogs, not because Edna needed these things but because there was nothing else to offer.

The men sat around the iron stove and talked with their low, buzzing voices about what to do. Everyone in town was desperate for something to do. The men didn't know where to put their hands.

No music played. Peter Miller had removed what had been the communal radio to his own house. It was his now, as was the quiet store. He leaned with his knobby elbows on the counter, half listening to the grief of the men as if it had no bearing on him. I had the impression that his older brother's death had also seemed far-off to him, as tiny as newsprint. Peter was nearing forty, and he had the noncommittal look of a man who was still waiting for his actual life to begin. He had still not met the better people who would eventually matter to him. He just leaned there with his narrow head turned away, like another feature of the counter that looked so sterile without the green water of the pickle jar.

"Lordy, here they come," one-armed Mike said.

We all watched the cars from Morgan come around the corner as if from a great stillness. Even I heard the doors opening, one of them with a squeaky hinge, and then the abrupt pops as the doors closed.

The men came into view with their straw hats on and their shadows hugging tight on them since it was the middle of the day. Five of them following Estel, who came out of the hardware store and led the way across the town square. All of them looked bigger

than him, or younger, or tougher. Two had shotguns. They walked with big steps like men about to do something. Their big strides carried them past the old pump and past the benches and the insulted rosebushes, and I wondered what mob or sea would not have parted to let them go by.

With their straw hats.

With their shadows tight and dark under them.

As they moved away on the other side of the square, finally looking less like giants, Martin Cranmer, who had ridden back from Morgan with them, walked in front of the window, just on the other side of the glass. He noticed the shapes looking out at him and he twitched his hand as if he were about to wave and then thought better of it. He passed with his head down and then he, too, receded off towards the woods where his home was.

THE YARD IN front of Miles Falmouth's dirty little house was full of women. A few men, too, but we looked ignored and dispossessed. The connection between the women was humid. Languid. The hive had been broken into and honey had been stolen so they buzzed and crawled all over one another like drugged things. The men were not needed in the yard with talk of posses and guns and hangings, so we stuffed our hands in our pockets and orbited groups of women, or we leaned against the mossy trees and smoked.

People ate and drank and talked, but nobody laughed and nobody smiled, and only this distinguished the scene in Falmouth's yard from a party. As I walked around the knots of women I heard

things like "shame" and "awful" and "the Good Lord," and then I saw Dora, and she came and draped herself against me, breathing in the smell of my chest and shirt. Her eyes were red from crying and her face was white and tired as if she had not slept, though it was only one o'clock.

I knew this face of hers. This was the face she wore through much of the divorce. How could things ever be right again? How could she face her students and tell them about fractions and the times table and Abraham Lincoln when there was a little boy chewed up under a tree? Only the sheriff had seen it and now the sheriff from Morgan and his men were looking at it, but the idea of it was planted there for all of us to keep forever. It didn't matter if the boy had been handsomely freckled or quick to smile, or good at baseball or hunting squirrels; in Whitbrow's memory his name would be henceforth married to the word murder. Not only would the boy never be a man; he would never leave the hole where the locust tree had been.

The dogs were baying behind the house like some bad engine coming to life and the lawmen were preparing to follow the dogs. Everyone knew the dogs would pull them into the woods, and they did.

The killer had come from the woods.

"I COULDN'T HARDLY stand them bastards from Morgan," Estel said, owlishly drunk now.

Dora brought us sandwiches, giving me a look that said, *As long*

as you know I'm just playing domestic for the sake of company; you're going to make me a drink and tell me what's going on as soon as this man leaves.

The sheriff continued.

"Joe was half decent, but them other'n was puffed up like too much shit in a sack. Hell, Joe, too. He run Miles and Edna through all the same questions I already asked em, makin Edna cry all over again, and worse, if that was possible. Didn't get nothin new. And they all shot their mouths off while we were runnin them dogs, sayin I hope we get that nigger by supper, and talkin about what they was hopin to eat and kiddin about how bad each other's wives cooked. When I didn't fun with em, they started funnin after me and I told em to shut their damn mouths. Joe said don't mind him, he knew that kid. Like it was some prize he was givin me.

"Well, them dogs had a scent, and they didn't like it. Lester knows how to run a hound. But they took us windin all around, finally up the trail and then where do you think? Martin goddamn Cranmer's house. Well, I banged on his door and he come out with no shirt on and scratchin that beard a his, stinkin like . . . Well, you know how he stinks. I said, you think you had a visitor last night? He says, how would I know, I was in the pokey. Good thing for you, I said, and I wonder if you knew that when you was tearin up them flowers. He said I ought not to be jawin with somebody I knew was innocent, that I was runnin them hounds so slow he could get away on a one-legged horse, so I said, you're right, I ain't got time for this. Normally I got a lot of patience with your smart mouth, but today I am not in the mood. I looked him dead in the eye and said, if I thought you knew something about who killed

that boy and you weren't tellin me, I'd come back here and burn your damn house down. And he knew I would, too. He took his ass back in his little hut and shut the door."

The dogs wanted to cross the river.

It's easy to imagine Lester holding the dogs while the other men boarded the raft and then settling them on it. Perhaps he spoke to the hounds, handsome reddish things with slightly looser skin on their faces than most dogs had, and called them by their names. He would have told them how well they were doing, how brave and good they were, and he would have let them take water from the river. Some, like his father, would have said Lester was the kind of man to spoil a dog, but Lester never saw dogs as property. They were friends of his, friends that liked to work and were grateful for instruction. Lester would talk sweetly to the dogs after his father whipped them. Lester would sneak a shirt-full of food to them and get whipped himself. If Lester had been a saint, his statue would have featured him kneeling, getting his hand licked through the slats of a fence, with one eye out for his father.

It took two trips to get all the dogs and men across. Estel said the men from Morgan never stopped "funnin." On the other side of the river one of them slapped at a deerfly on the back of his friend, but it was too fast.

"What the hell was that for?"

"Deerfly. Would a bit you."

"Well, it wouldn't a slapped me."

The dogs picked up the scent again and pulled them deeper into the forest, baying constantly. Lester had never seen them so disturbed.

They pressed on past the gouged pine trees and kept going for nearly an hour before they saw him.

The dogs went right to him.

He was picking blackberries.

It was a big, muscular black man with a closely shaven head.

He had a bucket half full of blackberries and his mouth and fingers were stained from eating them. His shirt was stained, too. He saw their guns and dogs and, because he felt he was expected to, he raised his hands.

The dogs were barking and howling now. They had their man. Gordeau trusted the dogs so much that their reaction to the blackberry eater was tantamount to a conviction in state court.

"That's him," he said.

The boys from Morgan started in immediately, asking him the questions that fit the circumstances. His name. His whereabouts last night. He would not speak. They cuffed his hands. One of them carried his bucket of blackberries and ate from it as they walked.

"Why don't you talk, boy?"

"Maybe he's a deaf-an-dumb."

"Hey, are you a deaf-mute? If you are, say somethin."

"Well if he is, how can he say somethin?"

"I was makin a joke, a funny joke. He couldn't hear my question, neither, if'n he was a deaf-mute, see? That's funny."

"Oh, he can hear us okay. He hears every word we's sayin."

Lester Gordeau would later say he knew the man was no mute, and no idiot either. He thought that he had seen him in town before, though maybe not since he was a little boy. He remembered

that in school he had learned about old-time sailing ships and how much work it was to pull those ropes and climb up all over the sails. When he saw the black man those ten or twelve years ago he thought he looked strong enough to be an old-time sailor. Walking behind him now, far behind him because the dogs still bayed after him, Lester thought that he still looked strong enough to pull sailor's ropes. He remembered being glad for the guns the lawmen wore.

Estel walked next to the man, looking at him intently. He was trying to look straight through the man's skull and into his brain to see if it contained the memory of the Falmouth boy. Tyson Falmouth looking up into this man's eyes. *He's going to hurt me. I'm too small.* Did it happen that way?

"Look at me," Estel said.

He did. Eyes so brown they were almost black. Intelligent eyes. He knew what was going to happen to him. The Negro looked forward again. Did he recognize him? Yes. He had sold something from the hardware store to a bald colored a few weeks ago. What was it?

He couldn't recollect.

But he remembered that face.

It was him.

"Why did you kill that kid?"

But it was over. The man had no words for any of them, and the next time Estel tried to meet his gaze by moving in front of him, the man looked right through him.

"Answer the man," the sheriff from Morgan said. When the captive did not answer, but only marched forward and looked

ahead with that passive look like paintings of Jesus, the sheriff from Morgan poked him stiffly in the ribs with the barrel of his shotgun. The man winced but said nothing. That was how the abuse began.

When they got to the river, three lawmen went across. Then Gordeau and the dogs with Estel pulling the rope. Then two lawmen transported the prisoner, one of them pulling while the other kept his revolver cocked under the black man's chin. They mistrusted his silence and felt that he would surprise them if he could.

They were right about that, of course, but they could not guess how.

"IT WAS LONG about five in the evening when we got to Cranmer's place the second time," Estel said.

"I beat on his door, but he didn't come out til I yelled, Goddamnit, I know you're in there and I ain't goin away. He opened the door buttonin up his shirt, with a big yawn on his face, and said you caught me nappin. Said he was dreamin of Mexican señoritas and we was a rude subsitute. I said I was just wonderin if this was a friend of your'n. Dogs seem to think he was here last night. He and the nigger looked at each other and he said, I'll tell you exactly what happened. I paid good money for this specimen, he said *specimen*, an it up an run away on me first chance it got. And then some more bullshit about thanks for returnin my rightful property and would we be good enough to help him tie it to a tree for a proper whippin, but I'd had enough.

"I grabbed hold of his greasy ass beard and yanked him out into

the yard, just meanin to shake him up, but that's not how the Morgan boys saw it. They thought I rung the soup triangle on Cranmer's ass. The meanest one, Alfred, he kicked Martin in the leg real hard, and the others moved in. But it wasn't gonna be easy. Martin yanked my thumb to get me off'n his beard, and damn near broke it. Quick as a snake he jumped over and socked Alfred so hard in the guts he went down on all fours and hacked like a dog. One of them slow moments happened then, where you see everythin at once. The rest of them was movin at him, and I seen his eyes cut at a axe in a treestump. My hand started movin towards my holster an he saw that, too, an didn't go for it. In that split second, the boys was on him, and they tangled his arms up from behind so all he could do was kick. But he did kick.

"His feet was bare, but he stomped his heel down on the foot a the fella behind him and then kicked up with both feet. Big Joe caught a toe in his eye and his hat come off his head. Then the man with Cranmer's arms and him both fell. All the rest come on him then, kicked the shit out of him, kicked him so bad the dogs was whimperin. The nigger was watchin it all like it had nothing to do with him. He could a run, but didn't. I do believe they would a kicked that man to death if I hadn't a jumped in sayin easy, easy, he ain't the one done it, you're gonna kill him. When they backed off, I looked down at him where he was still holdin his arms around his ribs and grindin his teeth, and I said I told you your smart-ass mouth was gonna get you in Dutch. I will be back.

"Big Joe asked Alfred if he wanted one last lick, but he was wheezing too hard, so Joe took the lick. As we left, I saw Martin look at the axe again, and I wondered if he was sorry he didn't use it.

"Said a funny thing then.

"'Sing, locusts. Just keep singin.'"

MOST OF THE activity at the Falmouth place had died away.

It was getting on towards evening and the women had begun to find their men and take them home, leaving only a few to keep vigil with Miles and Edna.

Estel was glad not to have a big crowd around when they brought the Negro behind the Falmouth property to the knocked-down locust tree. They showed him the pit under the tree although the remains of the boy had already been removed. The captive showed no interest in the tree or the pit.

They led him to the hog pen and the hogs did not like him. The men from Morgan watched his face to see if he would maybe break down and confess, weeping in that lamentable darkie way so they could at least hang him knowing for sure they had the right man. But he did not do this. He never broke. He used his silence to keep them in doubt, and, although they knew this, the doubt bothered some of them.

It bothered Estel.

What did it matter to the boys from Morgan if they were wrong?

Hanging the wrong man, if it was a black man, would cost Morgan nothing. But it just might cost Whitbrow another day like today, and Estel could not take another one.

I imagine Miles Falmouth stood bent over his cane. His un-shaven face looked raw and old although he was just forty. Estel

said he shook when he saw the captive. Edna Falmouth held him around his soft, beaten shoulders. They stood there together and Miles shook.

"I've seen this'n in town, though it's been a while. He's one of them squatters. He killed my boy."

Estel looked at Miles.

"You sure about it, Miles? Cain't be wrong on somethin like this."

Miles was sure.

"Hang this sumbitch or I'll shoot him."

Estel felt sick again.

O Lord Sweet Lord honey and milk are under Thy tongue, my love is like a goat that stands on Mount Gilead, and why did I seek this post?

Now Estel brought out a cigar, a cheap one by the smell, but that didn't stop me from taking a drag of it when he extended it towards me cherry first, like some cornpone Prometheus offering man the first glowing brand.

"But the dogs were sure?" I said.

A lynching. By God, I was sitting on my own porch in Georgia asking an officer of the law about what I was now sure would turn into the lynching of the black man. The one who wanted a pickle. The one who stared at Dora in the square. How did I get here?

"I asked Lester if them dogs was ever wrong an he said no. I never seen it, he said. I leaned down to him real quiet, like I'm

leanin down to you, and I said, would you hang a man over what them dogs say? Is it enough, Lester? And he didn't say nothing, so I said, you gotta help me.

"Lester closed his eyes and said, them dogs ain't wrong, but I ain't gonna sleep so good knowin a fella swung cause I said so. So I'm sayin I don't know.

"Now I saw that the boys from Morgan had got them a crate and some rope from Miles, and the nigger was watchin all this knowin what it was for but not lookin like he gave a rat's ass. What was he thinkin? An innocent man should a been screamin for his life, but then a guilty man usually made noise, too. Not that I know from hangins. Neither did Big Joe. He didn't know how to make a noose, so after a minute he gave up tryin and his man Alfred strung it. Then they took the cuffs off him and tied his hands with rope so nobody'd know the Law'd done it.

"Well, Blake, let's get on it, Joe said. I couldn't make my feet move. I said I didn't know about this no more. Miles screamed that is him, and I mean screamed it. What is this shit? Joe said. Did you see the way them dogs done?

"What are you gonna do? I said, Put the dog's paw on the Good Book an make it swear? That's why they ain't gonna be no trial, he said, but we all know this is the one done it, an if you ain't got the backbone to follow through, then the hell with you. I didn't say nothin, so he kept on, callin me a damn fool, sayin why don't I go back to my hardware store an polish my shovels.

"So I did leave.

"I walked all the way back to town an nobody who saw me comin stopped me to ask what happened. I locked myself in the

store and cried til it felt like there was nothing left a me but peel. I know they hung that boy. And I know something went bad wrong. And they ain't never gonna tell me what. An they ain't comin back."

I SAW THE men from Morgan leave.

Eudora and I had been sitting, holding each other on a bench in the town square. The sun was almost down now and the frogs and locusts took up their nightly chorus, but it was not a serenade. There was no love in it. It sounded terribly neutral. It was a sound that would go on unaffected by human grief or joy and, while it was possible to hear God in it, it was equally possible to hear His absence. The boy's funeral would be tomorrow. No waiting around in this kind of heat. And there would be no school.

We had bumped around town all day, now at the drugstore, now at Pastor Lyndon's house, now at the general store. She had pulled me home to make love around dinnertime, but we had not lain together long before we dressed again and came to the town square to escape the silence of the house. But it was quiet here, too, except for the locusts, and now the frogs, joining together in their agnostic hymn.

Just before we left the bench, realizing now the futility of paddling at the growing horde of mosquitoes, we saw the sheriff from Morgan and his men come up from behind us. They went around us, crossing the square towards their waiting vehicles. They walked with small steps and the ones who carried shotguns carried them like yokes. The sheriff, the one they called Big Joe, croaked

"Evening" at Eudora and he would have removed his hat if he had not already been holding it. Most of them carried their hats.

The sky glowed red and orange in the west when the men started their cars. How small and pale their faces looked behind the glass. Delicacies in a gourmet butcher shop.

The color of pâté.

I never saw them again, even when things got worse.

CHAPTER EIGHTEEN

DORA COULD NOT stand still. She paced the bedroom in her nightgown, running her hands through her hair while I sat propped up in bed.

Estel had left an hour before, staggering off down the road a little lighter for the actual poison he had ingested and the figurative poison he had disgorged; Dora had been percolating the whole time since. Now it bubbled up and out of her.

"Maybe it was the right man, but it makes me sick that they had no trial. Nothing. Somebody points a finger and that's it."

"I know," I said.

"He was such a sweet boy, too. Tyson, I mean. Oh my God, my God, I just want to pull my skin off every time I think about his

poor, sweet, freckled face. He wasn't one of mine, but I met him. Did you know him, Frankie?"

"He played baseball with us that first weekend."

"He had freckles," she said simply, and then something else too low for me to hear.

I asked her what.

"I said I hate it here."

THE DREAM DID not come until almost morning.

It started in the trench.

I was slogging through ankle-deep mud in the earthworks at the head of a column of soldiers. Ochre mud. Milky. Sky the color of pewter. When the column stopped marching I found that I was in a place where the trench was shallow and I could look across the mud and wire wilderness that lay between the allied defenses and those of the Germans. Barbed wire coiled out laterally to both horizons, and I could feel rather than see the Huns crouched in their trenches, slate-eyed behind machine guns, gloved fingers sweating at the triggers.

I noticed a figure caught on the wire almost exactly in the middle of no-man's-land, but too far out for me to tell what uniform it wore; all I could see was the whiteness of its face as it struggled to free itself. I clambered up the loose wall of the trench meaning to free the trapped soldier, and the other men clutched at my coat and trousers to stop me. They slowed me down, but I pulled their hands open and kicked at them until at last I was able to hoist my knee and hips up and scoot, sliming myself with mud. I got to my feet

and began walking towards the figure pinned on the wire. The silence bewildered me. Why were the Huns not firing?

I knew they were there, their breath steaming in the cold over their weapons, ready to send a rosary of lead that could make whole companies kneel. Ready to shred me like cheap pork with just one throaty *pop* from an anti-tank gun. But it did not come. I saw now that the squirming figure was German. It wore the grey. I saw the point on the helmet, outdated now, just the kind of thing you saw on posters, and the proud boots, somehow black despite the deep mud. The figure stopped struggling when it saw me approach and reclined in the coils of the wire as if on a couch. When I came to the first loops of wire I stepped through them. They caught at my clothes but could not hold me fast. I stepped decisively, and kept stepping, unmindful of the wire that nipped at me. The French and British always said the Yanks had a talent for getting through wire, and this was how it was done.

Now I could see the face of the German. I had thought that it would be the face of the boy from the trench fight, that this would be my chance to save him, that I would pull him free and carry him back to the German line on my shoulders, and the Huns would be so moved by my gallantry that they would cheer me, pass me their tin flasks of brandy and schnapps to drink from, shake my hand, pat my shoulders. Their greatest gift, of course, would be not to shoot me through the back as I left.

The dream remade itself then. It was not the German boy trapped on the wire; it was not a boy at all. It was Dora's face beneath the helmet. Dora's mismatched eyes. I was upon her now, standing over her. She tilted back her head so the helmet fell off,

freeing her bob of honey-colored hair. The redness of her mouth beckoned like a pomegranate and I tasted it.

The chill in the damp air receded and it became a warm dream, all kissing; I kissed the woman on the wire and snuggled in with her so I was trapped, too, hopelessly so, but it did not matter. All that mattered was the warmth and wetness of the kissing, the contact of our mouths, that the war might in fact end with this kiss, the feel of her tongue, her long tongue that pointed delicately, I loved to watch her lick stamps, taste ice cream, catch a drop of coffee running down the side of the cup, her mouth on mine in our different uniforms, bring the Kaiser to see it, bring Pershing on a stretcher, God and Jesus, her perfect tongue and Gabriel in the clouds above it all with a horn, a ram's horn tipped with gold, the music of the Hebrews, the kind that cracked Jericho, so now the horn sounded and the seams of the clouds split and lilies fell in a damp and lovely snow until everything was covered.

When I woke, the woman I called my wife had me in her mouth, had held me so for some time now. How like a Sphinx in her nightgown. Her hand working below her lips. Her eyes flashed up at me and the clouds split. And everything fell in a slow hail of petals.

TYSON FALMOUTH'S FUNERAL was well attended despite oppressive heat. Many in town had talked about going in order to show Miles and the remainder of his family that they were not alone in their loss.

But that family was alone.

They would be alone no matter who came or how much food was brought to the house afterwards. The father of a dead son, when that son had no brothers, must stand alone with his surname dying in his mind. The mother of a dead son must stand alone even among her sisters with the memory of that child's birth and the wasted milk of his nursing.

I saw Tyson's sisters trying to understand what had happened; all three were younger than their brother. The oldest of these was in a sort of trance and wore a blank face. The next one furrowed her brow with an expression of grim effort, as if by some precocious act of concentration she might understand the nature of death and unravel it; that she might shout *Eureka* and wake Tyson from within his closed casket. The youngest girl seemed the least troubled because, I suspect, her understanding was not mature enough to embrace the event. She seemed impatient with the droning words of the pastor and the pale faces of her parents, and perhaps with everything that would happen between now and the moment when her brother would stop hiding and come back.

I stood in the back holding Dora and looking at that awful little box that held a boy in it. It was covered in wildflowers that the girls of the town had gathered and plaited into a wreath. That the flowers looked too much like the ones the pigs had worn was a truth nobody needed to speak aloud.

MILES FALMOUTH SHOT his pigs that night.

Just leaned on his cane and shot every one of them, hogs, sows

and piglets. Nobody tried to stop him or ask him why. When the squealing and the gunshots were done, he looked at the faces of the several neighbors who had come and said, "Y'all can take what you want. Cut em. Smoke em. Make cracklins, I don't care. Just don't bring none of it round here. I got no more use for them sumbitches."

His wife and the girls stayed with the neighbors that night.

And the next night, too.

NEWS OF THE shooting of the pigs did not reach Dora and me until later because we got up and drove away. Not for good. Just for the day. We did not pack the car.

I proposed the trip while I brewed coffee in the kitchen and heated water for oatmeal.

"And exactly where are we driving?"

"North. As far north as we can go and still make it back by dark. I want to get this town off us for a couple of hours. Maybe if we do that we can make a firewall between what just happened and the rest of the year. God, I just want to wash it off."

She came up and hugged me from behind, kissing the back of my neck and saying, "Yes. Thank you, yes."

So we got in the car with the clothes we wore and a little money and an old wine bottle filled with water and we drove out of town pulling a cape of dust behind us. We drove north with no map and stayed on the highway past the intersection that would have led us to the mill town.

Not far past there we were nearly hit by an ice truck. It had been

swerving and going twenty miles an hour so I went past it with my hand on the horn ready to blow it if the truck lumbered over at us, which of course it did. I laid on the horn and the very old man behind the wheel of the truck guided its bulk back onto his side of the road without ever losing his expression of bewilderment. He never even looked at us. It wasn't in me to yell or make an uncivilized gesture at the old bird, so I just waved a little as I passed.

I felt Dora's small hand on my thigh. She leaned close and smelled my neck. "You smell like soap," she said, then rested her head on my shoulder. For just that little while there wasn't any other place I wanted be, and life was sweet and foreign like the taste of a mango.

It came to be two o'clock, the time at which we agreed to turn around, and I pushed it another fifteen minutes, doing nearly sixty where the road was good enough. But at last I stopped, as if an unseen leash had pulled taut. We came to a filling station and the attendant pumped gas and checked the oil and the water and found it easy to talk me into buying a bag of pecans.

We turned around then and I headed for a pretty, shaded place I remembered from the way up and we sat on the grass and ate, not saying much. The engine ticked under the hot bonnet. When we kissed, it was not like a married couple about to make love, but like teenagers not sure if they should go any further. We decided without speaking not to spend that heat, but to bottle it and take it home with us, so we petted awhile longer before I let her back into the car.

I turned the car around on the shoulder so we could look north one last time while the birds chirped and the hot wind blew and sometimes cars moved by us in one direction or another. Beyond

the horizon lay the Northern trees, whose leaves were ready to redden, and the Northern fields, preparing to go tawny and brown, and somewhere even farther the factories that made snow checked their tooling and their rosters, knowing it would not be so very long now.

Chapter Nineteen

It was near the end of September that Estel Blake's shovels were stolen. The thieves made off with some picks, too, as well as some kerosene and a few score yards of rope; but the notable thing was that they took all five shiny new shovels Estel had in stock at the hardware store that served as anteroom to the sheriff's office.

This was better, though, Estel said. Theft was better than what August brought. Even when the theft made little sense. The thieves did not open the cash drawer, nor did they force the door into the sheriff's office where Estel's Colt .32 revolver hung in its belt; the money one could get for that fine gun would buy a lot of shovels.

"What were they going to do," Estel wondered aloud at the general store, "build a canal? Go on a treasure hunt?"

At least the locks weren't damaged. This was because he almost

never locked his window. Even in hard times, Whitbrow was not the sort of place where one had to lock one's neighbors out. Still, it was apparent that the ease with which he had been robbed stung him.

Worse, something about this seemed ominous to him, made him wonder if it was connected with the Falmouth boy's death. Soon he was pressing his hand under his breastbone like his stomach was full of sour, hot water as he considered the possibility that the boys from Morgan had strung up the wrong man. Within half an hour he was sure a band of squatters had crept in here as quietly as weasels, confident they could bash the brains out of anyone unlucky enough to discover them.

"O Lord hear me, I pray they hung the right man," he said, as if half a dozen of us weren't sitting around him on the porch.

"Hear me in this, my Sweet Lord," he said again, then moved off towards the farms nearest the square to see if anything had been seen or heard the night before.

WHEN I GOT back home from my daily job of sitting around the general store pretending to be soaking up local color for a book I was too scared to do the real research for, I found Ursie Noble sitting on my porch next to my wife. They were chitchatting, so I refilled their lemonade glasses and joined them.

I noticed the girl's thick, Native American hair again, and the way she very consciously struggled to keep her legs in ladylike positions while she shifted around on her chair, now crossing them

awkwardly at the knee, now tucking them up beside her where they didn't fit under her hip because of her mannish boots. Ursie thirstily drank what had to be her second or third glass of lemonade, then thanked me, keeping eye contact for just that second too long. But how would I have known that had I not done the same thing? Jesus God! I laughed a little at myself and noticed I was sweating.

She's fourteen, you jackass!

It was as if she remembered her posture at just that second, and tried to pretend a string was attached between the top of her head and the ceiling. She darted an eye at me again.

Son of a jackass! Grandson of.

A cloud of flies, and flies for his eyes.

"So how are things going with the book, Professor?" Dora said.

It was hard to tell if she was amused, vexed or oblivious. Scratch the last one; Dora was never oblivious. She was smiling just a little.

I tried to gloss past the subject of my largely unwritten white elephant, but Dora wasn't having any; she focused her questions on the Confederate cavalry, provoking me into an impromptu lecture about which I felt very passionate until I could see that she had snared me into making myself boring to our young guest, who was now flicking around the flyswatter that had been sitting near her as if in mockery of the saber blows I had been describing.

"Have you ever seen a saber?" Dora asked Ursie.

"My great-granddaddy's is hangin on the back wall of the fillin station," Ursie said, now using the swatter to push her empty lemonade glass around on the table near her.

"Frank, why don't you use that flyswatter to show Ursie how a Southern gentleman might strike from horseback with a saber?"

I was game. I got up and took the swatter, crouching a little as if astride a charger, pretending to trot. Both of them started chuckling. Then I lashed out in a deep, pretty lunge and swatted hard at a housefly, which had been resting near Dora. She shrieked and jumped marvelously (although the fly buzzed off without even a bent wing) and then both girls laughed hard, Dora so hard she got a cramp under her rib, which made Ursie laugh more.

"Can your daddy do *that*?" I asked, making big bug eyes at Ursie.

"Oh, Mr. Nichols," Ursie said when she could talk. "You're much faster than my paw with a swatter. He ain't fast like that . . . Momma has to catch Sadie when she runs . . . Cause his belly's big an his legs is skinny . . . Oh my God, I cain't stop laughin."

Of course, that was the moment her father chose to come up the walk. I doubted he had heard any of that, but he was a somber, serious man, and must not have thought much of a grown couple horsey-laughing with his child. I had to bite the inside of my cheek to keep from braying again when I saw just how correct Ursie's assessment of her father's legs-to-belly ratio had been. With his knobby knees swimming in his trousers and his white belly pushing against the buttons of his shirt so one was open, he looked like Jack Sprat with a bun in the oven.

"Afternoon, Mr. and Missus Nichols. Hope you don't mind if I interrupt. Now, Ursula, you get on back home. You know I got work and your mama needs help. You come back on Sunday if you feel like a visit. Sorry about that, folks; we got pests enough without this'n here drinkin up your drinks."

"She's been a perfect lady all day long," Dora said, "and we'll be glad to have her over on Sunday or any other day."

Ursula went with her father, dragging her oversized boots in the dust as she walked, and she did not look back at us. She very consciously did not.

"SORRY I WAS flirting a little."

"You both were."

"You know I don't mean anything by it, I hope?"

"No. I think you probably draw the line at college sophomores. I'm just glad I squeaked in."

"You're wicked."

"Everyone's wicked. I was worse than her at her age. It's harmless enough. You're the best-looking example of what a grown-up man might look like in this town. And I guess she'd like to strap on my long legs and take them for a spin, but she'll find out pretty soon the boys will like her short legs just fine. Just the same, I don't think I'll want to make love tonight."

"No?"

"I don't think I will. I don't entirely like the way I feel just now. I'm not even twenty-five yet. I'm not supposed to feel old. How do you do that to us? How does every one of you manage to do that to every one of us?"

After school the next day, Dora went to see Mr. Woodruff, the father of Sarah, her most promising student.

I went with her.

Sarah had not shown up again after the Falmouth boy was killed, which didn't surprise Dora. Half of her students were still out, protecting the nest or being protected in it. Or just pulling up potatoes and okra because nobody cared about Manifest Destiny with Tyson's skinny little ghost howling by the locust tree.

Eudora didn't like this Woodruff man very much.

It had been he who told the class on the day that Tyson's body was found. Just came in without knocking, barked out the news without a sliver of discretion, and took his girl off by the arm. And in that drawl so thick it sounded like he had been dropped on his head as an infant.

It would be hard to get Sarah back from such a man.

She had her lips pursed and a worry line on her brow when I knocked.

Mr. Woodruff looked at us as if he were a bear who couldn't understand what a couple of deer were doing knocking at the entrance to his cave. The rain was coming hard, so he invited us off the dripping porch and inside. The porch with its puddles. The porch with its mosquitoes and mosquito hawks and moths and flying ants still crucified on the rusting screen, and gouges in the screen where part of it hung and made a lip. Perhaps the bugs had been left to warn others.

"How are you doing?" I said, offering him my hand, but quickly retiring it unshaken.

"I've come to talk to you about Sarah," Dora offered.

He grunted.

When he finally saw that we weren't going away, he let us into the house and we all sat in homemade chairs in the close space of

the front room. The air was thick and hot and damp. Sarah looked up from the chicken she was plucking in the kitchen and peeked through the doorway, but she did not risk a hello. I guessed she never knew exactly when to speak in this house, but with her daddy it was good to err in favor of silence.

"Well, talk then," he told Dora.

That drawl. He could have made a lullaby sound hostile.

"It's just that Sarah is very badly missed in school. She has quite a lot of talent and she likes to learn. She . . ."

"She has a talent for gettin in trouble is what she has. More time she spends away from home, more trouble she gets in."

Sarah kept plucking.

A horse whinnied somewhere out back.

Mrs. Woodruff appeared from another room and wordlessly poured a glass of tea, which she then brought to Dora. Just to Dora. No ice or sugar. Weak tea from the look of it; they were using their tea bags twice or more. I thought she might not have time to drink much before things with the father soured, but then I looked through the doorway to the kitchen and saw that Sarah was looking at Dora, grateful for any ally.

Yes, get me back in school, tell me about planets and clouds, and especially airplanes that fly all the way across the sea to France. I'll name the capitals of all the states right now if you will just take me by the hand out of this place.

"Mr. Woodruff, I assure you that she will get into no trouble while she's under my watch. She's such a good student. If you just let her finish . . ."

"What for? Ain't no work."

"Not now, but hard times come and go . . ."

"Ain't been no hard times like these. These is the end times."

"Maybe. But if not, and work picks up, you'll be glad to have a daughter who can get herself hired anywhere she wants, and not just in a mill."

"Please, Daddy," Sarah said from the kitchen. Quietly. Barely as loud as the rain outside. Oh, God, to be shut up in the house with this man smoldering all day like a fire that might lick out.

He grunted.

"The other students would appreciate it, too. She's so good at math she helps the others solve problems. Sarah really has a gift. She could be anything she wanted, a doctor, a journalist. She would have a good chance at winning a scholarship if you wanted to send her off to a women's college . . ."

"Now, just hold on. I ain't sendin her to no damn college while the other kids walk aroun bare of foot. They out back in the rain right now stickin their feet in the mud gettin ground itch is how much sense they got. We ain't for college, and college ain't for us. Besides which, I don't know if you got your head out a your books to see, but we got bad news aroun here. Niggers is killin our kids. Comin right up an killin em on they own land. Now, I ain't no cripple an I ain't no woman an I ain't no Yankee"—he looked at me for that—"and I ain't scared to shoot the head off nobody comin aroun if I don't know em. Sarah's watched over here. Don't seem she's so watched over at that school with jus you, or gettin there, or comin back."

"I understand your concern. But I promise you I won't let anything happen to her. Or anyone get to her. They'd have to go through me first."

That struck him as funny and he laughed in a gravelly little chuckle. It was the first appealing thing I had seen this man do.

"I know," Dora said, "there's not much of me to go through."

"No, you ain't much," he agreed, still chuckling.

Everybody was quiet for a while, letting the rain do the talking, until at last Mr. Woodruff said, "Alright, damnit, you women gonna worry at me like a tick. Go on back, Sarah. But you, you gonna keep her outta trouble, you hear? I got your word?"

"Yes."

"I do, now. I got your word."

We stood up to leave, and I saw that I would be the one opening the door.

"Thanks for the hospitality," I said, tipping my hat, for which Dora elbowed me soundly in the ribs once we were back outside in the warm rain.

CHAPTER TWENTY

THE PEOPLE OF Whitbrow wouldn't have to wait long to find out why Estel's shovels had been stolen.

I heard the knock coming from the front door downstairs and I knew it was bad news. Bad news knocks hard. I swung my feet over the edge of the bed, still blinking in the sunlight, and checked the clock. Almost nine thirty. "I'm coming!" I yelled, and I jerked on some pants and went down. When I opened the door I saw Saul Gordeau panting and sweating so it was clear the boy had been running.

"Been knockin for a while. You okay?"

"I'm fine."

"Sheriff wants all able-body men to go to the schoolhouse, Mr. Nichols."

"My wife, is she alright? What's happened?"

"She ain't hurt or nothin, but you best go to her. She's there, too. Bring workin clothes. I got to tell Mr. Noble."

And he ran off.

For just two or three seconds, watching the soles of the boy's shoes flash as he sprinted to the next house, I was abundantly grateful not to know what it was about.

I FOUND EUDORA sitting under the maple tree outside the schoolhouse. I went straight to her without stopping to talk to any of the others gathered there. No other women were being let as near the scene as she was, but she had already been inside so nobody insisted when she refused to be moved farther off. She just sat there holding a leafy branch like it was the only thing that could protect her.

Crows were cawing loudly all around. One walked around near us, quite fearless, looking like a tiny Burgermeister in black velvet pants. I offered her a hand to help her stand, but she shook her head, trying to smile though her face was puffy and red from crying and her eyes were too wide.

"I can't move just yet, Frankie, okay? I just need to sit here until I have enough strength in my legs to get up and then I'll help. I'll help, I swear, just not yet, okay?"

"Shhh," I said. "You don't have to do anything. Shhh."

I squatted down and held her head against my chest while she reached her shaking hands up to touch my arms. I held her head against me and kissed the top of it for a long moment and then I allowed myself to look up at what was happening.

People had war faces on.

Everything seemed tilted.

The men of Whitbrow had their sleeves rolled up and shirts tied around their faces so they could breathe while they hauled them out. More men were coming, saying "Jesus" and "Lord" and "I just don't believe this," and after each man said these things, he would roll up his sleeves, too, and find something to put over his face.

I put my shirt up over my nose without knowing why, but when I peeked in I was glad for the shirt, even though it wasn't enough. Tyson was there in the schoolhouse. What little there was of him. Raw and picked-over. Crows on him.

He was not alone.

Paul Miller was there, too. Bloated. Wormy. Coming out of his suit. There were others.

It was hard not to be sick.

Someone had exhumed the dead of Whitbrow and tied them sitting upright to the chairs behind the tables. Twenty of them. Some of them recent, some very old; the parts of these that would not bend had been broken off and placed beneath the chairs.

Dora had seen this, and past the shock I felt a shiver of rage that someone had left this for her to see. She told me later that she fought a small battle with the crows to get them out. She had done this with a branch she pulled from a young tree outside. It had not been easy to convince the crows to leave that room of plenty, but she managed better after she broke one's wing and then killed it.

It was then that she saw the writing. I looked up now and saw it. It was on the front wall behind where she stood to teach. It had

been written in dark, moist earth above the blackboard. Like a lesson for a dead class.

SEND THE PIGS

I steadied myself on the desk and saw the muddy footprints on the ground. People had done this in their bare feet. Men, but also at least one woman or larger child.

This was so deliberate, and so deranged. I was mad. I used my anger to push myself off the desk, roll up my sleeves and get to work. There would be an awful lot of work for the dozen or so who had answered Estel's call on blind faith. There was the removal of the dead. There was the placing of them in their boxes; these had been found stacked in a copse of trees not far away. There was the hauling of the dead back out to the cemetery. There was the sorting out of which bodies went in which holes; many of the older ones had to be guessed at. There was the shoveling under. Last came the cleaning of the classroom.

Many of those who helped got sick, but most continued even though their heads were light and their stomachs bounced. Pastor Lyndon did not speak as he worked. He became ill when, in the close heat of the classroom, the arm of a woman who was buried in 1910 came off in his grip and she fell.

"This is just the shell," I heard him mutter to himself. "She has gone home to glory and left the husk behind. This is not her, it is not. She is with God and she sings."

He had to run outside then, but he came back. Most of those who had to run outside came back, although a few did not. Pastor

Lyndon worked as hard as any of us. When we got the dead back to the cemetery, some of my fellow townsmen looked as if they were waiting for the good reverend to speak. When we put the last one beneath the marker and tamped the earth down, many were no doubt hoping Pastor Lyndon would give them some words to seal the matter. To tell them it was done and they had done good work and they should endeavor to keep their faith while God tried them. Since he did not, but only wiped the grime from his brow like the rest of them and sat down among them, some closed their eyes, and I have to wonder if they were making up his words for themselves, perhaps something about the Philistines or the false prophets or the trials of Job.

Someone asked Old Man Gordeau if he was going to run the dogs after whoever had done this.

"Cain't," Old Man Gordeau said, his voice tight. "Sons a bitches burned em up. Roasted em right in the kennel. Goddamn them to hell."

"You don't believe in no hell."

"I'm ready to build one to put them sons a bitches in."

"You see em?"

"I don't know what I saw."

"Sounds like you saw somethin."

"You'll think I was shinin."

"What'd you see, Gordeau?"

"Long hair. Some skinny-ass white woman with long hair. And a bare bottom, too. Least I think so. But she was gone so fast I'm not sure. I'm gonna put em in hell."

And then he walked off and stared at the ground with his hands

on his hips. He spat and watched it fall from his mouth. I had the curious idea that this was what he did instead of crying.

We sat around for some time with our muscles throbbing and our heads and stomachs sorely grieved, and then Sheriff Blake stood up to speak. He removed his hat, and for the first time I noticed how unflatteringly he was going bald; how much older and weaker he looked without his hat.

"If everyone could gather in and listen before you get to your homes. I know you're tired. We all are, I guess. I want you to go home and get what rest comes to you tonight, and say your prayers and amens real good. Cause tomorrow, come mornin, right at sunup, I want all men who can handle a gun to bring their weapons to the town square. I know some of y'all got dogs, but leave em. We are goin into them woods past the river; we are goin quiet and we are goin in force. If there is squatters in them woods, we gonna find where they livin and give them some. I ain't takin no badge this time, neither."

His voice sounded sure, and he had said the right words, but he rubbed the front of his pants while he spoke.

Many of the men nodded.

"You damn right," somebody said.

THAT NIGHT I had a Dan Metzger dream.

My dreams about the war come in several varieties, none of them pleasant, but some of the worst ones involve the death of my best friend, Dan Metzger, because they're not just frightening;

they're heartbreaking. I can shake off the fear of death; I can even shake off the guilt of killing; but when I wake up from losing Dan again, I'm all hollowed out inside. I had such a dream one of the first times Dora spent the night, in my tight little bachelor's apartment in Ann Arbor. I kept it together until I got to the kitchen, but then I cried for fifteen minutes after I broke a coffee cup. It says a lot for her that she didn't run for the hills.

In this most recent dream, the shell walloped us and there we were crawling around, looking for his glasses, and him all busted up. Then some doughboys came and buried him right then and there, and I was trying to explain to them that his mother was going to be mad at me. What's more, it wasn't fair that Dan was in the hole because he never hurt anyone. Dan got his nose broken for telling on older kids who tortured a frog. Dan aimed up and shot over the Germans' heads. Dan just wanted a wife who was nice to him, even if she wasn't smart or pretty, and he was owed that. They just shoveled.

I woke up with Dora shaking me.

"Honey, honey," she said, but so tired herself that her eyes weren't open.

"I had a dream."

"I know, my love. You're home now."

"Did I shout?"

"Yes."

"What did I say?"

"You said, 'Leave, go, let him up.'"

Chapter Twenty-one

I never got back to sleep, then I decided that was all right and I got my service pistol out of the desk drawer and took it downstairs to oil it. When I say I took it out of the desk drawer, I should specify that I mean the desk drawer in the office, not the drawer of the nightstand. Eudora didn't like guns in the house, but she was willing to tolerate them as long as the sanctity of the bedroom was respected. I had balked at that initially, but when she pointed out that I might wake up wrong from one of my nightmares and mistake her for Kaiser Wilhelm, I conceded.

It was good to clean the .45. It was good to keep my hands busy rather than dwell on what had happened the day before, or to consider the prospect of going into those woods. Drop the magazine out. Slide the rack back and check the chamber. Turn the bushing.

Then say "goddamnit" under my breath when the spring pops the spring plug loose and it hits the kitchen floor. I was on my hands and knees looking for it with the oil lamp in my hand when I remembered looking for Dan's glasses in the dream, and I wanted to curl up and sob, but I pushed that down and found the plug.

Several men were standing around in the town square when I got there at first light. Someone raised a hand to me as I approached and I saw that it was Buster Simms. People were standing near Buster because he was so big he made them feel better, as though he were too big to be hurt or to let hurt come to those who stood with him. His size made the lever-action rifle he carried look like a toy. I shook with Buster and Buster's hand closed around mine like the larger of two nesting dolls. His grip was strong, but he held strength in reserve. Paul Miller used to shake hands putting some extra squeeze in it so it was clear who the bigger man was. When Buster shook he reined it in a little, as if the other man had offered him some fine porcelain thing that might crack if borne down upon.

Estel Blake came now and stood upon a bench so everyone could see him and he could see who had come. It was getting light enough to see the color in faces.

There were more than he wanted here. He sent Old Man Gordeau home because he had a bad cough, and Gordeau fought him on it until Estel pointed out that his hacking would make it impossible to get the drop on anybody. He sent home a young widower who had kids, and he tried to send Saul Gordeau home with his daddy but Saul wouldn't have it.

"Now, Lester here is twenty and one and that's alright, but you ain't but seventeen and this might get rough. Probly it will."

"Reckon it already has," Saul said. "Sons a bitches burnt up my dogs and dug up my daddy's uncle."

He said it just like Old Man Gordeau would have and it got a yellow little laugh out of them.

"I'm just sayin you're young for this and it don't set well with me."

"Sir, I might be young, but I don't shoot young."

I noticed the rifle Saul carried was an American Enfield, the doughboy's rifle. My old rifle. Bolt action, six shots, deadly, deadly accurate in the right hands, and, since 1918, cheap. I later found out that no fewer than nine households in Whitbrow held copies of that rifle. After the war, a man in a navy peacoat had come around and sold them out of the back of his truck for ten dollars apiece. Harvey at the Drug Emporium had one, but never shot it. Hal the butcher kept his slung under the counter. It was the gun Tyson Falmouth had carried when he went to check on the pigs.

Saul looked like a child, but he was only a little younger than I had been when Uncle Sam had stuck an Enfield in my hands and nearly shut me in a coffin.

I had only been a passable marksman.

Not Saul.

Estel Blake assessed the slight blond boy who was standing with his feet planted, holding the big rifle like it was part of him.

"It's true," Lester said. "He's better'n I am or ever will be. You remember that rabbit he hit on the run when we went huntin last year. You were joshin him how it was luck, but I'm here to tell you it wasn't."

"Alright, young man," Estel said. "But if you change your mind out there and want to get on back, there ain't no shame."

"Same goes for you, Sheriff," Saul said.

We left.

We numbered fifteen.

"WE'RE LOST."

"We're not lost. I know I seen that before."

"Knowin you been somewhere before and knowin how to get back is two different things."

"Well, when did we leave the path? When was the last time someone saw somethin they knew was on the path?"

"Hour ago we seen them pine trees with the cuts in em."

"Yeah. Hour ago."

"Now, what is this? Anyone know if this has got a name?"

"Won't be hard to remember. Looks like that leanin tree is a ole man tryin to push that big rock uphill."

"Alright. We'll call this Uphill Rock. Let's keep walkin straight east. Frank, keep tight on that compass."

"Sisyphus."

"How's that?"

"Sisyphus. He was condemned to roll a big rock uphill every day, and when he got it to the top it would roll back down and he'd have to start all over again."

"Seems like I know that feelin."

"What was that fella's name again?"

"Sisyphus."

"Think I'll just call it Uphill Rock if it's all the same to you."

BUSTER SIMMS BROKE up a big, round wheel of corn bread his wife had made and handed some around to the ones closest to him, myself included. I was quickly sorry I took it because my mouth was too dry to eat it. Walking armed through the forest with a party of armed men, not knowing when there might be gunfire, was driving me apeshit. I had one foot in these Georgia woods and the other back in the Argonne. Birch trees reminded me of the birches there, with their tops missing and caked in mud from shell-splatter. I was straining to listen for sounds I was no longer capable of hearing; branches snapping, hushed words in German, the cocking of a weapon. I rubbed my hands on my pants and looked around, wondering if anyone could tell how hard my heart was beating. Nobody seemed to notice.

It was mid-afternoon now and the others were tired and hot and ready to see anything that would break up the routine of marching forward through these woods.

I hoped we wouldn't see anything.

My anger at those who had desecrated the dead and traumatized Dora had been eclipsed by barely containable feelings of panic and a strong desire to sprint out of these woods for good.

I felt that we were being watched, but then I second-guessed myself and reasoned that it was just the memory of that feeling kicking up silt. Gooseflesh went up my left side as I remembered what had been watching me the last time I was here. Jesus, was I just as scared of that creepy boy as I had been of stumbling into a machine

gunner's sights? Maybe. Even with a party of armed men around me, I didn't want to see the boy with no pants again. Not ever.

But there was no way I was turning back.

The watched feeling got more urgent.

I went up to Estel Blake and put my hand on his arm to get his attention. His arm was tensed and stiff like wood.

Estel turned and whispered something to me; I saw his mouth make the words *I know.*

He had heard something. I now sensed how tightly wound the others were and knew that they had all heard something. They were jumpy. And they were bunched up.

I touched Estel's arm again.

"Get these men in a line," I whispered.

"What?"

"Put these men one behind the other and space them out before they shoot each other."

Estel nodded and went from man to man until it was done.

But we went on like that for a long time before anyone fired a weapon, and only one of us saw what was in the woods.

IT WAS MAYBE half past three when we discovered the bones of the horse. The horse had died some time ago, and my first thought was that perhaps we had stumbled across the battlefield; that this was one of the many Confederate horses who died beneath or on top of their masters that day in 1864, its topsoil perhaps washed away in hard rain. But the ground here was high and the topsoil well

anchored by roots. And this horse had been eaten. The smaller bones had been cracked open and the marrow licked out. I saw the scowls on the other men's faces and knew that my face was expressing the same contempt. There's something in a man that loves a horse and hates to see one desecrated.

The sheriff was the most affected, and I can only venture that the sight of those gnawed bones reminded him too sharply of the boy he had so recently found beneath the locust tree. He muttered something to himself, or so I thought until I saw by the way he closed his eyes that he was remembering his Psalms again.

"What the hell is out here?" Lester said. "That ain't no dog. Dogs did not do that."

"I don't know," Estel said, "but we gonna find out."

He said it, but nobody believed him. Nobody wanted to meet what made those deep grooves. Not in his heart. Not if he was honest.

About four o'clock something moved and several men shot at it. Estel stopped them and they watched the smoke clear and several of them went in that direction to see what they had hit.

"What are you doin? Dammit, get back here!" Estel said, but they went anyway.

The brush was thick and soon the men were out of sight.

"Hey!" Estel said, but stayed where he was and the remaining men stayed, too. A long moment passed.

"Where are you?" a voice called.

"We're here!" the sheriff said. "Follow my voice."

"Here-here-here-here!" Buster said.

"Keep talking," a voice said.

"Here-here-here-here-here!"

The men came back and rejoined the group.

"Did you see anything?"

"Nothin."

"Who shot? Lester, did you shoot?"

He shook his head.

"Well, since you know how to keep your britches on, you and me are goin to walk up front. How about you, Mr. Nichols? You fire?"

"No, sir."

"Then why don't you take up the back."

"I would do better near the front. Man in the back needs good ears."

"That's fine, then. Buster, you shoot?"

Buster shook his head.

"Alright, you take the rear."

"I was afeared you was gonna say that."

It was only when Buster almost tripped over Saul's rifle that they realized Saul Gordeau was missing.

He had been the last man in the rear.

WHEN HE SAW that the boy was gone, Estel began to fall apart. We all knew that's what was happening, but nobody tried to usurp what was left of his command because nobody else knew what to do either. It was getting late enough so we had to leave soon if we wanted to make the river by dark. Everyone wanted to make the

river by dark. So we abandoned all pretense of stealth and shouted the boy's name until all of us were hoarse. We tried to retrace our steps. We saw no sign of him. He was gone utterly and did not answer his name. I think many in the party were quietly glad to be moving back towards the river, and as long as search and retreat were both served by the same heading, there was no contention in the group.

When some of the men felt they were near the place of the shooting they slowed down and began to look more carefully. I proposed that we should walk in an ever-widening circle and keep a close eye out for blood or dropped items, and Estel nodded his assent. We called the boy's name again and again until all the meaning washed out of it and it became like any other syllable, more related to salt or sod than to Lester or their father.

Estel touched his face a lot while we searched. I had the impression he was remembering flies, fearing to find another boy walked on by flies.

Nothing happened except that the light got weaker. One man suggested that the boy had gotten scared and headed back west. This made sense to other men who were eager to head home. A majority soon formed that professed to believe the boy had turned back, and would be waiting for them by the river or back in Whitbrow. Members of this same majority also pointed out that they had only one light, no food and very little water. By way of easing the general conscience, one suggested that if the boy wasn't already home they could renew their search tomorrow. Lester nearly hit the man who said that. Buster came between them, but argued Lester's part, saying if Saul was hurt they would be killing him to leave him out all night.

Estel spoke up then, saying, "He's probably crossed the river. I'm sure he's crossed the river home."

And if he hasn't, I can't bear to find him, I could almost hear him thinking. *My steps are heavy with the fear of bumping a foot into him; I will shake myself to pieces, Selah. Lord give me one night of rest before I see anything else that makes me see Thy throne empty and my own death close and final.*

Those who wished to leave grabbed at the sheriff's weakness, tried to hide their own behind it. They were sure the boy was home. They promised to come back tomorrow.

I was as scared as any of them, maybe more scared.

I have seen something in these trees, and something worse in others.

But still I spoke up and said,

The woods have not yet forgotten how to gobble men up

"Who volunteers to tell the boy's father?

that monsters got his youngest boy

or do we let Lester do that?"

"I ain't leavin without my brother," Lester said.

"Now it seems we got to all go or all stay," Buster said, "and I'm for all stayin."

"Me, too," I said.

"You damn fool, the boy's gone home," one man said. One of those who shot.

"That's right," another said. "He's waitin on us."

"Who's goin to tell our wives if we stay?"

"And if he ain't home, you gonna look your wife in the eye and tell her you left a boy in the woods? Cuz I will."

The man wanted to say something back to Buster but didn't.

His friend said, "Now, I ain't no coward, but I ain't no fool neither. Seems to me if they ain't nothin bad out here, the boy's alright. But if they is, they's goin to give us hell tonight an us with no light or nothin."

"I'd rather be a fool," Buster said. "If we start now we can pick good ground and make a fire. Camp here and start first thing in the mornin stead a wastin all that time walkin home and back."

I said, "Whatever we do, I agree that we should do it together. We've got good enough numbers now to discourage an attack, but if we divide, the smaller party will be . . ."

"Shit out a luck," Buster finished.

"Well, I ain't leavin," Lester said.

"And I ain't stayin," one of those who shot said.

I saw that the sheriff was gone to pieces and where a good leader might have kept the group together, there was none. God, I did not want to stay out if the group was going to split, but I saw that Lester would stay and I couldn't leave the boy alone.

The light was going.

"Seems to me we should all stay," Buster said again, but with less strength. I was suddenly sure that Buster would leave, too, and that's what happened. Ten left for the river. Then the sheriff, looking beaten. Then Buster said, "Come on, you two. If these sons a bitches won't stay."

Lester shook his head and I stood with him.

Buster handed off Saul's Enfield to me, saying, "Here, you might want somethin more than that piece on your hip."

"Thanks," I said, taking it. I hadn't held one since I was

nineteen, but it felt heavy and wicked and only too familiar in my hand.

"Hand down that light," Buster said.

"We gonna need it to cross the river," one of those who shot said.

"Hand down the light afore I break your head."

He did.

Then Buster gave the light to Lester.

And then he left, smaller than he had been.

WE HEADED FOR Uphill Rock because it looked like a good place to have against our back. While we gathered wood by the last of the daylight Lester thought he heard something, so we got our rifles ready and Lester called "Saul!" but nothing happened. I thought of the boy with no pants and then I made myself stop thinking about it. We got a fire started just as night came on. We smoked, but didn't talk more than we had to. We agreed to take turns sleeping but neither one of us could for the first part of the night, and then, near morning, both of us wanted to. Several times Lester heard walking and once he thought he heard voices and we pointed our guns, but we did not call out into that darkness. If the boy was out there, he'd see the fire and come to us. We were perfectly visible. I knew how easily we could both be shot with the fire going, but there was no question of staying in the dark. There were worse things than being shot.

I let Lester sleep for two hours but then I could keep my eyes

open no longer and I began to dream. In my dream, a naked woman walked to the edge of the firelight eating from a pig's head. Blood was all down her front and the pig's head was so fresh it jerked. I jerked, too, and woke startle-eyed. I shook Lester awake and reclined into the moss and earth, trying not to think of anything except pennies, which I counted in my head, seeing each one fall into a mason jar. I had seven dollars before I slept again and this time I didn't remember any dream.

Lester shook me. First light. The sky glowed dimly between the cane ash branches above us and the trees were alive with birdsong. The fire was out. We had both slept.

Lester leaned down over my face.

"They's a bell. I hear a bell."

"Like a cowbell?"

"Smaller. Tinkle-tinklin."

"Where?"

We readied our rifles and walked crouching as Lester led me towards the sound. It would stop for a while and Lester would stop and wait, but then it would sound again. Soon we saw the bells.

Three bells.

Saul Gordeau stood shirtless, stumbling in the brush, his skin very white against the dark foliage around him. He was blindfolded with what used to be a strip of his shirt, and gagged with a crab apple and another strip. His hands were bound behind him with rope. The most disturbing thing, however, was the cruel iron collar he wore, with three iron rods coming up from the neck, each ending in a small, tinkling bell. Had his hands been free, a padlock would have been necessary to secure the collar. As it was, only a

braid from a hank of rope held the contraption in place. Every time he bumped into something, or even moved, the bells announced his location.

The birds sang on with good cheer.

Lester walked straight towards Saul but I stopped him and made him hang back with the rifles while I went to the boy. When I got close enough for Saul to hear my steps, the boy started shouting hoarsely through his gag and whipping his head around so hard I thought he might injure his neck.

God forgive me, I was so tired and numb I didn't want to take his gag off; I didn't want to know what had happened to him.

THE BOY WOULDN'T talk for a long time after they got his bell collar off. I lent him my coat. Saul just sobbed and walked with us towards the river, Lester's arm around him. His tremors came in waves. When at last he spoke, he wanted to speak to me away from Lester because he didn't want family to know what he had to say. But he had to tell so someone knew what they were.

"THEY SO STRONG, the men and women. When they grab you it's like you's a little kid again. I saw a white woman with curly wild hair and a nigger woman and a white man. They was more, but they pulled my shirt up over my head quick, so I didn't see em all, an I didn't know where they was takin me. They carried me and

they went fast, but it don't seem like we went all that far. They smelled bad. Like animals that's been out in the rain or down in a burrow. We went down to a kind of cave cause I felt us go downhill and there was a echo. Everythin they said had a echo.

"They stripped me down and tied me down then and put their mouths to me. The men and the women. I didn't want to, I promise I didn't, but I came off and I never knew for who. One of them was the Devil. Had to a been. All them stories was true. He put my hand on his chest and changed hisself to a animal so I could feel the fur come in on my hand. I felt him drop to all fours and stand there pantin his stinkin breath on me and then he changed back. Said he could do that whenever he wanted cause he was old. But some of the others only did it when the moon came. That they had to then. That they liked eating pigs then, but they were gonna eat something, so why didn't we just send the pigs?

"They never let me alone all night. They was laughin when they carried me back. I don't know if they can die, Mr. Nichols, but I hope so, cause I have to kill em. I think they took my soul outta me and I'm goin to hell no matter what I do. So I might as well kill em."

Saul got himself together after that, at least from the outside. He had regurgitated it and settled on a plan, and I knew that plan. Deciding to kill somebody or something can be strong medicine for a while, but it burns. And it doesn't stop after it's all over.

I didn't know what the boy had seen. Not believing him would have been best, but you can't counterfeit reactions like his. It doesn't mean he hadn't hallucinated, but I wasn't sure he had, either; my parameters of belief were becoming more and more negotiable, and they weren't nearly done stretching.

The three of us walked quietly to the river.

When we got there we realized the raft was on the wrong side so Lester cursed and took his shoes off and waded in holding his rifle over his head. Then Saul went in, with me close behind him; I feared Saul might wilt and let the waters take him downriver.

It was soon after that we saw the new posse coming towards us. Only six this time. Buster looked so ashamed I thought he might cry.

The nine of us limped home and when we got to Whitbrow, nobody was waiting for us.

AT THE CANARY House, I found Dora sleeping in her clothes on the couch. When she heard I was staying out all night she had tried to keep vigil, but hadn't had enough sleep the night before. I leaned to her, and just when I was about to brush the hair at her temples with my fingertips, she woke and drilled her eyes through me. She had been prepared for something bad to enter the house, perhaps Estel Blake holding some item of mine and asking, "Did this belong to your husband?"

She sat up and grabbed me. The force of her embrace pressed from me the paternal feeling I had watching her sleep. It was like an Old Testament widow clutching her dead husband's brother. Her new husband.

"You have to get me out of here, Frankie," she said.

"You want to go up to bed?"

"No. Out of Whitbrow. We should go."

"Dora, I'm exhausted. You're exhausted. I saw things that I don't have the strength to talk about. Let's get some sleep."

"No, Frank. This is the time to talk about it. We have to go. I feel it in my bones."

"Go to what? To Johnny's house again? Do you want to stand in a soup line? It might come to that."

"Anything but this."

"What about school?"

"There isn't going to be any more school."

"What about my book?"

"You aren't going to write it. You would have already. Something in you, the part of you I love the most, knows the world doesn't need it. Another bloody general. Another corrupt, petty feudal lord."

"That's your opinion. You don't like history. Most women don't."

"There's a reason for that."

"I will write it."

"You don't mean it. You're saying that because you think you have to. When are you going to write it?"

"When this is over."

"*This*. What is *this*? When is *this* over?"

"I have to see it through."

"You're going to get killed."

"No."

"You're going to get me killed."

"Never."

"Fine. Just you, then. Is that what you want?"

"I don't think so."

"Are they going to put a statue of you up by the pump well? *Orville Francis Nichols, Yankee, who died that we'uns may live.*"

"You're being small."

"Is this your chance to die in the war like you should have?"

"Stop."

"You don't owe him that."

"I said let's stop."

"He wouldn't want it. Dan, right?"

"I don't like you talking about him. I don't like you using him to get your way."

"*My* way?"

"You want us to run out on these people. Something has to be done about *them*. The ones in the woods. They're so vicious."

"I saw."

"I saw more. They're so *bad*."

"We don't really live here, Frankie. Have you noticed? We don't go to church with them. You go to that store and play checkers and listen to their conversations like you were looking at them through a glass, the same way you would at a pub in London or a café in France. But you don't live here any more than you lived in France. And things are just as bad here as they were there, aren't they?"

"Actually," I said, genuinely surprised by my answer, "they're not."

"Not yet."

"And what you said about not going to church with them. That's not entirely true. We go to their funerals."

"Yes, I suppose."

"And we go to their town hall. Have you forgotten that?"

She was silent.

"This is happening because of the pig ritual. We voted to stop it. We came into town and you stood in front of them and spoke your reasonable, logical words. And I believed that what you said was right. And together we put our finger on the scale, and the scale tipped. Maybe it would have anyway. But we own it now."

She nodded a little, looking dazed.

"I suppose I see that," she said quietly. "But that's a principle. I don't care that much about principles. I don't want to find dead people in schoolhouses and wait around on the sofa wondering if you'll be carried home and laid out on the table for me so one of those good ole boys can tip his hat and say, 'Sorry, ma'am.' I want to have your babies, Frank. Big, healthy babies with your patient eyes and fine little wisps of hair just your chestnut brown, and I don't even *like* babies."

"Dora . . ." I said softly, and reached out to stroke her hair. She pulled away a little.

"I know I can't have that. I don't need you to tell me I can't have that."

"I wasn't going to."

"But I want to make love to you as if I could. As if every time you put your seed in me it might just take anyway. I want to lay with you every night and every day I want to work a job where I feel I'm doing some good. To hell with principles. I do the best I can and if it isn't enough I cut my losses. Sometimes you can't win and you have to change your plan. That's smart, isn't it? Aren't we smart people?"

I chewed on this for a moment.

"Alright," I said.

"Alright, what?"

"We'll go. I'll ring the movers in Chicago and get them to come down. And I'll ring Johnny and let him know he's going to have guests again."

She sobbed and gripped me tight again, saying, "Frankie, thank you, thank you, my love, thank you."

I NAPPED BRIEFLY on the couch but did not fully sleep. Dreams like muddy fish drew close, then darted off, and I was glad to let them go.

Where are your pants, my friend?

I thought about how good the boy had been at throwing stones. Did he hunt birds that way? He threw the first stone when I had pointed the camera.

But I did take that picture. It had been waiting in the guts of the camera for me to remember it and to have the courage to develop it.

I quit trying to sleep now and went to the little darkroom I had made for myself in the closet under the stairs.

It was nearly two when the picture came out. Blurry but identifiable. Just beginning to crouch for the stone, his right arm drawn across his body. Farther away than I remembered. Some part of me had hoped the image wouldn't come in. That I had dreamed it. But it wasn't so.

I would go to see Martin Cranmer the next day and I would ask

him who the boy in the picture was, or what. And if I got no real answer I would not speak to the man again.

I rang the movers that afternoon and found that they couldn't get a truck down to Georgia for a week. Dora was crushed, but a week didn't seem so long to me, especially since we would need time to pack.

"Let's use our time wisely," I said. "Let's go to the courthouse and 'git hitched' the weekend before they come."

"Really, Frank?"

"Really."

"No, I mean are you really asking me that standing up?"

I dropped to one knee.

"Marry me, Eudora. Give me the deed to that lovely little property below your navel, and let us live in sin no more."

"Yes," she said. "Gladly. After which you'll get me the hell out of here?"

"I promise."

She spat in her hand, I spat in mine and we shook on it.

Dora and I ate a big dinner that night. We laughed easily. I didn't feel the least bit guilty. *To hell with star-crossed Whitbrow,* we seemed to be saying.

Let it bury its own dead.

CHAPTER TWENTY-TWO

"THERE'S NOTHING IN it for me. Explaining that boy to you."
Martin had only glanced at the photograph before putting
it back down on the table. He drank from a bottle of gin.

"That is a curious statement," I said.

"Then here's one that makes clear sense. I mostly drink clear
booze because the rest of it looks like it's already been through a
gentleman."

So saying, Martin got up from the table and went to the work-
desk where he finished pulling the skin from a rabbit he intended
to have for his lunch. Smoke from the fire outside came in the
window and the smell promised good roasting. Martin poked a
stick through the animal in a way it might have found embarrass-
ing as well as uncomfortable if it still cared about earthly matters.

We went outside to the fire and Martin braced the spitted rabbit aloft over the fire using two Y-shaped branches planted in the ground.

"Wish you'd been here yesterday. I trapped some doves. Not much more meat than the heel of your hand on any one of them, but I had six and could have gotten by on three."

"I was already engaged yesterday taking care of the Gordeau boy. He thinks he spent a night at the Devil's underground spa."

"Did he see it?"

We had both been standing with our arms folded the way men do when they watch a fire or especially something cooking on a fire, but now I turned my head and looked at Martin.

"See what?" I said. "The spa?"

Martin looked inscrutably at the fire for a moment before he spoke.

"Anything interesting."

"Something specific and interesting? An *it* rather than a *who*?"

"You missed out on a fine career as a detective. It almost doesn't sound like you're interrogating me."

"And you almost sound like you don't know what's going on past the river."

"A check to the king! Black castles. Would you like a smoke?"

I took one of Martin's strong cigarettes and lit it with a twig. "So are you going to kick me off your ancestral lands again if I keep asking questions like 'Who is that boy?'"

"No."

"Who is that boy?"

"They're not ancestral. I picked this place for its vast, quiet

woodlands. But now they're not so vast and sure as hell not quiet and I'm thinking about pushing on."

"Funny, so am I."

"Brother, that wouldn't be a bad idea."

Martin went back into his house and fetched out the gin, spritzing a little on the rabbit so the fire sizzled.

"There's a fight coming and I don't want to pick sides. It's that simple."

"A fight between what and what?" I said.

"Let's go inside."

Martin shut the door and drew the iron bolt. He sat down at the table and looked up at the stuffed beaver and then at me.

"Between the easy to believe and the difficult to believe."

I waited.

"I like you, Mr. Nichols. Otherwise I'd have nothing to say. Every word out of my mouth is like a piece of glass I'll have to pick out of my supper later. Or maybe everything I don't say is going to hang over my bed later if something bad happens to you."

"Who is that boy?"

"He's a leper."

"A leper?"

"That's right. Or it's close enough. He's sick, and so are a few others."

"You can speak plain English to me."

"No, I can't. They wouldn't like that."

"Then speak to me in parables."

"They're sick and their illness makes them hurtful."

"Ah, the parable of the hurtful lepers."

"They prefer to hurt animals."

"Swine before pearls?"

"That's it. That's it exactly. But some horses' asses decided to stop what had been a convenient if expensive compromise with . . . well, with the improbable. And if you think the poor folk of Whitbrow couldn't afford to send the pigs over the river anymore, I promise you they can't afford what's happening now. If the situation doesn't right itself soon I'm going to have to give this little patch of land back to the weeds."

He drank. I winced at the amount of alcohol that went into the taxidermist's mouth, but when he passed the bottle I drank, too.

"Why won't you just tell me?"

"Have you noticed where I live? Geographically? Or maybe cartographically, I don't know. Anyway, mine is the closest inhabited dwelling to the river. I am between the river and the town."

"Jesus. You're saying you have contact with them."

"They're sick, I told you. There are fevers in those woods and fevers make people do things that are not polite."

"Whatever they are, they're dangerous and they should be gotten rid of."

"Someone with the Spanish influenza would be just as dangerous. But you don't shoot sick people. You contain them."

I reached for the bottle and Martin slid its cool glass into my hand.

"Besides," Martin continued, "it's not that easy."

"For God's sake, will you tell me what they are?"

"No."

"You infuriate me. You do it on purpose."

"But I'll tell you what they don't like."

"Alright."

"Conditionally."

"What's your condition?"

"Well, currently I seem to be enjoying the condition of a stool pigeon."

"What don't they like, Martin?"

"My condition."

"Jesus bloody Jesus, I see why you live alone."

"My condition is that you will not share what I tell you with anyone else in town. Because if you did, they might attempt to molest our sick friends. And if they were not wholly successful, the surviving . . . lepers would know where the good people of Whitbrow got their information. And they might come across the river to discuss this with me."

"So why tell me at all?"

"The very question I ask myself. And I answer that I would hate to see harm befall you. And I answer that everything is going to hell anyway. And I answer that I would hate to see pretty . . . what's-her-name?"

"My wife?"

"Sure."

"Eudora."

"I would hate to see pretty Eudora come to grief. It looks like you two have a good thing and you're both thinkers and your mission is to pollute the world with thinking children."

I did my best not to react to that.

"Swear on her legs," he said.

"What?"

"Swear on her exquisite gams—and I am nothing but proper and respectful when I call them exquisite. Swear on them that you will not spread the information I am about to give you to the good folk of Whitbrow, but that you will only use such information *in extremis* to protect yourself and those legs."

"I do so swear."

"Silver. They have a reaction."

"What do you do? Touch them? Stab them?"

"You don't want to be that close."

"Shoot them?"

"Shoot well. It's not likely to come to that, but if it does, shoot well. They don't just shrivel up and die. But silver's the only thing that hurts them so they stay hurt. It's the only metal that makes wounds they can't heal almost instantly. Anything else and you're just giving them a haircut. They come back, and quick. What else? Drowning would probably do it, if they stayed under a good while. Fire, of course. Fire kills everything. Even starfish."

He leaned closer.

"If you put one down, do me the favor of burning what's left so maybe they won't know I told you. But they will. They smell everything. There. That's all you get and I'm sure it's too much. I'm probably a dead man. Pass down the holy water, will you? All that squealing makes a girl thirsty. Oh, and on the subject of burning the remains, let's go on out and turn br'er rabbit."

"Has it been long enough?"

"No, I guess not."

THE STREETS OF the mill town held few people in the middle of the day. The people were hidden in the belly of the mill, seeing to the huge looms with the air loud around them and stinking of dye; they were gathering in the fields and turning wrenches at the auto garage; the people were mashing vegetables and spooning them into babies' mouths and wiping those mouths after; the people were drowsing in furniture stores or changing flypaper in kitchens. Things were not easy here, but they were normal. And the children were in school.

I could tell Eudora felt truant in her summer dress walking through town with me, as though it were obvious to any who looked that she was a teacher and should be in school. It was not her fault she lived in a cursed town.

In Chicago the mornings would be cool now. Seagulls would ride kinder thermals over the sailboats that still planed across Lake Michigan. I ached for Northern air on my face.

I caught Dora looking at the reflections she and I cast in the windowpanes strolling together on a day trip for the last time as anything but legal husband and legal wife. We fit together despite my twelve-year surplus. Nobody uncle-and-nieced us. Men stole looks at her instead of staring because it was clear her bed was already warm. When I went into the silversmith's to pick up a rather unusual order I had phoned in, I asked her to wait outside, and only then would the men from the shops across the street let their gazes rest on her. I saw through the window how one fat man

stopped his car at the corner and removed the cigar from his mouth as if about to speak to her, but she turned her face from him so definitely that he drove on pretending he had not stopped.

"What are you getting, Frankie?" she asked me as I emerged from the silversmith's.

"A present. I'm not at liberty to say for whom." She had not seen me pocket the clip from my .45 before we left.

My smile disarmed her. It had been a good idea, coming here to an unbroken town. The moving company had said they would come Monday, October fourteenth. We went to the courthouse and made an appointment with the justice of the peace for Saturday, the twelfth. It felt good. It felt right. If we took nothing else away from this place, at least we would leave it as legal man and wife.

We sat in the town square. Across from us, various posters adorned the brick wall of the boarded-up hosiery mill; the largest featured an enormous Little Orphan Annie staring out at the world with her dead, white eyes, holding up a mug of Ovaltine. "Here's Health!" the legend read. In the foreground, a bronze angel lamented Confederate dead, unconcerned with its veil of pigeon droppings. Dora fed sandwich crusts to the pigeons, which, she remarked, were smaller and meaner than the ones up north, who always seemed to make out, even when they had to compete with people for scraps.

OLD MAN GORDEAU spent the first days of October driving to other small towns in the county to buy dogs back from those he

had sold dogs to before. The cousins and sons and daughters of the dogs he had lost, but the same muttish, red breed with the same unerring nose. He rebuilt his kennel closer to the house, easy shooting distance from his bedroom window, and he started in training the new dogs. It would not take him long with his sure hand to get the animals ready to track and hunt. He would have work for them soon.

Lester kept the feed shop running while Saul and the hired boys saw to the farm and the goats and horses. Saul was not well, but he was not talking about it. Old Man Gordeau let it be known around town that he wasn't going to wait forever to go back into those woods, alone if he had to, and when he did he was bringing dogs and a fiery sword.

Dora and I started packing. It was a strangely joyful task, even more joyful than the unpacking had been. It didn't feel like defeat. It felt like a setting right of something that had spun horribly wrong. It felt like we had been pardoned by the governor just before some fatal hand yanked the switch. I didn't even mind that Paul Miller's jerk brother charged us too much for the cardboard boxes he reluctantly parted with.

Estel Blake spent a lot of time in the general store since it was within earshot of the bell on the door to his hardware shop. He sat with those who gathered there even though the place was quiet and sad now and there were always enough seats by the stove. He talked about how the men would go into the woods again, and other men talked about it, too, but they were all tired of hearing themselves.

Estel knew that the town needed a captain, but since he had no idea how to help things, he tried to better himself by spending the

hour before dark practicing with his revolver. As the moon waxed pale and chalky rising later and later in the daytime sky, he made the copse of trees behind his house shiver with gunshots. He got better than he ever had been at hitting small blocks of wood thirty paces off, until one day a neighbor showed him a bullet hole near the baseboards of his house.

The sheriff argued that the man's house was at a safe angle from the targets he shot at, but the man just closed his eyes and shook his head. It was probably the same way he shook his head when he had been asked to help bury the dead, and again when he was asked to go into the woods.

"Cain't no man tell which-a-way a bullet's gonna rick-a-shore."

Estel Blake fixed the board in the man's house; I can see him walking away with black soil on the knees of his trousers. And he never did shoot behind his house again.

So now he sat in the general store with the rest of us, playing checkers sometimes, but mostly just sitting, smelling summer dying on the breeze that came through the screen door. He did not know that he was waiting for the full moon to come, but that was what the whole town was doing. For the next few days, Whitbrow lay as still as a bride waiting to meet her husband.

CHAPTER TWENTY-THREE

ONE MORNING IN October, not long before our furtive, planned nuptials, Dora found a wedding dress in the second-hand shop behind the butcher's. She could not believe it was really there, even when she put its scratchy fabric against her cheek and smelled its smell of hot summers boxed up in cedar. It looked as though it might fit her, but she tried not to hope too much. The gift was too sweet and too unlikely.

When she asked about it she found out it had belonged to the widow Miller, who had cast it from her house with all the other trappings of her long marriage before they enfolded her and dragged her to the next world. The great and concave mattress bearing the stamp of Paul Miller's form slouched just outside the back door.

Yes, it looked as if it might fit.

When she brought it to the butcher's shop up front, Hal said, smiling, "You sure you want that? Bad luck to wear a widow's dress that ain't kin."

"And why would a Christian man like you sell bad luck?"

"Worse luck not to pay the ice man. And ain't you already married?"

He winked.

She said, winking back, "I get married every year."

I FOUND OUT about this later, of course. Dora kept the dress hidden from me until the day of our wedding. She folded it neatly into a suitcase and went to change in the ladies' room of the courthouse where other women came and went, some of them smiling at her; but she remembered one woman stared at her in the mirror while she fixed her hair. Dora in her white dress and lace. The courthouse was not a place for virgin brides. She stared back so hard the other woman left without even shaking her head the way she had planned to.

My fiery love.

When I saw Eudora floating towards me in the lobby of the courthouse I thought of Actaeon and how he must have felt to see the goddess Artemis naked in her bath, all light and the petals of every white flower on the water. Every face in the courthouse turned to see her where she passed. It seemed for one drunk moment that the gentlemen might begin to applaud and they must have felt

it, too, because that was what they did. It started with a musta-chioed youth getting his shoes shined in a wrought iron chair and it was mimicked by the black boy shining; then two suited men, probably lawyers, took it up, clapping around the hats they held in their hands; then a farmer put his hat in his teeth so he could clap more freely. It was genuine and good and when Eudora got to me, she was blushing hard behind the little bunch of flowers she held to her mouth and her eyes were wet and shining.

Several of the men waved at me and one yelled "Congratula-tions!" and another "Good luck!" and I waved back smiling and I walked with my bride into the courthouse.

We did it.

We said the words and did it.

When we left, we all but ran to the car through the warmth of the afternoon. Her suitcase came open and we squatted to gather up Dora's clothes from the morning, and since our faces came close together we stayed there frog style and kissed as though we had nowhere else to go and nothing else to do.

When I got behind the wheel of the car and started it, it occurred to me that the moment of the applause when I saw my wife coming towards me was the best moment of my life, that there never had been nor would be a better one. I wanted to slow everything down. I wanted to remember every lake-grey- and shallows-green-eyed glance she threw at me, pregnant as they were with what had hap-pened before and what we had now won through to. I wanted a camera when she climbed out of the car in her wedding dress to change in the washroom of the filling station.

As I drove home, I looked at her so often in the bronze light of late afternoon that she chided me to keep my eyes on the road, but she was laughing.

It was good.

I have never forgotten how good that day was.

CHAPTER TWENTY-FOUR

THE NOISE BEGAN around eleven that night.

My new wife and I were talking in low tones, too excited to sleep, but spent from our last union, while the candle sputtered and made shadows. The breeze from the window was cool now so Dora had unpacked our blanket for the first time in that house. I remember looking once past the curtains and marveling at how beautifully the full moon threw light over the leaves outside. The view from our window looked like a picture-show view.

When the screams came even I heard them. Neither one of us moved for a second.

They came again. Two women. The word *help*.

I sat up in bed.

"Was that the Noble place?"

She nodded, wide-eyed. Gripping my arm and holding. I removed her hand and threw off the damp sheets. I put my pants on and took my holster, belt and service pistol from the drawer of the bedside table. While my wife had prepared for bed, I had readied things because Cranmer's words had echoed in my head, and because I remembered what Saul had said about the moon.

So I'd seen that the doors and windows were locked and I had loaded the clip with the silver-tipped lead custom-made for me in the mill town.

Now I held that pistol and my sweat was on the grip because I sensed I would shoot it soon and my life would hang on how I shot.

And maybe Dora's life, too.

"Stay here!" I shouted at her.

And I ran down the stairs barefoot and shirtless, almost tripping, out into the movie-house night.

The moon and the wind were strong and the trees made dazzling shadows. My bladder, while not full, would have felt better empty. I ran hard, hardly noticing the stones I later found had bruised and cut my feet. The screams had stopped, but I still heard noises. I was about to see something bad.

The lights were on.

The front door was standing open.

It was bad.

Ursula Noble sat cross-legged on the floor of the kitchen holding one arm between her legs. Everything around her was knocked over or spilled or torn up and she had gotten the tablecloth off the table and had it wrapped around that arm and blood was all over

the cloth and all over her. All over her legs and face and I suddenly knew that she would die.

Her father was lying on the floor of the common room and he did not move.

She was crying and I went to her and pulled her arm from between her legs and saw that her hand was gone. I used a long wooden spoon from the floor and part of the tablecloth to make a tourniquet as best I could remember how. I did this barely looking at her, mechanically, just to get through it. Watching both doors, afraid of what might come through one of them. My sweat in my eyes despite the cold air. My hands shaking.

I heard the youngest crying in a back room.

When the tourniquet was on I went and found little Sadie sitting in the bedroom and crying with deep lungs. She looked unharmed.

I ran back into the kitchen, stepping over the father. I could see the man was breathing. A stain in the shape of a clover darkened the wallpaper. Everything upset and broken. It was too much. I went to Ursie and took her face in my hands.

"Where's your mother?"

She was sobbing too hard to make a sentence.

"Shook her" and "outside" were all I could understand. Her drool on my thumb. I stood up and she knew I was leaving and she opened her eyes as wide as they would go and tried to keep me there with her one hand but I tore away. I took the pistol from where I had set it on the floor and left, a saltshaker rolling under my foot spilling me so I hit my shoulder hard on the way out, but

never fell down. I had the impression the father was moving now, slowly rubbing his stick-like legs on the floor trying to come to, but I rushed out the door now and did not look back.

A shiver went through me and raised gooseflesh on my left side as I went out into the cold air and silver light again. A streak of blood on the front porch hooked left, betraying the direction in which the mother had been dragged. There was a bobby pin in it. I took care to step around it all and walked to the left side of the house. Softly and quietly now, straining to see in the patchwork of moon-shadow.

The woods were thin and I saw motion in a clearing sixty or seventy yards away. My lips began to move as I whispered *please please please* although I did not know what I was asking for or whom I was asking. I crouched behind a tree.

I could see two of them.

Pulling at her the way dogs would fight over a rabbit.

Like wolves but not wolves.

Bigger.

Using their forepaws in a mockery of hands.

Standing half-erect sometimes like apes might.

My heart beat so loud and fast I thought it might break the shelf of my chest. My breathing was so hard I was sure they would hear. I fought to keep still but shuddered anyway. I sighted down the pistol but didn't draw the hammer; I was too far away for a good shot and I knew I could not make my legs move closer. She was clearly dead but even if she wasn't . . . Not towards them.

I backed away from my tree, keeping an eye on them. Trying to

control my shaking. Crouching low, I made my way to the Noble house again and saw that the front door was shut. Sadie cried out but her cry was stifled. I went to open the door but as soon as I touched the handle I heard a loud *clap* and something stung my face and something else passed by my head.

Am I shot?

I ducked to the side and shouted, "It's Frank Nichols!" But another shot tore a chunk out of the door and would have hit me had I not moved.

Light came from the hole in the door.

Sadie cried now that her father's hands were busy.

The noise will bring them back.

It was then that I remembered my wife alone in our house and I ran. I sprinted through the night air bare of chest and foot with the pistol tight in my hand.

I only survived because I looked over my shoulder.

It was closing in at a full run, not ten yards away.

Its eyes like dim green lamps, its teeth bared, its wild pelt rippling. This could be my death. Now.

I thumbed the hammer back and pointed the pistol behind me, still running. The monster dodged right, meaning to flank me, but exposed its own flank for just that second.

Please.

The big .45 jumped hard in my hand and banged loud. An instant of bright flame and then smoke. It was powerful. It was good magic. The thing's hindquarters bucked sideways when the slug caught it and it spun out, giving a bark of pain and surprise. It

stopped to lick its badly injured haunch and I might have sunk one in its chest had I been willing to stop running and take a steady shot, but I kept running and shot again and missed.

I saw motion behind it, farther off but coming. How many of them? I had only seen one other but there was no way to tell if maybe half a dozen were threading their way towards the noise of my gun. I thought they could probably smell my fear, that it would smell bright.

As I ran I saw my bedroom window as a square of light bobbing past the branches of the young trees along the road and I moved so fast now it seemed the balls of my feet barely nipped the ground. One was moving in the trees beside me. I glimpsed its shoulders as it ran. It was bigger than the other one and darker, maybe black, but it darted back into the brush when I raised my weapon and kept pace with me, just too far off for a good shot. I wanted to make sure one was not gaining on my other side but feared to take my eyes from this one. They were quick.

As I got to the porch I put my back to the wall and tried the door with my left hand. Open. I had forgotten to tell Dora to lock the door behind me. I got it open and leapt inside and saw my wife in the kitchen wide-eyed and small, holding a knife.

"Get upstairs and shut the door! Lock it!" I said, and I bolted the front door and dragged the heavy sofa and two packed, taped boxes in front of it.

Something moved past the window.

Please please please.

I ran into my kitchen, which was wild with the shadows of branches swaying on the floor. I grabbed Dora's silverware from the

drawer. Some of it fell and clattered to the floor as I took the stairs two at a time, moving past the shut bedroom door and into my study. The front door downstairs began to rattle as something strong tried to force its way in. Then three hard raps came.

Is it knocking?

They came again.

"Frank?" Dora yelled.

"Stay in there! No matter what you hear!"

I took the small cannon from its place in the corner of the study and poured powder in it, but the powder went everywhere. Now I perched it on its carriage. This was taking so long. If my hands weren't shaking. If I had a little time. Tore one pocket out of my pants for wadding. Quarters and nickels from my pocket—I remember how ridiculous it was to see a buffalo going down the hole—but not dimes; dimes were too light. Only butter knives and those delicate forks fit in the narrow aperture of the weapon. This was taking too long! Now the other pocket so the load didn't fall out when I pointed it down. More like a large shotgun than a small cannon, made to shred horses and men.

Why is it so quiet?

When I had it loaded I moved it to the hallway and pointed it down the staircase so that nothing could get up them without facing it. I had choked off the upper floor.

Or so I thought.

They're planning something, too.

I laid the pistol next to me.

Glass broke in the kitchen.

"Frank?"

"I'm alright, love. Be still."

I poured the priming.

It walked into the living room below.

Not the black one. Reddish. I saw it through the railing at a hairpin angle from the stairs. When I saw it my hands began to shake so badly that I could not light my lighter. I felt my testicles turn to ice and crawl up inside me.

It came around the corner with its yellowed teeth bare and its tongue hanging. Teeth like Turkish knives. It saw me and reared up to consider me, its ears nearly brushing the ceiling. It was not impressed. Back down on all fours and started its run up the stairs. Its smell coming hot before it, my skin tingling, anticipating the grab of those awful teeth.

It happened fast, I know that, but it seemed very slow.

Jesus God please please I'll do anything so sorry heartfully just let it THERE yes THERE please you GOD!

The lighter caught and I touched it to the priming, which issued a short *sst* and then a hard and final *BANG* that rattled every joint in the house and broke out a downstairs window.

At the last moment, when it saw the flame of the lighter and understood that it was going to be hit, it half turned away and caught the brunt of it through the ribs and middle. The effect was appalling. It was almost sawn in half. It panted hard twice through what was left of its lungs, blowing an awful bubble, then shuddered, caved in and died.

The recoil of the gun knocked me from a squatting position and onto my back; the carriage had slammed across my shin, laying it

open and all but breaking it. It was some time before I felt this. Or my badly burned hand.

My wife screamed my name.

I picked up the pistol.

I ran to the door and when I found it locked, I laid my shoulder into it and it gave.

The monster, the black one, was attacking Eudora where she had backed herself into the closet, kicking at it. It looked up at me as I burst into the room, and even as I raised the pistol it leapt on the bed and broke it and jumped out the window. My shot hit the headboard. I turned to see my wife. She was sitting on the floor of the closet holding her wounded foot aloft. It had bitten deeply into the meat of her heel and her blood ran and dripped.

"Frankie oh Frank help me it got me but I think I'm alright I just need help getting up oh my God what was it what the hell was that?"

"Just sit here and let me see it."

I stopped her bleeding with the top sheet of the bed. My hands were still shaking.

"That was the cannon."

"Yes. We'll have to clean this out."

"Oh God, we should have left. Why didn't we leave?"

"We'll leave now."

"It hurts. I'm sorry I jerked my leg. You're just trying to help and I can't stay still."

"I think you'll be alright. It's not as bad as it looks."

Dora rarely cried but she did now.

"I want to leave, you have to take me home. I don't understand what's going on here but it's so bad. Take me home, Frankie, anywhere."

"I will. I promise."

That was what I said.

Even though both of us knew it was too late now.

CHAPTER TWENTY-FIVE

D O YOU KNOW him?"

"No."

The sheriff stood with me on the porch in the cool of the morning.

I thought he looked grey and ill, and he was probably thinking the same thing about me.

"I'm supposed to take you in."

I nodded.

"If the best explanation you got is that you shot an animal and in the morning it wasn't."

"Please don't."

"I don't guess I will. A lot goin on I don't comprehend. No animal I know could have done that at the Nobles, and no man neither."

His voice faltered as he choked back a sob.

"What are you going to do with him?" I said, nodding towards the staircase inside. I had covered the two biggest parts of the naked man with sheets and towels. What was left of the back and shoulders suggested an acrobat. Small man, but strong. His face had been spared. He had an Irish look about him with his auburn hair and friendly cheeks and when I had thumbed his eyes shut he seemed to be frozen, laughing at the best joke he ever heard.

"Bury him in a potter's field. I don't know what else."

"Shouldn't somebody look at him? The other sheriff?"

"Ain't nobody comin."

"I don't understand."

"They said it's our bed to lie in and they won't come."

"What about . . . I don't know, the FBI?"

"You want to tell your story to the FBI? The wolf-man story? They'd lock you up in a sanatorium and then lock me up for not lockin you up. I need time to think. About everything. It's too much."

"I know."

"I guess you do. How is she?"

"Dr. McElroy stitched her and put ointment on her for infection. He's worried about that because the bite's so deep."

"I hope you put something on that eye, too."

I nodded. He meant my eyebrow, which had swollen up badly. The night before I had noticed it hurting and found a dime-sized piece of pine from the Noble's door wedged under it.

"Did he want her in the hospital?" he asked.

"He said that hospital's only good for dying. You go in for a hernia and never come out."

"That's about right. But he sent poor Ursie there. Oh my Jesus."

That half-choked sob came out of him again.

He put his hands on his hips and bent forward at the waist, trying to collect himself. I put my hand on his back, and as soon as I felt the warmth of his skin through his shirt, the gesture seemed invasive and awkward. I withdrew it and he stood up.

He reached for a tin in his shirt pocket and put a pinch of tobacco in his mouth.

"We're leaving town," I said.

"Maybe me, too. Let's see about movin him off your stairs."

IN THE PICTURES, gangsters spray bullets and the victims shut their eyes and fall asleep. Killing isn't like that, of course. I found that out pretty young. But killing someone in your house is different from doing it on a battlefield. On the battlefield, you might have to throw a body into a shell hole, or hide behind one, or share a trench with one until the shelling stops, but that's it. When it happens in your house, you have to clean it up. All of it. And then you have to keep living there.

It was a huge, awful fucking mess. Endless pieces of bone and tissue on everything, endless pumping at the well. I scrubbed the walls and floor until my hand and arm were numb, except for the hot pain where the flash had burned the back of my hand raw.

But the floors and walls.

I thought the sponge would run pink forever.

When that was finally done and the sheriff and Lester came by

for the dead man, I drove into town to get supplies. Estel gave me the keys to the hardware store and told me to take what I needed and not to worry about paying.

As I drove, I passed the carpenter's house and saw him hammering in his open work shed. The whole town could hear it. Everyone knew it was for caskets.

When I got back home, I was grateful to do a different kind of work. It was easier to strip burned wallpaper and board up windows and dig warped nickels out of the wall than to do what I had done before. And it was better to work than to sit and think.

Between tasks I saw to my wife. Once the downstairs was clean, I sat her pillow-propped on the couch and fixed the bed, then carried her back upstairs warm and dreaming in my arms.

Anna Muncie, the teacher of the younger grades, came over with cookies for Dora. Anna's face was swollen from crying. Dora did not have much appetite nor did she speak much, but Anna sat with her while I worked and then near dusk she made a dinner that she herself ate most of.

When it was time for bed, I left a candle burning in a glass bowl and I set my pistol on the nightstand. Dora slept quickly. I watched her breathing for several hours before I, too, succumbed and entered yet another troubled sleep.

I DREAMED ABOUT the trench fight, only this time when the German boy ate my fingers sitting in the mud with me, he then ate my

hand up to the wrist, got up and left me in the mud. Soon stretcher bearers fetched me, all suited up in gas masks, and hauled me to Chicago, on Halstead, I think, near a manhole that was also like the door to an oven. It was Hell. They wanted me to jump in since it was against the rules for them to push me. I refused. They explained that they had no place else to go and they were quite willing to wait. I remember the fire reflected in the eye plates of the mask. I remember the heat from the open hole.

It was from this stalemate that I awakened and found the sheets damp.

Dora was as hot as a brazier.

"Dora?"

She moved her face back and forth a little. I held my hand to her forehead and frowned.

"Eudora."

She made a small noise in her throat and then opened her eyes halfway.

I gave her water to drink. I made her take aspirin. Three of them. I put damp towels on her head and neck and she warmed them up so fast I spent half an hour doing nothing but wringing and replacing and fetching more cool water in a pan. Through all of this, she watched me with moist, cloudy eyes. Moonlight lit her face and she looked so beautiful I was afraid she was about to die, like in some painting of a saint's death.

"Honey, how are you feeling?"

"Foggy. Froggy. Not good. Heel itches."

I sat up and watched over her while she slept the night through.

When I finally began dozing, it was not yet light, but somebody's roosters had started anyway.

That morning I sent for Dr. McElroy, who put a thermometer in her mouth, then hissed when he read it. He offered to ring the hospital to tell them she was coming, but she sat up in bed and refused.

"Mrs. Nichols, your temperature is so high I'm surprised you're lucid."

"I heard what was said about that hospital. I'm not going."

"How do you feel?"

"Bad. But not as if I'm going to die."

"Light-headed."

"Yes. Exactly what was my temperature?"

"Maybe I got a bad reading. I'm going to take it again."

He did.

"Well?"

He paused before he spoke.

"You may not feel that poorly, but I believe that you may die."

"Then I'm not going to do it in a hospital."

"That hospital being what it is, I am disinclined to argue. I'll do what I can for you and pray about the rest. Let me change the dressing and get a look at that heel. With this much fever, I'm sure it's gone septic."

When he had the heel unwrapped, Dr. McElroy held it in one hand and blinked at it. He picked up Dora's other foot and looked at it. Then he blinked at the first heel again.

"Did I dress the right heel? Of course I did. Where the hell is it?"

"What, Doctor?"

"The wound."

THE MOVERS CAME that day. I had forgotten all about them. Instead of the broad-faced jovial black man and his smaller colleague, the company sent two humorless white men.

"We've had some bad luck," I said.

Neither of them spoke.

"My wife is taken ill. She can't be moved. We'll need to reschedule."

"You should have called."

"I know. I've been upset."

"Sorry about your luck."

"Thanks," I said.

Then he handed me the bill for the move that hadn't happened.

I took it and got my checkbook.

"Is John still working for your company?"

"John?"

"Or maybe James."

"Jimmy? Big, black guy?"

"Yes."

"In jail."

"What . . ."

"I dunno, mister. I don't really know the guy."

"Hit his wife with a crowbar," the other guy said. "Paralyzed her."
I wrote the check.

I WAS ONLY peripherally aware of the events that occurred in Whitbrow during the next few days, the days of Eudora's fevers. I did not go out to see what was barking when Old Man Gordeau used his new dogs to find what was left of Mrs. Noble, nor did I attend her funeral. I saw a mule-drawn cart full of furniture bump its way up the road, but I did not care who was leaving. My wife was my only business.

She stayed mostly in bed at first, weak and glowing like a coal, sleeping sometimes eighteen hours in a day. It was getting cooler. I saw to the opening and closing of the bedroom windows to keep her from stifling at midday or catching chills at night. When a hailstorm hit and raked the leaves and knocked shingles from the roof, I sat with her and read to her while she drank the tea I'd brewed. I took walks near the house and kept her room full of flowers. My best find was a patch of sunflowers near the end of their season, and when she saw me enter the room with a bundle of them, her smile turned my insides into a powder that shifted in me the way dunes shift.

At first she did not eat and it was all I could do to keep tea or water moving through her, but then her appetite came back, slowly at first and then with a startling urgency. I went to the general store and the butcher's almost every day. She drank water by the pitcher. She craved organ meat so I fried chicken livers and gizzards or beef liver when I could get it. She asked for soup with beef joints for stock,

and she gnawed on these when the bowl was empty. Hal the butcher saw so much of me that he asked me if I were breeding greyhounds.

Dora got stronger.

She took longer and longer walks during which I held her elbow. Although no sign remained of the bite on her heel, she complained of pain in that foot and leg reaching all the way to her hip.

Her color got better. At first she glowed with a feverish beauty that recalled the consumptive women of romantic literature, but that beauty soon lost its fragile quality and became a glow of unapologetic vigor. Her fever and pain persisted and she had dreams that made her thrash and clutch the sheets and moan. But when she awakened, her vibrancy put off my worry.

"What were you dreaming, love?"

"I don't want to tell you."

"Why not?"

She sobbed once, both laughing and crying.

"Because I was killing you in it, silly."

It was from Anna Muncie that I learned about Ursie.

Five days after the attack she died of the same rolling fevers that punished Eudora. Dr. McElroy had gone to visit her and the doctors there told him that she was gone and that they had never seen anything like it. Not just the persistent fevers, they said, but the wound itself. They had never seen a hand try to grow back from a stump before. They showed him the little fingers, like an infant's fingers with their tiny nails, sprouting from her wrist. An X-ray

revealed fine hand-bones knitting at the end of the radius. She pushed her IV needles out, too. The punctures kept closing up.

The director of the hospital was a religious man and, after she was dead, he saw that she was cremated along with her records.

SHERIFF BLAKE DID leave town.

Buster Simms told me about it.

One-armed Mike had called on Sheriff Blake the second Monday after the attack and found his house standing open. He called his name and knocked for a long time but he so hated to enter anybody's house without permission that he left and got an ice cream at Harvey's.

He went back afterwards.

It had been more than half an hour and the door was still open.

Mike had a bad feeling. He stood on the porch and said "Estel?" another three or four times before setting a shaky foot over the threshold.

Everything was so still in the house. Leaves had blown in. Not many, but enough to crackle under his step. When he went into the kitchen he saw Estel's pistol and holster and badge sitting on the table, as well as a note:

MIGHT BE BACK

BUT GET A NEW SHERIFF

THE LORD HAS TURNED HIS FACE FROM US

AND I AM NO GOOD

Mike stood there a long time just staring at the note. He thought about where the sheriff might have gone. He checked the whole house starting with the bedrooms, and he squinted as he entered each one because he was afraid the sheriff might have hung himself. He had not. At least not here.

The house was a mess. Estel had been eating his meals in the bedroom for the last few days and the dirty plates were stacked in one corner. Flies buzzed around these. Dirty clothes lay about nonsensically. He had stepped out of several pairs of pants and just left them. The mirror had been struck and cracks webbed out from its center.

Mike went downstairs and sat on the porch.

The sheriff had been his best friend, and now he was gone.

He had to tell someone.

But whom?

In the end, he told everybody he could find.

WHEN OLD MAN Gordeau saw the note Estel had left, he knew the town was in no shape to elect a new sheriff, so he decided on Buster as the best man to take over as acting sheriff, a temporary post. As mayor of Whitbrow, Gordeau had financial and civic duties, and had final say on big issues. It was always the sheriff, however, who took matters in hand. The mayor might be the source of the town's wisdom, but the sheriff had to be its strength. Its daddy. The one who held the belt.

"Buster," Gordeau had said when he went to recruit the big man, "you're as big as a damn bear and cain't nobody from here to Atlanta lick you."

"A man's size ain't gonna matter against them things."

"You're missin the point. If people think whatever's out there has to get through your thick hide first, they're gonna feel better about stayin, and maybe fightin. Long as you do somethin."

"Like what?"

"Well, seems to me that now we got dogs again, we ought a go back in them woods and hunt."

Buster told me about these events in the course of his visit with me the next day, as he scoured Whitbrow for men with enough spit in them to go into the woods again. It was a thin harvest.

When he came to my door, he had his hat in his hands so the wind toyed with his thick halo of hair.

"Mr. Nichols, I know I got no right to ask favors of you after I went with those that left you and Lester in the woods. But I am askin a favor. A big one."

"About what happened across the river, I want you to know . . ."

Buster stopped me by waving his hand.

"You're a good man and you're gonna say somethin generous about it, but I done what I done. And nothin you say's gonna change the fact that I run out on you, and that don't sit well with me."

I nodded.

"We are goin back out there, but this time we got dogs. And we will find them."

I felt my heart beat faster.

"Do you know what's out there?" I said.

"Do you?"

"Have you got time to talk?"

"I'll make time."

I told him.

I told him everything. The boy in the woods. What Saul Gordeau had seen (most of that, anyway). What happened at the Nobles'. How the silver in my gun had wounded one and chased off another. I told him how I killed a monster on my stair at night and in the morning pried up a man.

I knew I was breaking covenant with Martin, but after the attack on my wife I was ready to betray any number of taxidermists to strike out at them. The man-wolves. Ursie with the tablecloth on what was left of her arm. If Martin felt squeamish about harming his "lepers" across the river, I did not.

When I was through, Buster nodded, sorting through it all in the no-man's-land between belief and disbelief.

"I'll come with you into the woods on one condition," I said.

"I'm listenin."

"Someone's got to go to the mill town, and I mean tomorrow, and get bullets made for every gun we take with us."

"Silver?"

"Silver."

"Ain't no way we can take that much time fore we go out there. Besides which, won't nobody else believe this."

"You do."

He nodded slowly, looking at his boots.

Then he shook my hand and left.

It turned out he went straight to Pastor Lyndon's house and asked him for the big, silver collection plate he had used so long to pay for the damned things' dinner.

WHILE THE NEW sheriff went to the mill town to have bullets cast for the posse and in the days before those bullets would be ready, Whitbrow settled again into the spell of waiting it had learned so well these past months.

Stores and houses were put up for sale as refugees continued to limp away from the hurt town, but nobody came to buy. Some didn't wait for buyers. Those who left went as far away from Whitbrow as their money would take them. Some to Morgan, but more to the mill town. One family to Nashville. Several to Atlanta. All of them were glad when they got on the road. Poverty and hunger were not as bad as what they left behind, and when they got where they were going, I doubt they talked about Whitbrow.

Sarah Woodruff left her father's house on a clear night when the stars raged overhead, taking one change of clothes and a sack of books she could not abandon. Charley Wade saw her walking out of town with the boy who talked about the army; she walked with him all the way to the bus station in Morgan. Like my mother, she got out of this place; I hope she did a better job getting it out of her.

EUDORA BEGAN TO sleepwalk on the same night that Sarah ran off. The same starry, cool night.

I woke up when I realized my wife was not in her bed. I ran a hand over the plain of warmth her body had left and I rolled over and smelled her scent on the pillow. Her new scent, alive with

beeswax and trees. I lay diagonally across the bed, stomach-down, feeling the beginnings of an erection and meaning to ambush her with it when she returned from what I presumed to be a trip to the outhouse. I began to drowse again and then sprang awake when I realized it had been a very long time and she was not back. I rolled over.

"Dora?"

I sat up in bed and unraveled my feet from the top sheet. A glance at the clock told me it was three in the morning.

I swung my legs over and stood up nude in the cool room, trying to feel rather than hear her.

She was not upstairs.

"Eudora?"

I had a premonition that I was rehearsing for something unpleasant, that I would find her this time but that eventually I would be left alone in this or some other house. I went out of the room and stood at the top of the stairwell, reminded of the view from behind the cannon. It was then that I saw her, standing where I had first seen the monster, at that hairpin angle where the common room led to the kitchen. The light from stars and a crescent moon outside were so weak I had to strain to make her out. She just stood there, naked like me.

I walked down the stairs, squinting at her.

"Honey, what are you doing?"

I got close to her and saw that she was not awake. Her eyes looked through me and she swayed as if she were trying to find her land-legs. Her lips moved gently. A hand twitched.

Was it bad to wake a sleepwalker?

I seemed to remember hearing that. So I sat on the overstuffed sofa watching her. Until she moved again. Into the kitchen. She put water in the teapot and set it on the stove even though there was no fire. Stood swaying in the kitchen. Then she went to the back door and tried to open it but could not figure out the latch. She walked back to the spot I found her in, and I was tempted to speak to her but did not interfere with her until I saw her go to the front door and unlatch it successfully. It swung open, letting a chilly breeze in, and she walked slowly onto the porch.

I called her name and went to her then, putting an arm around her. She responded by moving her face towards me, but did not wake up. I steered her around and directed her back inside, latching the door. I guided her back up the stairs one by one and when I put her in bed I tucked the top sheet around her so tightly I would feel it if she got up.

By and by I slept.

Just before dawn she made love to me drunkenly, the strength in her legs pressing at my hips while she rode me. I thought she might break the bed again. I was not sure she knew who I was.

After, I watched her sleep while daylight bled into the sky.

For the first time I was afraid of her.

IN THE MORNING I wanted to hear music, so I went to where I had moved the gramophone for easy loading into the moving van, not far from the front door. I ran my fingers over the walnut casing to see if it had been nicked or gouged by the shrapnel that had

coned down from the stairwell when the cannon went off. The wood was cool and smooth to my touch. The old Aeolian Vocalion. My father's last birthday present to me. I imagined my father's spirit as a falcon mantling over the gramophone to protect it from the shrapnel. A sleepy, slurring falcon with reading glasses on. I chuckled and opened the hood. Touched the brass arm holding the needle. The little brass arrow of the volunome. The guts of the thing.

I thought of France and all its smashed houses, the litter inside them. Everything made to be enjoyed for a little while and then broken. One day this, too, fractured like pot shards under a city.

I put a record on the turntable and then fitted the brass crank into its port and turned it. I was rewarded with the slow, sweet jazz a colleague had sent me from Berlin. A woman chided her faithless lover in German, sending goose bumps up my left side. This song always moved me. German usually sounded like a chisel to me, but this woman turned it into a paintbrush.

Dora walked barefoot down the stairs.

"I'm sorry. It's loud, isn't it?" I said.

"I'm glad it woke me. It's nearly noon. Honestly, I seem to be sleeping my life away."

"It's this place. You'll come back to yourself in Chicago."

"Have you eaten, Frankie?"

"No. Nibbled."

"I'm starving."

"There's still some of that smoked ham in the icebox. How do you feel otherwise?"

"No, I finished the ham while you were sleeping. I don't feel

half bad. Foot's a real pill and my head's not clear, like we went to bed tight. But we didn't touch a drop, did we?"

I shook my head.

She came and draped her arms around my neck.

She spoke into my ear.

"Music's nice. I remember this one. What's she saying now?"

"That he will learn about sorrow. Someone else will take him to school the way he did her."

She moved against me so our embrace became a dance. I took her hips in my hands and swayed with her, bending my head down to her.

"You with your shoes on," she said. "I feel so short."

"It's about to end."

"Start it over."

I did.

We danced without speaking the second time through. Her strange smell in my nose. I held her tightly, but not as tightly as I wanted to.

The next several days passed as that day did, full of dreams and whiskey and sleep, the sleepwalking of my wife, her hungry love-making, her greedy belly.

And then I went back into the woods.

CHAPTER TWENTY-SIX

IT WAS THE last day of October.

Halloween, but nobody celebrated it here.

Although Dora and I had never joined the people of town in their Sunday devotions at the church (covering ourselves with the tattered rags of my Catholicism), I could almost hear Pastor Lyndon intoning, "If God wanted you to have a false face, He'd have given you one."

Funny that flower-bedecked sacrificial pigs struck him as Christian, but only heathens made jack-o'-lanterns.

We met at the cemetery just before dawn.

Buster Simms handed bullets of silver out to each man in the requested caliber. The gunsmith in the mill town had gouged Buster terribly for the work because the metal was so much harder

to melt and fashion than lead, with the result that most men could afford only a few rounds—although Saul had paid for twelve with his daddy's money, enough to fill his rifle twice. He had insisted on fitting the bullets into the casings himself and had stayed up all night measuring and re-measuring the propellant, seeing to his father's and brother's .30-30 shells as well. They took five each.

I requested seven, enough to fill the clip with one in the chamber. These slugs were solid silver; the ones I had gotten from the silversmith were lead with filings in the nose, capped with wax. I had no way of knowing if they would do more than hurt. I thought so, but I was glad to have the solid rounds. The four weaker slugs went last into the clip and in the chamber; the more potent ones, four of them loose in my jacket, would be the last rounds I shot. In case the first ones didn't do it.

I would have liked to have heard the conversation between Buster and the gunsmith; the silversmith had asked me if I was shooting at haints. Once he explained to me what a haint was, I said he wasn't too far off.

Buster looked at us, the men he had gathered. He had stood himself near the freshly turned earth beneath which Ursula Noble's ashes rested in her mother's jewelry box. This box sat atop the coffin containing what remained of her mother. Buster wasn't good at talking to groups of men so he let that mound of black dirt do the talking for him. It would say the right things to make of us the vengeful men he wanted, men who would have the strength to go into the country of our enemy and act. Ursula's father was the first one to speak. His eyes were dry and hard. He snugged his .38 into his waistband and said, "We goin?"

"Yep," Buster said.

And that was how it started.

Nine men went into the woods.

Myself. Buster Simms. Saul, Lester and John "Old Man" Gordeau. Dr. Harlan McElroy. Arthur Noble. Lawton Butler. The young carpenter Charley Wade.

Three dogs went also.

Lester had these dogs leashed, dogs his father had seen whelped and sold, but had now bought back. Even though he had only worked with them for less than a month, Lester knew these dogs and they knew him. The female, Delilah, was the biggest and best behaved. The boys, Mustard and Shep, had long since tested her and found themselves lower on the rope, so what she did they did.

The Gordeaus had taken these dogs to the Noble place to get their talented noses full of that smell. *Their* smell. It was strong to the dogs. They hated it and yet they pulled towards it, wanting their masters to extinguish its source. I was sure the dogs knew more about what was in the woods than we did; they had read libraries in the musk and saliva and hair left at the murder scene, and only Delilah's faith in Lester's divinity fortified her to drive the other two dogs towards those across the river.

We kept a good pace on the first leg of the journey. We crossed the river pulling the raft across in groups of three. Nobody said it, but all of us sensed that this time was for keeps, and that our hunt would turn around on us if we had not come back across by sundown.

As labyrinthine as those woods were, it was hard for me to see how we would.

We stopped at Magi Rock long enough to drink and to let the animals drink, and then we kept on. Summer was over now and the cool air let us push long and hard without rest. We had left the trail hours ago. None of us knew exactly where we were, but I got the idea that the dogs had been chasing something in circles, or, since we always seemed to be on new terrain, in a sort of broad, lazy spiral.

Looking up, I saw how yellow the trees were above us. Were we on higher ground? It was colder here than in town. Autumn was moving faster here.

It was a little like the Argonne, but for once I was afraid of something besides nonexistent Germans. The fear was almost good this time. There was a reason.

The dogs, who had been pulling us forward with purpose for many hours, were now becoming frantic. Lester had no gloves, so I'm sure even his callused hands were becoming raw from the strength in the leashes.

"Somethin's close," he said.

Time slowed down for me as it always did in the moments before some event. I looked down and saw my feet moving towards whatever was out there. One of my boots knocked the top from a mushroom. Sweat trickled in my shirt despite the chilly air. The air smelled clean and good. I opened my mouth to try to hear something besides the baying of the dogs, but I could not.

I marched forward with the rest of them.

Movement in the trees made Saul stop and raise his rifle, and the rest of us raised our weapons, too.

Something in the trees off to the left.

One of them.

I felt a tremor in my hands but willed it to stop. I rested my thumb on the hammer of my pistol.

One of them.

The dogs knew.

I knew, too. Which one of them it was. Knew it as surely as I had known my father was dead that night my telephone rang near midnight.

Where are your pants, my friend?

A flash of red in the trees.

"Show yourself," Old Man Gordeau croaked next to me, then Buster said it louder.

The red flash again, faded cloth.

Pale yellowish skin.

"Hold your fire," Buster said. "It's a little girl."

I moved sideways to get a better look.

I saw the dress, an old dress, faded nearly pink in places, hung on a small, thin figure standing in the brush fifty yards out.

But it wasn't a girl. It was a mulatto boy of about thirteen.

The same boy.

The boy with no pants.

The dogs were losing their minds, barking with wide eyes, spittle flying from their mouths.

"God," I said.

"Come over here to us," Buster said.

But it didn't move.

"Watch her," Old Man Gordeau said, shouting over the dogs.

"I think that's a boy," said Charley Wade.

"God," I said again.

It put its thumb in its mouth like a small child might, but there was no innocence to it.

I found my voice.

"That's one of them. I've seen him."

Saul raised his rifle.

"What do I do?" he said. "I don't want to squeeze on no little boy."

He said this mostly to his father, but his father didn't answer.

Buster moved towards it, and it moved back. Coy like a little girl. The familiarity of the game raised the hairs on the back of my neck.

The whole party edged forward to catch up with Buster.

When Buster moved forward again, it retreated, keeping its distance exactly.

Calmly.

"Shoot that thing," Arthur Noble said.

Buster said, "We won't hurt you. It's them we want."

"Didn't you hear Mr. Nichols? It *is* one of them. Shoot it!"

"No, Arthur. Not no kid."

It was at that moment that Delilah yanked her leash out of Lester's hand, startling him so that the other dogs got free, too.

"Hey!" Lester shouted after them, but it was too late. The three dogs charged hard at the boy. It ran farther into the woods. The dogs ran after it. We began to trot now, too, much slower than the

dogs or what they were chasing. Just before the thing in the red dress fell completely out of sight, the dogs caught up with it and dropped it to the ground. I assumed from the thrashing in the ferns and leaves that the dogs were tearing the boy apart.

Then one of the dogs made a sound between a yelp and a scream and ran back towards us. The thing in the red dress was up now and running, far away in the trees.

I could see that it was *chasing the other dogs.*

Away from the party.

They vanished from sight.

The remaining dog was running towards us, trailing its leash behind it and shivering and crying pathetically. While the rest of us just stared, Lester went to the dog.

"Mustard?" he said, though how he recognized it I did not know.

The dog's face was covered with blood, its own blood. Its nose had been bitten off, and one eye was out. It sat on its haunches and scooted away from Lester, trying to wag its tail and crying, bobbing its ruined head. Lester knelt to the dog and moved his hands around impotently, wanting to help it but afraid to touch it, just saying "Goodmustardgoodmustardgoodmustard" in a hopeless paternoster.

"Do it, boy," the elder Gordeau said.

But Lester knelt there, wringing his hands.

So Old Man Gordeau shot the dog.

"Just let me see that goddamned thing again," Saul said, whiteknuckling his rifle. "Just let me see it."

He would get his wish.

WE TRUDGED FORWARD, following the tracks of the boy and dogs as best we could. Blood showed on the lighter leaves near the boy's bare footprint, but soon gave out. Odd drops of blood had fallen here and there, and Lester would have other men stand at them, then rotate forward so the line of travel could be established.

Soon they came to a dip in the land with pooled blood and more torn and stamped-down grass and fallen leaves, and then the dog's tracks stopped altogether.

Lester found other human tracks, larger ones, in a patch of bare soil and on lichen-covered rock nearby.

He groaned and tears formed at his eyes as he scouted the scene.

"Them dogs is dead," he said, "and someone come up and took em. They went off that way, but the boy kept on ahead. Which do we follow?"

"That damn boy," Saul said.

Buster nodded, and we kept on.

WE KEPT ON much too late.

The first stone hit just after dusk.

The sky was smoky purple above the canopy of trees, and then the canopy gave out as the posse entered a small clearing. The waxing moon was trying to shine behind thin clouds. I suspected Lester was wondering whether to tell everyone that he had lost the trail, and he pulled out a plug of tobacco, stirring his finger around in it to get the last crumbs.

He was putting the pinch in his cheek when he saw something flash just in front of his nose, making him start and inhale.

The stone caught Charley Wade hard and he went "Ah!" and bent over double, cupping his free hand over his ear and holding his revolver awkwardly in front of him. Lester spasmed and coughed while the rest of us crouched and shouted and pointed our guns in all directions. Still coughing, Lester pointed his rifle from the hip and shot blind into the trees.

Another stone bounced off my shoulder and then Buster ducked a third one that hit the doctor square in the teeth. He jerked and shot his .32 at the trees even though his shot wasn't clear. Buster shouted *God-DAMNIT* while more stones fell and more men shot.

Saul broke right and scampered towards cover; I went with him, as did Buster and most of the rest. Arthur Noble ran off left, followed by Lawton Butler, who held on to the back of Arthur's overalls.

Saul got small behind a tree and sighted down his rifle, waiting. I crouched behind him, then realized Charley was still bent over in the clearing, getting hit again, saying "Ah!" I ran out and grabbed Charley's hand, catching a rock that felt like it might have broken my collarbone, and I yanked Charley back into the trees. Charley lurched and fell, slinging his gun into the trees and out of sight. The doctor covered his head ineffectively with his hands and ran for the gun, but a stone hit him so hard in the cheek he turned right back around and took cover again.

He shot his own gun dry and I shot once at what turned out to be a dead tree.

Yelling and shooting off left.

Panic.

Buster said, "Red dress!" and shot, then slipped and fell against me. A stone had grazed his head.

Buster's hand on my white shirt left a bloody print.

Lester, still coughing, was about to shoot another bullet, but his daddy grabbed the barrel and pointed it down, saying, "Stop shootin til you can see somethin."

I saw one, a Negro woman with wild hair, and I shot twice at her before she ducked behind a tree. Her stone just missed Saul's head, and Saul turned his rifle towards where it had come from. When she broke cover, she ran so fast I barely saw her. Saul's shot rang my better ear, and the woman fell.

Everything got quiet after that.

I put my gun away.

"Goddamnit," Buster said again.

No more stones came.

The woods seemed to exhale.

Lawton Butler stumbled across the clearing, holding his head. Bleeding. "Arthur's dead," he said quietly.

Then he said it again.

DR. McELROY WIPED his hands on his pants.

"I've seen cancer as big as a catcher's mitt. I've seen a woman with a fishhook in her eye. But I never thought I'd live to see a man stoned to death."

"Like in the Good Book," Lester said.

"Sometimes I wonder how good a book can be that's full of such as this."

Arthur Noble lay where he had been trying to cover his head. He had run out of bullets just before Lawton had been hit hard enough to lose consciousness. The pile of stones lay all around him.

"When I come to, it was all over," Lawton said. "I ain't made for this. I'm sorry."

But the doctor was still staring at Arthur, who might have looked like he was about to sing, except that his jaw was wrong.

Buster said, "Doc McElroy."

He looked at Buster now where Buster was holding a handkerchief to his side, just above his belt.

"I did that," the doctor said.

"No hard feelins. Just tell me if it's bad."

"Don't take this the wrong way, but it just hit fat."

Buster smiled a little at that.

"Put whiskey to it if you got some. When we get back, I'll go in looking for shirt."

"You should put something on that face, too. You're a mess."

Dr. McElroy pulled out his brass cigarette case and squinted at it, but it was too dark to see his reflection now.

"When we get home," he said. "If we get home."

SAUL HAD STAYED watching where he'd shot the woman, worried, perhaps, that she might get up again or that one of them might

come back for her. Now Buster said, "Let's have a look," and we all went forward.

She was a black woman of thirty-five or so with a shaggy, tangled mane of hair that was just going grey. She wore men's dungarees and an old-fashioned ladies' coat that had flapped up to show the bare skin of her back and her narrow waist. There appeared to be no fat on her, but abundant muscle.

Saul had hit her squarely in the head, and her mouth was open and the blood under her could fill a sink. The doctor leaned over her and covered her back with her coat. Everyone kept his weapon on her just in case she grabbed the doctor's wrist.

She did not.

She was dead.

"WE CAIN'T LEAVE Arthur," Charley Wade said.

"What about her?"

"The hell with her," Old Man Gordeau said. "If they want her buried, they can do it. They got all the damn shovels."

Buster said, "We ain't got time for buryin. We got to hunt or run. I say hunt, but we gonna vote."

"What do you mean, vote?" Lawton said, still holding his head, which was bleeding less, although his drunken slur and difficulty focusing suggested he had a concussion.

I said, "Lester, can you find them?"

"Not in the dark, not without dogs. But maybe with the light."

"That's good enough for me," Saul said. "Hunt."

Old Man Gordeau said, "Hunt."

"Run," the doctor said.

"Run," Charley said.

"This isn't even worth a vote. We're beat," Lawton said, quivering his lip like a child about to cry.

Buster said, "I'll take that as 'run.' Three each. Two left. Mr. Nichols?"

I put my hands on my hips and looked down at my feet for a long moment before I spoke.

"As soon as this is over, I'm putting my wife in the car and driving out of here for good. This is your town. I thought maybe it could be mine, too, if I fought with you, if I planted my feet and stayed. But it's not. I won't run out on you tonight. I'll do what you say. There's eight of us. Seven should vote so we don't split down the middle. I abstain."

"No," Lawton said. "No, no, no, no, no."

"Who's left?"

"Lester."

Buster looked at him.

Everybody looked at him.

He was about to say "run," but when his daddy shifted his weight from one foot to the other, Lester looked down and the word "hunt" came out of his mouth so quietly I wasn't sure what he said.

"No. Do what y'all want. I'm leavin."

Then Lawton Butler turned from where he stood near Buster and walked slowly away.

"Hey!" Buster shouted at his back, but Lawton kept walking.

He had only gotten a few steps when Buster trotted up behind him and spun him around, trying to be gentle, but the man's balance was bad and he fell into Lester Gordeau's leg. He crabbed up to his feet and looked wide-eyed at Buster.

That was when he made the mistake of pulling his pistol out of his trousers. He probably only meant to back Buster away with it, but Old Man Gordeau, who wasn't five feet away, didn't wait to find that out and shot him in the chest with his deer rifle, just left of the sternum. When his heart stopped, Lawton Butler shrugged his shoulders and made a sound like a man about to throw up, then raised his pistol, shot Gordeau once in the stomach, and fell down dead.

The old man sat down hard with a groan and said "Jesus" through clenched teeth as his sons clutched at him and everyone else, even the doctor, stood fish-mouthed at what had just happened. Gordeau kept saying "Jesus" until he passed out and that was when the spell broke and Dr. McElroy came over to him, felt his neck and lifted his shirt.

"He's not dead, but the way he's bleeding, he'll die."

"Ain't there no chance?" Lester said.

"Maybe in a hospital. Not out here."

"I just changed my vote," Lester said. "Let's get out of here. Please."

THERE WAS NO good way to carry Old Man Gordeau.

In the end, the Gordeau boys used the hand-axe Charley Wade

had brought and cut down saplings to make the frame for a crude litter. Saul stripped the jacket from Arthur Noble and the pants from Lawton Butler with little hesitation (even when Lawton's eyes opened and the dead man belched, causing Lester to jump back as if from a rattlesnake), and the brothers stretched these between the poles.

Charley Wade asked about the propriety of abandoning their friends, but nobody wanted to haul them, not even Charley, so they stayed. Handkerchiefs over their faces were the only funeral rites the two of them got; Dr. McElroy, covering Arthur, said "Poor Sadie" in lieu of a prayer.

Buster took Arthur's gun, saw that it was empty, and tossed it into the trees. Lester, whose rifle was almost dry, took his daddy's six bullets. Each man checked his remaining load. I looked in Lawton Butler's pistol and found it empty. The bullet in Gordeau's belly had been his last.

We looked where Charley had slung his gun as he fell, but it was too dark and the brush was too thick. The gun was gone.

For the first hour, Gordeau came in and out of consciousness as his boys carried him along, groaning when his litter bearers encountered a root or shifted his weight clumsily. Dr. McElroy's improvised dressings had soaked through and there was nothing clean for which to swap them out. The old man only spoke once; he looked at Lester tight-lipped and said, "Boy," but then seemed too tired to say the rest.

He died some time soon after that.

When it was clear that he was gone, the boys set the litter down, as they had already done several times to rest their arms, and Lester started to cry. Saul looked away from him.

"Quit that," he said. "Daddy wouldn't cry over you."

"I guess not," Lester said.

But then Saul cried, too, less for his father than for himself; for what had happened to him, what would likely happen to him yet.

Nobody suggested they leave Gordeau behind, though all of them wanted to. I could see in Charley Wade's eyes that it was all he could do not to sprint for the river.

The boys picked Gordeau up and moved along.

I was the one who recognized the trail.

I spotted a fallen log with two gnarled branches reaching up like someone asking to be lifted, an image I had noted in our last excursion. We found the path back to the river just on the other side of that. This cheered us, and, even though it was getting near midnight and the river was an hour away, Buster thought it might be smart to rest.

"Sit a minute, and smoke if you got it. We still got a ways to go."

I accepted a cigarette from the doctor.

Lester and Saul, who had worn themselves out carrying their father, sat against the same large tree and napped, each holding his rifle in his lap, their heads nearly touching. Buster asked Dr. McElroy to look at his pocket watch and tell him when it had been fifteen minutes. He and I kept our eyes on the still, cold woods around us. Charley Wade melted against the fallen log with the outstretched limbs. The doctor sat next to him and smoked.

Nobody saw it happen.

"Time," the doctor said.

Buster roused each man separately, quietly.

A moment after Saul awakened, he started and stood up fast.

"What is it?" Lester said.

"My rifle. Lord, my rifle."

Saul was holding a branch with rotten bark.

He had been sleeping with that on his lap.

His gun was gone.

ONLY CHARLEY WADE saw where the first shot came from.

He was halfway through the words "Look out!" when the *BANG* of Saul's stolen rifle bounced in the woods. Chips of bark flew near Lester as he scrambled to his feet.

"Gimme that!" Saul said, reaching for Lester's rifle, which he held out to his brother, but Saul's fingers had just brushed the stock when the next shot from the woods rang out and Saul fell down, grabbing his jaw. Screaming womanishly. I had heard this noise before.

Got the one behind Jesus God I'm next

The rest of the party crouched and ducked and now opened up, firing madly in the direction the shot had come from.

The half-moon had come out, throwing pale light down through the trees.

I saw that we were obliged to shoot over the body of Old Man Gordeau, whose face was bare and drawn in the moonlight.

Another muzzle flash from the trees; it had relocated. Or there were two. We kept shooting. I reloaded the clip with the shells from my pocket, fired two at a silhouette, then got a stove-pipe jam. I cleared it, then stopped shooting. The doctor flinched as a

bullet passed quite near his head. He was otherwise frozen, holding his empty pistol in front of his face for no good reason.

Lester emptied his rifle and said, "I'm out!"

"Me, too," said the doctor.

Buster said, "Shut up!"

"I think they shot six!" Lester said. "If all they got's the Enfield, they dry, too."

"Could be they got my gun. They's still three in that," Charley said.

"Shut the hell up about how many bullets you got," Buster yelled.

It was hard to be heard over Saul.

He was shrieking, hoarsely now.

I had two bullets left.

I resolved then and there not to use them unless I was within ten feet of one; to save them until I was certain I would die unless I shot. My resolution would be tested very soon. I looked around at the group. Lester had his shirt off, his white limbs bare to the cold; the doctor had dropped his empty gun and now held Lester's shirt bunched and pressed against Saul's jaw, muffling his cries somewhat. Lester was looking around to see if there was a dropped gun he could shoot, but he could see none, and nobody was firing now. We all panted, crouching behind trees, our breath pluming.

Lester saw something and fixed his gaze on it.

I looked where he was looking.

The red dress. The boy with no pants walked out almost nonchalantly into the moonlight. Buster stood to fire, but the boy saw him and crouched low, fast, just as Buster squeezed. The bullet

whined off into the trees. The boy now bent down and grabbed Old Man Gordeau by the pants legs and began pulling him across the trail to the trees on the other side. Lester Gordeau broke from where his brother thrashed and groaned and ran to the trail, grabbing his father's arms.

"Let him *GO!*" he shouted at it, but it pulled grimly, stronger than Lester, jerking at the dead man's legs in a series of short, hard tugs like a dog pulling at a knotted sock. Lester was losing ground. He dug in and tried to pull harder. He knew it was staring at him but he would not look at its face.

The moon went behind a cloud again and it got darker.

I wanted to shoot the boy but would not part with those last bullets; nor could I make myself run onto the trail to help Lester.

"Let go, Lester!" Charley yelled.

"Lester, get back here!" shouted the doctor.

That was when the boy in the red dress dropped the old man's legs and walked up to Lester, who stood stupefied, holding his father's arms. He didn't even move his head away when it reached up like a magician about to do a trick, and grabbed Lester's ear. The boy yanked Lester's ear off.

Lester yelled and dropped his father.

Both brothers yelling now.

The boy tucked the ear in his mouth like a piece of candy. I sighted down the barrel now, arguing with myself about whether to shoot the boy; that was when Buster grabbed Charley's axe from his belt and ran at it.

It didn't even duck.

Buster swung hard and hit true.

He buried the axe in the boy's head as if in a soft tree stump; I knew the sound it was making even though I couldn't hear it, knew that Buster was *feeling* that sound in the bones of his arm. He let the handle go. The boy staggered backwards until he hit a tree, then slid to the ground as his legs buckled under him. Every man stood still, holding his breath.

A gout of blood poured down the boy's head.

Then stopped.

The axe fell out of the boy's head and onto the trail. And then the wound was gone. The men who were close enough to see it gasped. The boy wiped the blood out of his eyes with the hem of his dress and stood up, picking up the axe.

Buster backed up a step. I walked onto the trail and stood next to Buster, my gun pointed at the boy. Not ten yards away. Despite my shaking hands, I was sure I would hit him.

The boy dropped the axe.

Grinned his sharp-toothed grin.

Then started to shake.

The doctor might have thought it was a seizure from the head wound, but that had not just been a wound any more than this was just a seizure.

Buster and I backed away.

The boy changed.

Quickly, tearing the red dress.

The moon came back, shone on its dust-colored fur.

It stepped out of what was left of the dress.

I remember smelling urine and thinking Buster's bladder had loosed. Turned out it was mine.

I sensed Buster turn and run beside me, so I turned and ran also, still holding the pistol with two shots left in it.

I believe all of us ran.

All except the doctor, with Saul's head in his lap.

I never saw them again.

Or Lester.

BUSTER AND I ran together until we could not run. Twice I hit trees, once so hard I almost lost consciousness. When we could no longer run we trotted, and then we walked. Buster wore the expression of a tragedy mask and, at times, made a sound between panting and sobbing. I put my arm around the big man's shoulders but Buster didn't seem to care; just clutched his hands under his chin like a child saying grace and made that sound.

I don't know how long that went on. I know we were making for the river, and I have no idea if we were heading in the right direction. I was sure we wouldn't get there. I was right.

When strong hands took my arm and spun me, I didn't resist. I had no fight left. "This one?" said a small-eyed Negro with an unevenly trimmed woolly head. A white man said, "Yeah. This'n shot me. With this." He had already plucked my pistol out of its holster. He had permanently matted long hair and a huge mustache. They were both naked, as was a white woman with a curly brown mane, who moved past us and made for Buster. Thankfully I didn't see any more. The men hoisted me on their shoulders like a rolled-up rug and started running with me.

Behind me I could hear Buster screaming hoarsely, "Stop! Stop! Stop!"

Not about the men running with me; about whatever the woman was doing to him.

I knew I was going to die.

And something odd happened; I relaxed.

And it all got funny.

The white one, the one with the cowboy mustache, was running in front with my legs, limping, favoring his right side. I remembered now shooting one of the monsters in the haunch the night my wife was bitten. The right haunch. I started laughing.

Then I realized that I recognized his mustache.

He was one of the hobos who came through town looking for work. I sat next to him while he ate ice cream at Harvey's on that hot summer day. The colored with the bad haircut had been with him. It was also possible that Curly Woman was the pipe-smoking "Polish" woman. Jesus, they had our number. They hadn't been angels looking for honest men; they had been devils making maps.

I laughed harder.

The colored with the bad haircut, who was holding my upper body, laughed, too, and said, "Sound like young marse got a joke to say."

I thought about Dora, alone in the house, and I stopped laughing. I clawed and tried to dig my fingers into the black man's eyes. He didn't yell, just made a sound like *ack*, twisted out of it and dropped me. Because the other one had my feet, my head hit the ground. Now my feet were dropped. I opened my eyes just in time to see the black one straddle my chest fluidly and sit down on me

like an anchor. I remember the moonlight on his blousy but thread-bare shirt, how old and dirty it was, and his stink. It was the not-unpleasant smell of a Negro's skin and hair corrupted with something feral and something coppery like old blood. I had smelled it while he ran with me, but now it washed down over me.

"You need a bath," I said.

He blinked his small eyes in surprise.

"Lawd, you got a mouth on you," he said admiringly, then hit me with incredibly hard open hands until I blacked out.

I think it was twice.

CHAPTER TWENTY-SEVEN

I WOKE UP in a cage, naked, outside.

It was morning. It was cold. My head hurt like it was sitting in a socket of cold, broken glass. A curious chicken just outside the iron bars cocked its head so it could see me with its preferred eye.

"Good morning," I said to it.

I sat up, noticing first how white my legs looked and then that they had rust stains from the bottom of the cage. I had a very civilized and unnecessary urge to cover my private parts, but there was not so much as a handkerchief in the frigid cage. There was not enough room to stand, or to fully extend my legs.

I looked at the chicken again.

"Would you please tell management that I would like to be moved to a better room?"

It walked off disinterestedly.

"I'll have your job," I said.

I knew where I was, though I scarcely believed it.

I knew where I had to be.

Despite the murderous pain in my head, I looked around and took stock of my situation. A grey, ancient smokehouse sagged just to my left. Near it stood a sort of round wooden disk. The fact that everything was blurry informed me that my glasses were gone.

To my right, a low stone wall defined the limit of what appeared to be an overgrown garden. Past that were rows of dilapidated shacks, swarmed over by kudzu and impaled by young trees.

This was all somehow familiar to me.

When I turned around and looked behind me, I knew why.

I saw it.

La Boudeuse.

The plantation of Lucien Savoyard, my great-grandfather.

Of course.

I turned around and looked at that wooden disk again, noticing this time the leather straps and buckles. Yes. This was the wheel on which Savoyard's slaves had been flogged and tortured and spun until they were witless. I noticed that it was not overgrown.

"He awake," a voice I recognized said. The Negro from last night. Not the strong, bald one. Bad haircut. He came over with a chipped bowl and stood over my cage with it.

"Open your mouth."

I was thirsty enough to oblige and I drank as best I could the cold water he poured through the bars. I was shivering.

"I think the man cold," he yelled back at the house. He seemed genuinely amused by this.

"Why are you doing this to me?" I said.

He looked at me.

He said the next thing very slowly.

"Cause we know who you are. We smell who you are. But don't worry none. We's the forgivin type."

He stooped for the chicken that had been eyeing me and snatched it up by the neck, taking it inside with him, unconcerned with its beating wings. It took a moment for that to sink in. How fast he was.

It rained.

I had been testing the lock to the cage, bracing myself as best I could and pushing with both feet, hoping something might give. Something did, but it wasn't in the door. I hurt my back.

"Goddamnit!" I said. That's when I felt the first drops. "Goddamnit, goddamnit, goddamnit."

Soon it was pouring.

I hugged my knees, watching the rain splashing in the muddy yard, trying to focus on that instead of the cold that was creeping through my body and the dull, tight pain above my right hip.

I saw a white foot tread in a puddle, and I looked up the leg and at its owner. The woman with the curly hair. Curly and matted. Naked, like me, standing in the rain. There was dried blood near her ear.

She had killed Buster.

"You're handsome," she said.

"Thanks," I said.

She just stood there.

A beautiful woman with a wide, abundant thatch of hair on her pubis.

Slightly deflated breasts with huge nipples and brown areolas.

Someone's mother.

The house was behind her, with its cupola and its balconies and mad growths of ivy. One of the upstairs French windows was open.

Then I saw her.

Eudora.

Her pale figure perfectly framed in the darkness of the interior.

Holding a bedsheet wrapped around her.

She looked out at me for a moment. I couldn't make out her expression. Then a black hand was on her shoulder and she turned under her own power, and she went out of sight.

"She's Hector's," the woman said.

"I see."

"Good," she said, and opened my cage.

She crawled in with me, entwined her limbs with mine, with her animal stink and her wild, tangled hair.

At first I tried not to let her, but it was like she was carved from warm oak. Her grip was unbreakable, even working against the thumb. She kissed me with her full lips and her rotten, hot breath, and I kept my mouth closed against her until she used her hand to force my mouth open. I bit her lip so hard my canines touched through it, and she jerked away from me, ripping the soft tissue open so a little part of her lip hung; the wound bled onto her chin in the rain. She laughed softly, like we were kids hiding in a tree house with a dirty secret. Drops of her blood fell on my chest and

mixed with rainwater. She licked at where I bit her, taking her blood back into herself, and soon the bite was gone.

"You tryin to make me bite you back, huh? You want me to turn you? I might, pretty man, 'cept he said not to. But I will do this."

She broke my ring finger.

I think she would have broken my little finger, but I didn't have one on that hand.

I was so numb and cold and crazy it didn't really hurt.

It didn't matter.

She started putting mud all over us. It was smooth and sticky, more like clay. She warmed it on her crotch, then used it to get me hard.

She stuck me in her dirty like that and rode me until I came.

Then she slept on me and I was glad to be warm.

It just didn't matter.

It got to be near dark and Mustache brought me dinner and a horse blanket. I had the impression somebody had a powwow and decided I might die of cold, and, for whatever reason, I wasn't wanted dead. Not quickly, anyway. Dinner was roasted chicken, no doubt my friend from the morning. The funny thing was, I was so exhausted and deranged that I felt emotional about it. Like the chicken had suffered despite its innocence. I cried and ate it crying. It was poorly cooked and red near the bone. It occurred to me that perhaps they weren't used to cooking things here.

When it was full dark, Curly Woman came and got me.

"He wants to see you."

I wrapped up in the blanket and went with her into the big, wrecked plantation house, noticing now the flaking paint and bullet holes and how there was no glass in most of the French doors. We came in through the dining room. Candles burned and spilled wax on a once-magnificent table where a carved peacock's jeweled eyes had been knifed out, probably by Union soldiers. I noticed that the candle-holders were rusted Civil War–era bayonets jammed into the wood. She removed a candle and used it to light my way past the stairs now; I noticed a depression where the steps had been stove in by a cannon-ball at the end of its momentum, then crudely replaced. A groove in the fine wood floor betrayed its trajectory, how it had skipped like a giant skee-ball. The Yankees who occupied La Boudeuse after the slave uprising had shelled it for sport when they left. This was like a temple to madness.

In the hallway, we walked past rotted tapestries and, because I looked at them, she graciously stopped and held the candle so I could see the motif. Eighteenth-century laborers hardly laboring at all. How different must have been the scene out the window that gave onto the fields; slaves toiling bent-backed in the sun, tearing their fingers on the rough plants while, inside, in dyed silk, French shep-herds lolled on rocks under shade trees. The master at his desk, the mistress at her loom and the house nigger pulling on the fan cord.

HE WAS IN the library. The big, bald colored from the town square. The one who sniffed at me and stared at Dora. The one they had

gone to lynch. She squatted near him now, at his feet, not looking up at me at first. Then she did and her eyes filled with tears and she looked down again, wiping her eyes with the end of her dress. Her own dress was on her now, but unwashed. His concubine. I saw my pistol on the small table that also held his ashtray. He was smoking a cigar, wearing a silk robe. The robe was opened on his broad, muscular chest, and I noticed that he was branded. A fleur-de-lis inside the lower loop of an *S*.

Savoyard.

"You were right," he said to the woman. "He is pretty."

I clutched the blanket tighter, afraid they were going to strip it off me.

"I want you to look at me, nigger," he said to me. "You are most definitely my nigger now. I think you know that. But I mean to make sure. You are too young to have known your kin, Old Marse Savoyard. But I knew him. I belonged to him. And I killed him. But killing doesn't end some things."

"He was evil," I said. "Now it looks like you are. Hector. That's your name, right?"

"He was more than evil. He was turned. I figured it out. But I was turned killing him. With that."

He pointed with his cigar to what looked like a small harpoon hanging above the bookcase. It had a shiny tip.

"And my name is Hector, but you won't call me that again. My name is not for you. I'll take a tooth out of your head if you say it. I got pliers I made myself. I was your kin's blacksmith."

Blacksmith. I looked down at his arms and hands and noticed the burn scars on them.

"He ran niggers out in the woods on the full moon and chased them, cause you have to chase something. Man and a woman every month. People around here thought he was a speculator, buying slaves and selling them again. But they didn't go anywhere. Just out in those woods and in his belly. We used to sing hollers about the moonshine killing us, but called it the sunshine so Marse wouldn't know what we were singing about. We knew it was a monster killing us. Knew there were two of them. Him and this boy that stayed out in the woods. We were all scared of the boy. Used to come lookin at us through our windows at night and we'd say if the yellow boy caught your eye, you were next to die.

"But one day I was talking to the house nigger who said how Marse ate with brass spoons and forks and I got thinking about why he wouldn't use silver like everyone else. Some of the slaves was Creole, from New Orleans, had belonged to his daddy. They said he *was* his daddy, his own daddy. Said the boy in the woods was his boy, followed him from Louisiana, and my nose tells me that's true. Said Marse was real old, two hundred years or more, that he came from France. He liked to fight in wars because he was hard to kill. Got to be a hero instead of a monster. Paid the doctors to cut his wives barren so he could pretend to die, then show up as his son and inherit his own money.

"He didn't mind having bastards, though, cause bastards don't inherit. Like your granddaddy. Like the boy. Funny, though. That makes the boy your kin, too. Your yellow little great-uncle who spends more time on four legs than two."

This struck him funny.

I wasn't in the mood to laugh.

"Why are you telling me all this?"

"Because it's going to get bad for you, and I want you to know why. I hope you appreciate what a gift that is. So much happens in life and the reasons are hidden from us. But you're mine now and you're going to understand why your life is given into my hand."

"I don't understand why you hate me so much. I never did anything to you."

"Nigger, I don't hate you. I hate him. But I can't hurt him no more."

"The boy's his kin, too."

"The boy's one of us. Even if he keeps to himself. Once you're turned, you're one of us. You want to be one of us?"

"No."

"That's good. Because if you said yes, I was going to make you beg me to turn you. Then if you did, I was going to eat your eyes out of your head because you were already broken. You still have a little spirit, so you get to stay alive awhile. But I was thinking about that silverware. I knew Marse would run me. One day I tested him. He was back from the war, and wouldn't turn loose of us. He had fought Uncle Billy's soldiers off and I thought maybe he was planning to kill us all and run. He came to see his horse, which I had just shod, and I gave him a silver dollar I had hoarded up. Said I found it in the ground, but it was his ground, so it was his dollar. He put a glove on before he took it and I knew Holy silver could kill him. Used my other two dollars to make that sticking pole up there and got preacher to pray over it. Put silver on pitchforks, too. And a scythe. All of us went, women, too. He shot four dead. If I had a pretty gun like yours, I wouldn't have had to get

that close. He wouldn't have bit me dying. None of this would have happened."

"If it's worth anything, I wish none of it had," I said.

"You know the best word I got from all Marse's books? *Alas.* That is a good word. Full of helplessness and beauty. And that is the word I have for you. Alas. Now you will go back to your cage and I will enjoy your wife again. By the way, I think you should know that she came here alone. I was going to go into town and take her. But she knew what she was now. And she came to be with her own."

THE NEXT DAY I had what a historian of the States' War might regard as a unique and completely undesirable opportunity to study the past firsthand; I was flogged with a bullwhip. Hector oversaw it, but I could tell he wasn't going to swing the whip himself. The black man with the bad haircut tied me to a tree while Hector smoked a homemade cigar and chuffed foul clouds about his head. He was almost genial, asking me where I was born, did I have any brothers. I thought about Johnny. I didn't answer. The other man turned me and tied me and Hector whistled appreciatively at the shrapnel scars on my back.

"Where'd you get these, boss?"

"Potato masher," I said.

"What's that?"

"What, don't you mash potatoes down here?"

"Alright. That sass is alright. But you had better be respectful

when I ask you to say the names of the ones your great-granddaddy put down. Because I'm feeling generous, I will only give you one lash for every dead friend."

"Say Mittie," he said.

Silence.

The Negro hit me with a bullwhip, making a sick, wet sound and hurting as bad as anything I can remember.

Whack!

I whimpered.

"Nigger, this man's gonna hit you til we get through twelve names. And that's just today. Miss Mittie died of fever cause Marse's overseer wouldn't let her rest when the corn had to come in, and didn't let us chop wood and make a fire cause he wanted us strong for the corn. Now say Mittie like you miss her, too."

"Mittie."

Whack!

"Say Oscar."

"Oscar."

Whack!

"Hey, that was good!" the man whipping said. "I almost feel like he mean it. Don't worry, nigger, I don't know no Oscar neither."

And so it went.

In the end, I got fourteen lashes, and the skin was lain open. It felt like my scars had split. Then they shackled me to that god-damned wheel and spun me until I was half nuts. I was making noises I couldn't reproduce now if I had to. I was talking, but I don't remember what I said. This went on for a long time. When

they were ready to take me down, some of my wounds had begun to dry. They had to peel me off the wheel. Then they stuck me back in the cage where I put my belly down on the rust-flaking iron and sobbed until I passed out, thinking that at least I was at the bottom of it.

The very bottom.

Well, if God is up there, He's a real card. He must split His Holy paunch laughing when one of us speaks in such superlatives. Because the bottom can always, and I mean always, be lowered.

I WAS AWAKENED by burning.

Mustache was standing on my cage pissing on me.

I just lay there, laughing under him.

He laughed, too, then he said, "My laughin's cuz it's funny to piss on somebody. Maybe you laughin cuz it's funny to get pissed on. I don't reckon to find out. Now wait for the shake. Alright. Sweet dreams, punkin."

Then he left me alone and it got dark again, and cold.

I didn't even bother with the wet horse blanket.

I focused all my energies on a new and important mission.

But, try as I might, I couldn't die.

IN THE EARLY hours of the morning, I was visited. I came to slowly, then started shivering so hard I could hear the cage rattling a little.

I was aware of a presence, and I cocked my head and saw that the stars were cut out in the shape of a strong man with a bald head. Hector. He was like a field of darkness, sitting Indian style.

"Why did you come to this place?" he said.

"What place?" I said in a pathetic little croak.

"Georgia."

"I was writing a book."

"About what?"

I couldn't remember. Then I could.

"About you. About the slaves. Killing my great-grandfather."

The end of his cigar glowed as he drew in, then let out a puff of smoke that made the stars shiver.

"Maybe I should let you go write that book. Would it be a good book?"

"Yes. It would have been."

"But you weren't there. It would be lies."

"It still would have been good."

He grunted and drew at his cigar again.

"How would you imagine that he died? Bravely, or like a coward?" Hector said.

"I don't care anymore."

"Guess."

"Both. Like everybody."

He grunted again.

"Yes, both. Bravely until he felt the silver burn him. Then he turned wolf and ran. But we had him cornered. So he turned man again to die. And even though the spear was through him, he bit my face. So I could be this. His gift to me."

"Why don't you fall on your spear?" I said. "Like a noble Roman."

He drew on the cigar again, then casually moved the burning end towards my eye. I turned at the last second and he only burned the skin near my eyebrow. I moved to the other end of the cage.

"It was a pleasure speaking with you," he said.

And he was gone.

CHAPTER TWENTY-EIGHT

I DON'T KNOW how long I stayed in that cage. Days. I wasn't whipped any more; they said they'd wait until I was stronger. But I didn't get stronger. Although I still accepted water, I stopped eating. My back was in agony. It rained. It dried out. The cold was a constant. Hector visited me more than once, but he didn't always speak. He was watching me rot. Presiding over my slow dying. It was so slow. Every time I closed my eyes I hoped I wouldn't open them again.

On the last day I dreamed about my mother. I was just a little boy again and she was sad and beautiful and pregnant with Johnny, and she was trying to clean something off my face. The washcloth hurt. I wanted to squall, but had to hold it in because there was a monster in the next room and if it heard me, it would come and

take the baby out of her, and it would be my fault. Despite the fear in the dream, it was so much milder than the reality I woke up to that it didn't feel at all like a nightmare. I didn't want to let go of her face, such a hard face to remember but so clear in the dream. It was awful to wake up in a cage, but worse to remember she was still dead.

Then I was confused.

I couldn't understand why I smelled smoke.

I opened my eyes and saw that there was a fire in the wild brush up against the side of the house, and someone was shouting.

La Boudeuse was catching fire.

Something rushed towards my cage and I shrank from it.

A man. A short, bearded man with a hatchet.

He smelled like kerosene.

With three loud blows, he busted the chain that held my door shut, and swung it open.

"Mr. Nichols, you made bail. Let's go."

Whose voice was that?

"If you don't get out of there now, I'm going to leave you with your new friends."

Not Southern.

"Move your ass!"

Martin Cranmer.

I moved my ass.

As well as I could, at least; my legs felt like they were made of wet, sodden lumber, and my back was so tight I couldn't stand up all the way. Another figure moved towards us, fast, and I croaked "Look . . ." because "look out" was too much to say.

"It's alright, she's with us," he said.

Eudora. My beautiful, ruined Eudora, barefoot, in a nightshift. I smiled.

She had my gun.

Martin hoisted me up over his shoulders the way you're supposed to carry the wounded, and he ran. That kerosene smell again, and woods, and beeswax. And I understood. He *was* one. He had always *been* one.

He ran with me on his shoulders faster than I ever could have run unburdened; he leapt over fallen trees and cut through rotten ferns and he never stumbled, and he made little noise. Dora kept up. He stopped once to cough, horrible hacking coughs, but he shook it off.

"Remind me not to smoke so much," he said, but then picked me up again and we kept on.

That stuck with me.

That his lungs bothered him seemed important to me, but I didn't know why.

Daylight broke and a cool dawn turned into a temperate morning. The woods rushed by full of birdsong and falling leaves. We were going by Uphill Rock now, and he put me down and told Dora to be ready with the gun.

After we were past it, he hoisted me again and we made for the river.

"If you were going to ask what that was about, save your breath," he huffed. "There's a cave entrance near that rock, and that's where they sleep when they go on four legs. They always go there after they carouse on the full moon. I would have preferred to wait until

the day after the moon, when they go down there and sleep like the dead; it's the one day you know where they all are. But you wouldn't have made it that long. The house is their house, and that's their den. I wouldn't visit, if I were you. Nothing but hides and bones down there, the kind of shit they love. And not just pigs' bones, either. The boy stays there sometimes, but I guess he's at Sunday school today."

I smiled weakly, thinking about how Lester and I had made camp there when Saul was missing. Right on top of their lair. No wonder I dreamed of women eating pigs' heads. Maybe I hadn't dreamed it.

When we got to the river, I didn't recognize the crossing point, but that made sense. If I were them, I would try to ambush us at the raft.

This was a wider, shallower part of the river. I waded it, supported by Martin on one side and Dora on the other. I thought about how pleasant it would be to die right there, to slip from between them and let myself fall into those cold waters and forget everything.

While we were crossing, I said into Dora's ear, "Are you still my wife?"

"If you can stand it."

PAST THE RIVER, Martin was hacking terribly, too tired to carry me any farther. Dora went to pick me up, but I wouldn't let her.

Martin stepped in front of me, and whispered evilly, between

muffled coughs, "They're coming. Four of them, maybe five. I never thought I'd say this to a man, but get on your wife or I'll coldcock you."

Martin helped her get me into the easiest carry, and we went on.

We made the cabin.

Martin bolted all the windows and doors while Dora put me on the bed.

"Do you have any trousers?" I said.

"What for?" Martin said. "We've already seen it."

Dora almost laughed.

He threw her a pair of filthy denims and she helped me get my legs into them. When she saw how much leg stuck out the bottoms, she did laugh. I could barely button them.

"Can you handle that thing?" Martin said to Dora, indicating my .45. She shook her head. I sat up and took it from her.

Just then the front door banged, hard enough to shake the little house. Dora started. I pointed the gun. I looked at the black iron reinforcements and the inch-thick drawbolts. The door wasn't pine. It was oak.

It banged again, hard.

Martin said, "Look, I know you're as strong as three fellows, but it would take ten to break that door. You're seven fellows short. Go home."

Now the bolted shutters banged, and I saw that the bolt was smaller.

"Don't worry," Martin said. "They're barred."

The shutters banged again, then gave. The black one had used a log. Now he wrapped his hands around the bars, getting ready to

yank for all he was worth, but Martin jumped and cut three fingers off him with his hatchet, hitting the bar so hard it made a spark. The man howled and jerked himself away.

"I'm gonna git you for that, Cramma."

"I thought you were already gonna 'git' me. What, are you gonna 'git' me worse? Grow your fucking fingers back and try again."

It got quiet.

It stayed quiet.

Martin grabbed a rough little stub of a pencil and wrote on the wall near me,

HOW MANY SHOTS IN THAT GUN?

I wrote,

2

He wrote,

DAMN

"Do me a favor," he said.

I nodded.

"In case they get in, save your last bullet for her. You they can kill. Her they can keep alive. You get me?"

"No."

"How'd you like to have your hands and feet cut off every day?"

"Jesus Christ, Martin."

"Don't 'Jesus Christ' me, that's how he thinks. The school was his idea."

"What about you?"

"Not me," he said, grinning impishly in his beard. "They can't get me alive. They know that."

Something occurred to me.

"Where are you from, Martin?" I said.

"Harrisburg, Pennsylvania."

"When?"

"When what?"

"When did you . . ."

"Let's just say that wasn't the first plantation house I've burned."

I grinned at him. Some part of me was treating this all as a fever dream. Nothing could surprise me. Or so I thought.

I heard the fat *pop* of glass breaking against the side of the shack.

"Oh shit," he said. "We're in the stew now."

"What?" Dora said. "Why?"

"I had a few jars of moonshine outside."

"Alas," I said.

Another jar broke.

"Well . . . maybe they won't have fire?" offered Dora.

"No," Martin said. "That was Hector's Zippo being opened. And lit."

A cloud of strong cigar smoke drifted in the window.

"It's been nice knowing you kids," Martin said.

"Likewise," I said.

Two more jars broke.

"Jesus," Dora said. "How much did you have out there?"

"Plenty," said Martin, opening a jar that was on his table and drinking from it. He offered it around, and we all took communion.

Another cloud of smoke came in the window.

"In case you were wondering," said Hector's deep voice outside, "we were unable to save the house."

I was tempted to shoot through the wall at him.

"My guess is you didn't try hard enough," Martin said. "Maybe you should go back and form a bucket brigade. Perhaps the good people of Whitbrow would help."

"You have burned my house, Mr. Cranmer. Worse, you have burned my library. I hope to inherit yours when you are dead. Will you come outside now, or must I light this fuel?"

"You know what?" Martin said. "You're a killer, a savage and a poor housekeeper. Maybe my books would be good for your education. Yes, why don't you take them?"

So saying, Martin poured moonshine of his own on his bookshelf.

Dora looked at him wide-eyed.

"What would you like first? How about *The Return of the Native*?"

He struck a match, lit the selfsame book, and pitched it through the bars.

"Not a fan of Hardy? How about Walt Whitman?"

He lit and threw that one too, but it was the last one.

The outside of the shack's wall went up and a wave of heat came from it. Martin helped me to my feet. He unbolted his door and at

just that instant the black one with the bad haircut launched himself through.

I shot him in the mouth. It was awful. It hit just under his nose and seemed to blow every tooth out of his head. He wasn't dead immediately, but he wasn't feeling combative anymore.

Now Martin lit his bookcase on fire and picked it up and charged out the door with it, pitching the whole flaming lot into the white man and woman, who were bowled over by it. Dora jostled me out the door. Hector rushed at Martin, but Martin flipped him heavily into the wall. The white man's arm was on fire. He must have gotten shine on him pitching jars of it against the shack.

"Run!" Martin said.

He was on fire, too.

I was lining up to use my last bullet on Hector, who was starting to shudder, but Dora grabbed my arm and yanked me off into the woods with her. I looked back over my shoulder, feeling like Lot's wife. I looked just in time to see Curly Woman get up, and I realized she had a gun.

I thought she would shoot Martin.

But she was shooting at us.

We weren't very far away.

Pop pop pop!

Then the gun was empty and something moved fast behind her.

The second to last thing I saw back there was Martin Cranmer partially on fire beating that woman with a flaming board.

The last thing was Hector dropping to all fours and turning into an enormous black wolfish thing.

Dora scooped me up on her shoulders again and ran with me.

I know the three of them killed Martin.

But he hurt them.

All of them.

Enough to slow them down.

And Hector never got his books.

CHAPTER TWENTY-NINE

DORA COLLAPSED JUST outside of town.

I had been in and out of consciousness myself, but the rough landing in Miles Falmouth's unkempt patch of acorn squash jolted me into the here and now. Dora and I both struggled to our feet. I saw now that her nightshift was drenched in blood, and she was holding her hand over her abdomen.

There was so much blood.

Her white legs were covered in it.

"I'm sorry, Frankie. I guess she shot me. I didn't feel it for a while, but oh God I do now."

"Is it . . . is it going to heal?"

"It burns too much. I think it's silver."

Charley Wade's gun. The bitch had picked up Charley's gun when he dropped it during the stoning.

We leaned into each other and rested with our foreheads together. My mind raced. Eudora was bleeding to death and I didn't know where to take her. Dr. McElroy was surely dead and Morgan's hospital was far away and dangerous. Oddly, I noticed that it was a pleasant day. The brilliant blue sky and tawny fields behind her seemed incongruous with the mortal danger she was in.

I wanted to laugh. I wanted to lie down with her so we could die together nestled like teaspoons.

"Who's out there?"

I looked at the porch of the sagging house and saw Miles Falmouth leaning on his cane, holding his rifle. I couldn't see clearly, but it seemed he had a beard now.

"Thank God," I said, then shouted, "It's Frank and Dora Nichols! We need help!"

He was silent for a moment.

What was he doing?

Fussing with the gun.

He pointed it now and screamed insanely at us. "GIT ON OUTTA HERE! I know what she is now. Maybe you, too. GIT!"

"She'll die," I said.

"Good," I heard, then he shot above our heads.

He drew and slapped the bolt, and aimed again.

"Next time I start tryin. GIT!"

I remembered my .45, which was still in my waistband; Martin's pants were so tight, the gun had stayed wedged in. I had the presence of mind not to actually put my hand on it now.

We limped together through his field. It was taking forever. He watched us down the barrel all the way off his property.

Now we were in the Gordeaus' corn, but there weren't any more Gordeaus. Crows were flying all around, a few at first, then many. A proper murder of them. We made the street. A dog was barking somewhere.

The town square was deserted as we went through. We limped near Harvey's Drug Emporium, and I banged on the door but found it locked. Harvey was moving inside. He pulled the shade.

"Please," I said, and banged the door again.

Nothing.

We moved away.

I looked at the wrecked tea roses.

I looked at the flaking town hall.

I looked down and noticed that we were both leaving bloody footprints on the sidewalk.

I felt woozy for a minute, and went to lean on Dora, but she was leaning too much on me. Her head was starting to droop. I reached deep inside me and pulled up what was left. I had to be strong for just a little while longer. I helped Dora towards the general store, but before I even got close, Peter Miller came out and waved us off.

"Keep away," he said. "Nobody here wants what you got."

"We're dying," I said.

"We don't want it," he said again, and went inside and locked his door. I looked around. Curtains jiggled and shadowy figures moved in windows in all directions. We were a spectacle. We were lepers.

The door to the hardware store opened, and for a wild moment

I thought Sheriff Blake was going to come out. He did not, but one-armed Mike did. He had a wheelbarrow. A fucking wheelbarrow.

"Get away from there," somebody yelled at him.

He dragged it behind him, unable to push it with just the one arm. He helped me put Dora in it. Then he went back to the hardware store and shut the door. He waved out the window at us. He was crying.

Staggering, praying, stopping to heave, stopping to rest. Somehow I got us home.

I piled Dora into the passenger seat of the Ford and then stumbled into the house to get the key and my spare pair of glasses, whose frames were slightly bent. I didn't bother locking up as I left. As I opened the driver's-side door, I saw my reflection in the glass and didn't recognize it for a second. Beard nearly full grey now. Sunken eyes. Crooked glasses. A ghoul was trying to get into my car.

I pulled the gun out of my waistband and sat down. The car seemed strange to me, like I had forgotten how it worked. I had to think my way through every step. Key in the dash, turn it to On, check the gas, clutch in, stick in neutral, spark lever up (this hurt my broken finger), throttle down, choke, then the starter button. Spark lever down. Let her warm up. Don't pass out. Brake. Reverse gear. Check mirror. Foot off brake. Now we're moving.

I backed the car out.

Right into a throng of women.

Nearly hitting Mrs. Woodruff, Sarah's mother. She was holding a large, mean-looking wrench. The other women had makeshift

weapons, too. And at least one gun; a woman I didn't recognize had a rifle.

Mrs. Woodruff's face was tight and determined. She slapped her hand on my window. Her ring nearly chipped it.

"You open that window and talk to me!" she said.

Proceeding on the theory that angry women with wrenches rarely have nice things to say, I stepped on the gas. I believe I ran over her foot. A hoe flashed and broke a headlamp. The woman with the rifle shot, but I don't know how many times because I was also honking the horn as I sped off. I can't say why. I believe it was a reflex. One of the shots hit the body of the car, but I could only assume it didn't damage anything important, because we kept moving. Now I saw Mr. Woodruff coming up the road on a horse, holding a pistol. God knows how the maenads had beaten him here; maybe he had gone ahead to try to cut me off.

He pointed the pistol, and I laid on the horn again, making straight for the horse, an ugly mottled thing. It did what I hoped it might do in ruining his shot, but then it surprised everybody with a proper rear and pitched the ignorant bastard into a tree.

And that was how we left Whitbrow.

I didn't know where we were going, but that's just as well.

We wouldn't have arrived anyway.

A BABY WAS crying.

I was on my stomach.

I opened my eyes, but this took some effort; they were crusty

and they hurt. Everything hurt. I saw words, and I tried to focus on them.

TALMADGE OPPOSES ROOSEVELT ON CCC

I didn't understand why this was important, why it was right in front of my eyes. I picked up my head a little and it felt like an ice-skater slid to a stop on my back and then wiggled there.

"God," I said, and shut my eyes again.

The baby kept crying.

Why wasn't Dora hushing it?

Why should she? She couldn't have any.

Where was I?

"Gramma, that man awake now."

"I told you he was fittin to wake up."

"I thought he dead."

"No, chile. Lots livin that look dead, and lots dead that look livin."

"Can I look him in the face?"

"Sure enough, he won't hurt you."

I felt a small poke on my right arm.

"Dammit, Horace, I didn't say you could touch im."

"His face was agin the wall."

I opened my eyes again. I saw that what I had looked at before was a newspaper that had been pasted to pine boards. Moving my head a little, I saw that there were others, covering the whole wall.

I was confused.

Where was my Dora?

"Don't you roll over and mess up my work, now," a woman said.

I edged up just a little on my forearms and looked to my right. Just about the cutest little black boy ever was staring at me with big eyes. Behind him was a huge older woman with a kerchief around her head, trying to bounce the bad humor out of a squalling baby in a burlap gown.

"You might just live," she said.

"My wife."

"I think she gonna live, too, but if you got any prayers, pray em hard. She bad hurt. She ain't woke up yet."

I saw something fall off my shoulder and wriggle on the fabric near my face. It was a maggot. I groaned.

"Horace, put that back under the man' dressin, and mind you don't kill im."

"Yes'm," said the boy, and he pinched it carefully between his little fingers and tucked it somewhere on my back. I felt sick.

"I know they ain't pretty but they eat all the bad out. I'm a take em off today an put honey to you. Moss, hosstail, onion juice an comfrey, too. An you gonna drank hosstail tea. Do that an them licks gonna close right up. Don't an you gonna be in the groun by Friday. What you think, can you drank a little tea?"

"Yes, ma'am."

"One thing you owe me to tell."

"Yes, ma'am?"

"Somebody lookin for you?"

"Maybe."

"Well, you better live, cause if you die I'm a dump you in a hole and never tell nobody. You come from Whitbrow?"

"Yes, ma'am. Where am I?"

"You didn't get too far. You in Chalk Ridge. We poor as blue-jays, an twice as loud, but you better off here. The Good Lord done forgot where Whitbrow was a long time ago."

"Gramamma?"

"Yes, chile."

"I don't like he face."

"Hush with that. Somebody put a bullwhip to you, you make a bad face, too."

I WAS WITH sharecroppers, poor tenant farmers who were working another man's land for barely enough to survive. He could kick them off anytime he wanted. They bought their mules, tools and tankage from him at very unfriendly prices. He made them grow corn, cotton and tobacco, and the corn went right up to the door. No room for their own garden, but my benefactor, Miss Matilda, grew a few things in the pine trees near the road. When the crops were big they broke even and when they were small they went further into debt. Eventually the landowner would evict them, seize their tools and livestock and sell them to the next bunch foolish enough to move in. God bless America. We had abolished slavery and reinvented serfdom.

I spent the next two days on my stomach, except for trips to the privy, helped there and back again by different members of the family. Miss Matilda had five grown sons, four daughters and so many grandchildren that I couldn't keep track and I was impressed

that she could. Despite their lack of shoes, monotonous diet (almost nothing but corn and lard) and dew sores, the children were lively and game. Horace was my most loyal companion; I guess he had adjusted his position on the quality of my face. He would share with me from a big bag of white clay I was supposed to eat; it tasted gritty and foul to me, but the boy loved it. All of them ate it. They seemed to crave it. It wasn't chalk, but it was just that white; I wonder if deposits of the stuff had been responsible for the town's name.

Horace sat on the side of my bed, which was really just an elevated plank and a sack stuffed with corn husks, while I told him stories like "Jack and the Beanstalk" and "The Three Billy Goats Gruff." We had a fine old time. But what he really wanted was a ride in my car.

Apparently the car was in good shape. I had blacked out and driven it into a ditch, but Matilda's son, who had driven the landlord's farm truck, used a mule to get it out, then started it with no problem. He moved it back behind the shacks where it couldn't be seen from the road.

I promised Horace I would give him a ride.

Three days after I came to, Miss Matilda helped me walk five shacks down where her daughter Samma lived; Samma's husband was dead, and, in the name of Christian charity, she had given her bed to the dying white woman who, as it turned out, had decided not to die.

"She woke up at all?" Miss Matilda asked Samma.

"Say a word sometime, then go back asleep. Mostly say 'Frank.' S'pose that be you."

"At your service," I said.

"Yeah, I guess you in my service now."

"We in Jesus' service, girl. Don't let me hear you talking small again."

"Yes'm."

Dora moved her head side to side, then lay still again.

"Samma, go see to Horace an leave me alone with Mr. Frank."

Samma obliged. Miss Matilda moved over to a spool table and picked something out of a bowl. She brought it over for me to look at. It was a slightly misshapen silver slug.

"What you gonna tell me about this?" she said.

"What do you want to know?"

"Don't play no 'what you want to know' with me. My boy Egger brought you and that woman lookin like two dead cats out of that car, and you got better like I thought you might. But I was sure she was goin to Jesus. Now I ain't so sure it Jesus she was goin to. She pushed this outta her. It came outta her lady parts, and now she's getting better fast. I ain't never seen nothing like this. But I heard about it."

"What did you hear?"

"She a Look-a-roo. Look just like us but change into a boogey when the moon come, and nothing kill em but silver. They tell that story to scare babies outta they fussin. But she is one. Whitbrow had bad trouble these days, like when the Look-a-roo was comin roun after the State War takin chilluns. Now you come outta there all beat up and shot up. Mister, you go ahead an tell me I'm wrong, if you can do it without lyin."

There was nothing to be done. There was no lie to be told and no more running to do. I just nodded.

"I'm a keep this silver," she said.

"Okay."

"They say the Look-a-roo come here to punish Massa for havin slaves, and that's why it stick on Whitbrow but leave us alone. But that moon's comin up brighter every night and I don't want her nowhere near us when it big. You promise me you git her outta here and leave us be. We got the Lord right here in Chalk Ridge and don't deserve no more trouble than we got."

No, I agreed. They didn't.

Dora woke up that night.

Two days later we left, with a gallon of hosstail tea and a bag of corn bread. I had a good, homemade shirt and a tattered coat. Dora got one of Samma's two homemade Sunday dresses, and Miss Matilda nearly had to beat her to get it from her. Miss Matilda was too proud to take money, but Samma wasn't. I called her over to the car and gave her a hundred and twenty dollars, and her eyes just about fell out of her head; that was two months' worth of teaching pay, and almost the last of the money my aunt had left us.

Now Samma's eyes narrowed.

"Man who got this much got a lot more besides. You'd a died, we'd a got it all. Give me twenty more."

I did.

"Hmph," she said, and hid it.

Before we left, I had a promise to keep. Horace and his younger brothers, sisters, cousins and friends, everyone who was too young to be in the field, all piled on and into the Ford. The sun was rising red and pretty in the east. I drove in slow, wide circles in a field, raising a cloud of dust, careful not to spill any of my squealing

freight. There were little hands on my arm, little hands leaving smudges on the glass. I saw a bunch of crows picking around and steered for them as one girl with her hair in lots of little red ribbons screamed, "Git them crows! Git them crows!" and laughed good, high laughter. The last weeks had been awfully short of good moments, but that was one.

That was definitely all right.

CHAPTER THIRTY

WE DROVE NORTH.

I hugged the steering wheel to keep my back off the seat.

She seemed nearly well.

We didn't speak much.

We had plenty not to talk about.

I had no plan beyond getting as far north as I could before the moon rose full that night. I thought, quite reasonably, I believe, that more conventional issues like how to deal with infidelity that may or may not have been voluntary could wait until after I knew if the full moon would, in fact, change my wife into a murderous beast.

Are you still my wife?

If you can stand it.

Northern Tennessee was vivid and cool. The abundant trees on the hills had mostly gone red or brown or butterscotch, or that rare warm yellow that looked gold when the light came through it. Sometimes the wind would knock loose a shower of leaves that would cascade over the road like a premonition of snow and Dora would smile and squeeze my leg. If only our days in Whitbrow could be shaken off and scattered like that.

I stopped at a filling station just over the Kentucky border on US 27 so Dora could use a telephone. She wanted to call her father and tell him we were coming for a visit before we cut west to Chicago. Her family's hatred for me was as unreasonable and unassailable as their illusion that Eudora had been the picture of wifely devotion before I came along and bewildered her. Small potatoes, now. I would gladly suffer their bald references to her legitimate husband and I would grinningly eat the beef stew her mother made on Sundays, knowing she had dipped less meat for me than for anyone else at the table, if only she and I could leave this gruesome summer behind us. Perhaps the father could hold the daughter down with his disapproving gaze and dare the curse out of her. Perhaps the father and son-in-law would mount a ladder to the moon and carve just enough out of it so no one could call it full again.

Anything.

The wind blew up, showering the car with leaves as I paid the attendant for pumping his gas. He was a man my age with a deep

scar that changed the shape of his chin. Everything and everyone was damaged. I gave him an extra nickel as a tip.

"Thanks, young man. God bless."

The attendant did not recognize me as a peer because Dora had made me shave my grizzled beard last night. My face felt naked in the cold wind.

I went around the corner of the building, past a table where a slightly cross-eyed girl was selling Indian artifacts I suspect she made herself, to find Dora.

She sat against the wall next to the pay phone with coins spread next to her as if they were seed for birds to come and feed on.

"I love that awful coat on you," she said, looking at me with moist eyes.

"Did you call? Are you alright?"

She shook her head.

"Are you cold?"

"That nice young girl changed a dollar for me, but I hurt myself. Frankie, I can't touch the coins. Just the pennies."

"Eudora."

"I don't feel good."

"Do you want me to dial?"

She was crying now, shaking her head.

"It's all real."

"It was for them. Maybe not for you. Maybe not away from there."

"My jaw hurts. My joints."

"You were shot."

The Indian artifacts girl had good ears. She turned around at that and I glared at her until she faced the road again.

"They said it would hurt. That it would take a long time the first time and that it would hurt."

I helped her up.

"They said the longer I lived the easier it would get, until I could do it whenever I wanted. That I could even choose not to when the moon was full. Like Martin. Poor Martin. He never changed anymore, never wanted to. Just got sick when the moon came. But that took years and years."

"Just give me a minute to think. Please. Do you want me to help you dial your father?"

"We can't go there. I can't."

"Let's at least get to Lexington."

"I won't make it that far. It's soon. *I'm so scared.*"

I held her against me while sobs shook her frame, her hands small and white against my lapel. A man in a fishing cap came around the corner to use the telephone but thought better of it and went away.

"So what do we do?"

"I don't think I would be able to open a strong door. A strong, locked door. We never saw them do that."

She looked up at me with heartbreaking love in her eyes. She always said it was unfair that I was so tall; that I was framed by sky when she looked up at me but that she always had the ground as a backdrop.

"What are you saying, then? Lock you up?"

I felt her nod against my sharecropper's coat.

"Where?"

"I don't know, Frankie. Find us a place. Lock me up tight and don't look in no matter what you hear."

"This won't happen. Not to you."

"Then we'll have a good laugh in the morning, won't we?"

THE SYCAMORE TOURIST Village was the one that fit the bill. The property was just south of Somerset, Kentucky, offering SOLITARY CABINS, NEW FLUSH TOILETS!!! and DAILY BUSSES TO BEAUTIFUL CUMBERLAND FALLS. I checked in under the name Zachary Taylor, at which the clerk did not raise either of his caterpillarish eyebrows. I asked to be away from neighbors.

"Why's that?" he said.

I didn't say anything so now he looked up at me.

"Well . . . we're newlyweds," I finally offered.

He chuckled and nodded his head at that.

"You kids want a radio? Five-dollar deposit."

I paid him. He filled out a slip and handed it to me, along with the door key on a carved wooden sycamore leaf that bore a number. I handed it to Dora.

He went in the back room and came back with a badly scratched and cigarette-burned tombstone RCA radio.

"Is that a six or a nine?" Dora said, examining the key.

"Nine. Stem goes down. I keep meanin to underline em. Yer next neighbor's in five, but sometimes they come late, so no promises."

WE COULD SEE our breath as we walked from the car to cabin nine. The smell of autumn was heavy here with its undertones of smoke and rot. I set the radio down just outside the cabin and Dora handed me the key. We looked at each other as I fit the key in the door, but then I let the key hang and took both of her hands in mine. I looked down at the stump of my little finger, the badly healing ring finger. The ring was still on. Hers was, too. She took a deep breath in and out. Everything was going to be different soon, and we both knew it. I looked up again and let myself swim for a moment in her gorgeous, mismatched eyes, letting where we had just been and what we were now headed towards fall away. For just that moment she was my true wife and I was in love with her and the door was not yet open.

THE CABIN ITSELF was almost perfect; the separate bathroom had a sturdy door with a real lock on it. The only drawback was a window in the bathroom, above the clawfoot tub. It didn't look big enough for one of them to get through, but it was hard to be sure. On closer examination, it proved to be painted shut. Yes, this just might do.

She shuddered.

"Oh, that's bad. That feels really bad. The light's getting weak," she said.

"I can't believe I'm about to lock my wife in the toilet."

She hugged herself cross-armed and paced the floor.

"God it hurts. Would you draw a bath for me, Frankie?"

"Hot or cold?"

"Hot for the joints, cold for the skin. I don't know. You pick. Hot. Please. No, cold. The skin's getting worse than the bones."

"Dora, I should get you a doctor."

"You know better. Hurry, Frank. God it itches."

She took Samma's dress off so roughly that one button popped off and rolled across the wooden floor.

I started the bath.

"Where's your gun?" she said.

"In the car."

"Make sure you get it."

"No," I said, turning the spigots on.

"Frankie, if I get out you have to shoot me. You have to."

"Absolutely not," I said.

"You've seen what they do."

"I know."

"I want to do those things, too. Somewhere deep in me, but it's rising. I want to hurt. I want to eat something that's still alive. And if I do, I can't go back. I'll like it too much."

She went into the bathroom then and I locked the door behind her.

"Don't open it, no matter what you hear. Promise me!"

Not completely her voice. A hint too low.

I pulled the key out and looked through the hole. Her eye met mine.

"You can't look at me like this. You can't let me out. Even if I tell you to. It won't be me. Promise!"

"I won't open it."

"Swear it!"

"I swear."

"Go away."

I left.

I went into the bedroom.

I thought I heard groaning.

I heard water splashing in the tub, or maybe the memory of that sound from before my ears were hurt. I felt insane.

I paced the room, jamming my hands in my pockets, thinking how like some grotesque of an expectant father I was. I went to the east window of the cabin and parted the curtain to survey the horizon. No sign of the moon yet, although the sky had gone pink and lavender where the sun's last gasp lit the clouds from below. I could barely make out the individual shapes of trees. How the last yellow leaves clung here and there as if an artist had used a fine brush to hang them. A hint of Naples yellow against all that grey and umber.

I opened the window and let the cold air jolt me. I watched the tree line where I thought the moon would rise and I waited for it. As a child I had loved to go to the docks and watch it rise as if born from the waters of Lake Michigan. My brother had always claimed he could see it move, but I would correct him, explaining that one could *almost* see it move. Before I lost my religion, I thought of God that way. A presence one could nearly but not quite verify.

"Eudora?"

No answer.

I turned my gaze back to the window. A rosy glow appeared

through a stand of sycamores and I knew I would see it soon. It would crest through the trees red and lovely, older than love, neither cruel nor kind.

"Eudora?"

My fingers tightened on the sill and my breath came faster, pluming out into the cold air. There would be frost on the ground in the morning.

It came.

Just the lip of it, glowing through the branches.

She screamed.

"Dora!"

She screamed again.

The scream broke the word in me, my given word not to look. The part in me that responded to that sound was older and stronger than the part that made promises, even stronger than the fear of injury and death. I ran to the bathroom door and fumbled for the key. Dropped it three times before I got the key in, but I didn't turn it.

I heard another noise then, so deep and threatening it stopped my hand. I felt the sound as much as heard it, felt it in the fingertips that rested against the doorjamb and in the ones that held the key.

I pulled the key out.

I looked through the keyhole.

I never should have done that.

She was in the tub.

She was halfway through it.

Her body had become long and canine. Her breasts were still hers, and they had multiplied. Her skin kept splitting and re-forming itself, so blood and tissue dropped from her. The worst part was her face. Because it was still her face, only her mouth was full of horrid, sharp, outsized teeth.

How like a Sphinx.

Then she spoke, only it wasn't her voice at all.

She could barely speak through those teeth.

She panted between the words.

"You let me out . . . You let me out NOW."

I mouthed the word "no" but no voice came out of me.

She looked into the keyhole.

Blood was welling in her eyes.

Still a woman's face on a monstrous body.

"I hate you. Everything. You're afraid I liked . . . I liked. Let me out and I'll tell you . . . about it. You let me out . . . you sorry fuck. You sorry, sad FUCK."

"No," I said.

"You . . . can't keep me here. You're not. Strong. Strong enough."

Then her mouth changed and she couldn't talk anymore.

She banged the wall and went into a fit.

Saliva poured from her mouth. She shook her head and her snout got longer. She shook it again and her ears grew. She turned her eyes up to the keyhole again and they were like lamps, both greenish, one more grey than the other. She bared those wicked teeth and snarled, utterly without recognition. I backed away from the door.

I went to my car and got the .45.

I peeked through the keyhole again just in time to see her rear up and swat the overhead bulb. It exploded. It was dark in there now.

The front door knocked.

"Y'alright in there?"

"Yes! Thank you!" I yelled.

"I heard screamin, so I thought I'd ask."

I hid the gun behind my leg and opened the door a crack.

A man in red and black flannel. The neighbor from five.

I don't know how I said this so calmly, hoping another god-awful sound wouldn't come from the bathroom, but I did.

"I appreciate your concern," I said, my voice cracking, my heart racing, "but we need to be alone right now. I'm afraid my wife's about to lose another baby."

"Lordy, Mister, I'm sorry. I got a car if you want a lift to the hospital in Somerset," he offered.

"They can't do anything. She's just going to have to get through this. I'm sorry about the noise."

"No, I'm sorry. Y'all take care. God bless."

"God bless," I said.

Nearly as soon as I shut the front door, the bathroom door banged again, so hard that a little bit of plaster fell from the ceiling. I turned the radio on and mostly got fuzz. One preacher talking about rum. Then jazz. I couldn't believe it. Good jazz in Nowhere, Kentucky.

I latched what was left of my sanity onto that.

I turned it up.

I sat on the bed.

The noises from the bathroom seemed to get more infrequent, and eventually stopped. My vigil began to relax. I probably lasted until ten o'clock before pure exhaustion overtook me and I fell asleep.

Night.

Cold.

I was lying on my side on a strange bed in clothes that weren't mine.

My crooked, spare glasses were on my head.

My gun was in my hand.

A radio was on, just playing static.

I reached beside me but Dora wasn't next to me.

Everything started coming back to me, and I sat up with a start.

Jesus.

I looked at my watch and saw that it was nearly three a.m.

Dora.

Was she sleeping?

I got up quietly and peeked through the keyhole.

There was a breeze coming from it.

I realized then that the bathroom was empty.

"Goddamnit," I said, really frightened, and grabbed the key. I opened the door. Moonlight and cold air were coming through the window, which had been knocked completely out of its frame. The curtain rod was still hanging by one support and the flimsy curtain blew in the night wind. Glass and plaster were everywhere. One piece of glass reflected the full moon at me like a trapezoid eye.

"Goddamnit," I said again, watching my breath curl potently out of my mouth.

I went and sat down on the bed again, running my hands through my hair, feeling insane, feeling worse, if possible, than I felt in the cage. There, at least, there was nothing to be done except to endure. Now I had to do something, but I couldn't imagine what, and lives hung in the balance. I briefly considered shooting myself. I decided not to, but gave myself permission to reconsider the question later.

At last I gathered my reserves, wrapped the blanket around me, and set off into the night to find my Eudora. My adulteress. My leper.

This was coal mining country. Small shotgun shacks sat well removed from one another. I saw tire swings and fences and cows and I got lost. Good and lost. I kept the gun under the folds of the blanket. I wandered by the highway, looking, no doubt, like just another vagrant on his way from one hard-luck situation to another. I laughed, because I supposed that was in fact what I was.

"Get out of the road, ya idjit!" someone yelled at me.

I was pretty sure this was US 27, but I didn't know. I was pretty sure I was going in the right direction. But the sun came up on me and I still had not found the Sycamore Village Tourist cabins. My feet were bare and I couldn't feel them anymore. I might lose toes! That struck me funny. Frost glittered on the grass by the side of the highway, achingly beautiful in the peach-colored dawn.

A sheriff's car pulled up to me. The officer inside was young, maybe twenty-five.

"Mornin to ya," he said.

"Good morning," I said, grinning.

"You doin alright, mister?" he asked, pushing back his hat in a gesture of effortless dash and goodwill.

"I'll be doing better if I can find my hotel. This US 27?"

"Yessir. Have you been drinkin, sir?"

"No," I said, "I'm an opium fiend."

He nodded thoughtfully.

"I have never seen an opium fiend in this county, but I do allow that you look like what I might imagine one to look like. Do you need a lift somewhere?"

"Sure," I said, "that's very kind of you."

I have a gun in this blanket!

I told him where I was staying and showed him the key.

He took me there without saying anything. I didn't blame him; I wouldn't want to say anything to me either. I'm sure I looked like a lunatic. I kept a shit-eating grin on my face and a white-knuckled grip on the gun so it wouldn't bounce out during the drive.

We pulled over at Sycamore Village and he reached across me to open my door.

"One other thing," he said.

"Yes?"

"My pa's a eye doctor in Somerset. Name's Dr. Murray. I'm Clint. Tell him you know me and I reckon he'll tighten those spectacles up for nothing."

I WALKED SLOWLY into the cabin.

The radio was playing jazz again.

Something was in the bed.

Eudora.

My Eudora was in the bed, with the sheet clutched all around her.

My first reaction was overwhelming relief, but my heart caught in my throat when I got a better look at her. She had blood matted in her hair. There was no small amount of it on the sheet, but I hadn't noticed at first because the sheet was a flowered print with lots of purple.

Dirt on the floor.

O sweet God let that be her blood please please please

I walked around and put the back of my hand to her cheek, as if I were checking her for fever. Her cheek was warm, but not like when she was ill.

I felt my heart fill up with love for her.

Yes, even this. I can even live with this.

That's what I thought.

But then I stepped in it.

Her vomit.

Just in front of the nightstand.

There was a lot of it, a heap of undigested meat.

So much her human stomach couldn't hold it.

It stank.

There were objects in the mess, too.

A button. Hair. A piece of cloth.

And something else.

I reached down for it.

Chewed up and bloody.

It used to be white.

It took a moment for me to realize it was a baby shoe.

It was heavy.

I put it on the nightstand.

She kept sleeping.

She had crawled into some coal miner's house and yanked an infant out of its crib in the night, like some fairy-tale horror. Like the angel of Passover. Some faceless child I didn't care about. My beloved Dora. She knew what she was.

And she came to be with her own.

Frankie, if I get out you have to shoot me.

So I shot her.

At least that's what I meant to do.

I crawled on top of her and straddled her chest, wrapped the blanket around the end of my gun and pointed it at her head.

Her gorgeous eyes opened and met mine, without emotion.

She knew what was in the blanket, and it seemed she neither wanted me to do it nor minded if I did.

I pulled the trigger.

The report was very loud in that small room.

The end of the blanket caught fire a little, then went out.

But here's the thing.

I missed.

As God is my witness, I meant to blow her brain out the back of her lovely head and then go find a river to pitch myself into. I didn't miss on purpose. Not in my mind. It's possible that the blanket and my exhaustion somehow caused me to angle the gun

wrong, but I don't think so. It really wasn't such a complicated thing to try to do.

I believe now that my wrist jerked.

Something in me refused the command.

A small mutiny.

I don't know what else to believe.

The end result was that the gun went off, she flinched and yelped and I blew a big hole in the pillow next to her head. A few goose feathers blew out and settled slowly, ridiculously, to the floor.

I got off of her and stood by the bed.

I popped the slide release and closed the gun.

I put it on the nightstand, but then remembered I might like to shoot myself later, so I put it in my pants.

She lay there shaking, but kept her eyes on me.

The jazz song came to an end and the announcer wished his listeners a happy Armistice Day.

I backed out of the room, taking the keys.

I walked to the car, breathing hard, my breath like locomotive steam in the cold.

The man in cabin five peeked white-faced out of his window, white as a fish-belly, then shut his curtain when he saw me look at him.

I started the car and left.

The clerk tried to wave me down, saying, "Mr. Taylor, Mr. Taylor!" but I kept going.

I expected Clint Murray, the optometrist's son, to pull me over and take me to jail for destruction of property and attempted murder.

But it never happened.

I kept going all the way to Chicago.

But not for good.

I did go back to Georgia.

Just one more time.

And not alone.

CHAPTER THIRTY-ONE

DECEMBER.
I was standing in John "Granny" Giangrande's apartment with my shirt off, facing his pretty window that gave on Lake Michigan. He was behind me, inspecting my back over his tiny glasses. He whistled.

"Goddamn, Nichols. I thought your back was fouled up before."

"Yeah."

"Do you plan to tell me how you got these?"

"Later."

"And where's Dora?"

"Later. Let's drink."

LATER, WHEN MY shirt was on and the night was black and bitter cold outside, and a little snow had started sticking on the window, we sat on his couch and drank his good wine. It was the kind of wine a guy who works on State Street and has no kids drinks.

About midnight, our dead friend Dan Metzger came up, like he always did when we were alone and had a bottle, which was part of the reason we rarely saw each other alone with a bottle. Funny thing was that I'm the one who saw it, but Giangrande's the one who always cried first. It's important to understand that about Granny to know why he did what I asked. It also makes more sense when you know how badly he was picked on at St. Ignatius and how many fat lips and busted heads I got standing up for him. It makes more sense yet when you remember that he sat stateside with a research job while Dan and I waded in the mud and got whiz-bangs and 75s chucked at us. That wasn't his doing, of course, and it's nothing I would Lord over him, but I knew it worked at him and I was quietly glad for anything that might sway him.

Men who want revenge have no dignity.

They have already died and sold everything.

I told Granny what happened only after I had sat with him long enough for him to remember how much he loved me and to hear that I wasn't nuts. I'm not saying I was sane. But I was demonstra-bly not nuts. So I told him what happened. But there was still the matter of what I wanted. I only told him what that was when we were both good and pie-eyed, and when, if not belief, something other than disbelief sat on his face.

"I don't need to tell you how dangerous that stuff is, do I?"

"No."

"Or how much time I'd do for making it?"

"No."

He was swaying on the couch.

"I will say yes, but provisionally. I reserve the right to say no tomorrow."

"Agreed."

"And I will say yes not because I believe you, but because you believe yourself. Which is good enough for me."

"Thanks, Granny. Thanks so much."

"And because you've never asked me for anything."

"This is big."

"Yeah. But maybe lots of little things every time I needed them sat in the bank and gained interest."

"You're talking like my father."

"I know. And the fact that you and I are becoming old men and still know how each other's father talked, that's a reason. I'll do it, Frankie. If this is some big joke you're pulling, then I'll be your patsy. And if you're dragging me to hell, like Father Patterson always said, then fuck the Jesuits."

I hugged him to me.

"Have you told your brother any of this stuff?"

"Not much."

"I wouldn't."

"I won't."

"You know who else?" he said, struggling to light a cigarette.

"What?"

He swayed and closed his eyes.

"Might go. Eicher."

KARL EICHER WAS another vet.

He was also our friend from high school years, but not grade school. During grade school he had run with the neighborhood kids who bullied us for being Catholics. His parents were harsh Lutherans and he hated them and hated how poor his father was and always had something to prove, but he was a guy who always needed to be part of the dominant tribe. His allegiances against the neighborhood Catholics began to shift as more Poles, Italians and Slovenians moved in, and shifted completely by the time the war broke out in 1914 and everything German was suspect. Karl Eicher became an unfortunate name to have. Now he was a minority. Now he needed the three awkward guys with glasses who went to the hoity-toity Catholic school.

He was a good guy to know, though.

He could get dirty pictures.

And he loved to fight.

When I went to find him, he was in Gary, Indiana, standing with the other day laborers by the docks. Right where Granny said he would be. He looked rough. He looked like the last guy you'd pick for anything but a cheap killing. I guess that's what I was after.

His face lit up when he saw me, not from affection, but because I was dressed decently and he knew he'd get a beer and a sandwich.

He was right.

Karl Eicher.

I hadn't kept up with him the way Granny had.

I lost touch with him in 1917.

In the war, he went with the Marines and, because he was little and mean, they used him to go into dugouts and tunnels. He ended up with a Bronze Star and a Purple Heart in Belleau Wood. I think it was a high point for him.

Granny told me how rough things had been for Eicher; that he had twice hit Granny up for money and that he had sent it. The war had sat on him hard and he couldn't keep work long. He sailed for a while, then went to D.C. with the bonus army in '32 and got teargassed with the other vets looking for the money the government owed them.

I had nothing to lose telling him what happened.

He had nothing to lose hearing me out, nothing but the rumble in his stomach.

He chewed his pastrami and nodded noncommittally, washing it down with the last of his beer.

I got up and got him another one.

Then I did what Granny suggested.

"You don't have to believe me, Karl. But if you come along and do what I ask, no matter how crazy it sounds, when we come back, I'll give you my car."

THE TRIP SOUTH seemed short. We were all glad to see the snowy farms of Indiana and Ohio behind us and to be able to crack the windows to smoke. We didn't talk very much at first, but by the time we hit Kentucky, Karl Eicher and I had become drinking buddies; we drank Old Crow out of a bag until we started swerving

and Granny made us stop for coffee. He drove us into Georgia, but I took over when we got close.

Then the mood changed.

We all felt it.

WHITBROW WAS DEAD.

Those across the river had killed it.

The toe of the corpse was the Nobles' filling station, overgrown with brown weeds and stripped of anything valuable. White, painted letters on the busted window advertised:

FREE PECANS WITH FILL-Up

The last p had been made smaller to fit because the painter had not measured it. Ursie Noble had not measured it.

The Canary House had been vandalized.

It had not been burned, as I expected, but all the windows had been busted out and the doors taken away. All the furniture was gone, even the porch swing, and someone had been using the living area as a dump.

A family of raccoons were nesting in the pantry, the doors and hinges of which had been stripped.

Upstairs was worse.

Upstairs was personal.

Someone had written WHORE on the wall of our bedroom and left the bones of a pig on the remains of the mattress. The mattress

had been cut to shreds. Some prudent scavenger had made off with the headboard.

The office wasn't as raw, but it was still hurtful. My rolltop desk was gone, of course, and the bottle of Drambuie I had stashed in it had been drained and left upside down on the sill. Someone large had taken a shit in the corner. I hope the SOB really mashed his thumb moving that desk.

What was truly funny about this was that I didn't know if the monsters in the woods or the good citizens of Whitbrow had done these things.

Granny helped me clear out the living room and get the pig out of the bedroom, and, before I could propose another remedy, Eicher shot the raccoons.

Granny and I scowled at him, and left him to pitch the bodies out himself, which he did, muttering all the while about filthy little cunts and rabies.

He didn't need silver bullets to kill them, but that's what they got.

That's the only kind of bullet we had.

And we had a lot of them.

We got our sleeping rolls and camped and waited.

I STAYED OUT of sight in the house for the next few days. Granny immediately went to Atlanta for supplies, then came back and sequestered himself in the cellar, working practically round the clock. Eicher took a stroll through town. Eicher told me that it

looked like the Huns had been through; everything was boarded up and overgrown and he never saw a soul.

Not a soul.

Someone had written GOD HELP US on the courthouse.

Whitbrow had ceased to exist.

FIVE DAYS AFTER we got there, it sprinkled, and then that turned to snow that didn't last. Granny was already done with his awful work in the basement lab he had built, and it was just a question of waiting for the full moon.

When it came, we got out of town for the night. Rented a room in Morgan's only hotel. Drank bourbon. Played poker for silver bullets. Talked crassly about neighborhood girls. You wouldn't think we were all pushing forty. It was so good to be with old friends, to have something to do, to be in motion.

I actually slept well.

WE GOT UP early that morning and had a stroke of luck.

It warmed up.

A hard rain came and looked like it meant to stay.

We left Morgan, passed Whitbrow and drove to a point in the road that the survey maps I had ordered showed would give us quicker access to Megiddo Woods than going through town. We parked the car and got the gear out, but we didn't suit up until we

were out of sight. Three men in surplus army gear and gas masks will tend to attract attention. Especially when all of them have rifles and pistols and shovels and one of them is carrying a rack of mason jars on his back.

Six mason jars full of brown, oily liquid.

Mason jars filled with mustard gas of very high quality, brewed up by the youngest of the men who helped perfect its use as an American weapon in 1917.

THIS IS HOW the idea came to me.

After I left Kentucky, I had checked myself into a Southside Chicago flophouse and filled the bathtub with beer. I promised myself not to leave until I had died or drank it all. I didn't tell my brother I was in town. I sat with my .45 on my lap, listening to the radio; before long I nibbled on the end of it and might have squeezed the trigger, except that I wanted to finish Hector and the others more than myself.

That's when I figured it out.

How to kill them.

Silver was too hard to deliver; they saw you coming. They smelled you. They were fast. And silver was dicey; Dora had survived a gut-shot. But burning would work. Martin said fire killed them. Martin used fire when they cornered him. And Hector had a brand on his chest, and burns on his arms from his days as a blacksmith. None of that had healed back.

The last piece of the puzzle came while I tickled the beard on

my chin with the barrel. I laughed! I set the gun on my nightstand and paced around in the frigid room.

Yes!

Martin's cough from those damned strong cigarettes. His lungs weren't healing themselves. Their lungs could burn and they could die that way. I could make them cough and drown in their own fluids, like those poor wrecked bastards in the gas wards. Even if they lived, they would never be right. They would be easy hunting.

That was when I checked out.

That was when I went looking for Granny.

I didn't even drain the beer out of the tub.

Now WE WERE marching through the woods in the rain like three ghosts from the AEF. Tin hats and all. Enfields and 45s packed with silver bullets. Even if we couldn't steal a march on them, even if they saw us first, I wanted them to see the big, soulless eyes of the gas masks and the silhouettes of the helmets and to know that something worse than they were was after them. I wanted them to be scared now. I wanted to give those fuckers bad dreams.

But those damned masks.

I had forgotten how much the nose clamp hurt.

Using the maps and the compass, I got us to Uphill Rock. The same tree leaned against the same big stone like Sisyphus at his hopeless labor. The rain was good. Even though it soaked us, it hid our scent, hid our footsteps.

Eicher went to pull his mask off so he could whisper something

to us, but Granny wouldn't let him; he insisted that we stay geared up whenever we were around the mustard, not to take a chance. By the time you smelled that sweet, garlicky smell it was too late.

Eicher motioned that he saw something.

The entrance.

Like a frowning mouth in the rock, half covered over with leaves.

Jesus, this was it.

Eicher motioned for us to cover him, and he put his rifle down and crept around to the side of it, slowly. Slowly he positioned himself and peeked in.

I guessed there would be four. Five if Dora had returned. I held up four fingers. He shook his head and held up seven.

Goddamnit. They had propagated.

Now he backed off the entrance and Granny came up.

The two of them were supposed to chuck while I covered.

Not so different from clearing a machine gun nest.

I got ready.

But Granny wasn't ready. He was shaking, bad. I wondered if the jars were rattling. Thank God for the rain.

Eicher took three jars off Giangrande's back and handed them to him. He took the other three.

He put up one finger.

They would pitch on three.

He put up the second finger.

Granny shook his head.

He couldn't do it.

But Eicher could.

He threw his three jars one after the other, then he took Granny's away from him and threw those, too. He pulled Granny back and got his rifle ready. Granny went to his position and took his rifle, but he just hugged it to him. He was in full panic.

A naked man walked out of the cave, blinking his eyes. He looked familiar, but I didn't have time to figure out why. Eicher shot him. He didn't understand what was happening to him. Then I shot him, too. He crumpled.

Granny looked like he was going to be sick. He went to pull his mask off. I dropped my rifle and went to him, stopping him from doing that, but he broke away from me and staggered off in the direction of the car.

More shots rang out.

I started after Granny, but then went back to help Eicher.

He had shot another man, who was holding his stomach and bellowing, collapsing awkwardly against the rocks. He shot him again.

There was motion behind him.

Two naked women running away.

Curly Woman and another one I didn't recognize from the back.

He shot that one, and she twisted and fell. Curly kept going. Eicher dropped his rifle and took out his pistol, running up quite close to the wounded one. She was pointing at him as if he were a bad child and saying "NO!" while he shot her three more times. It must have been a reflex. If it weren't so horrific and heavy with pathos it would be funny. It was Anna Muncie, the teacher of the younger grades, and she died scolding her killer.

This god-awful scene transfixed me, or I would have been faster.

The black one came out of a hole in the ground.

Hector.

The biggest one.

In wolf form.

He was all over Eicher, and now I didn't have a shot. Not until Eicher was disemboweled. Then something hit me from the side, hard, and I went into the ground and had the wind knocked out of me. My rifle went flying.

Even as it was happening, I groped for the pistol. I wrenched onto my back just in time to see Mustache jumping on me. He must have thought he was in wolf form still because he tried to bite me. He was salivating. His eyes were wide and insane and I saw his open mouth over my face, felt his teeth on my eye plates, felt his hand grasping the edge of my helmet, trying to wrench it off me. If there is anything worse than being attacked by a huge, supernatural wolf, it must be being attacked by a very powerful naked man who believes he's a wolf.

One more good wrench like that might have broken my neck, but he tried to bite me again. Saliva ran out of his mouth all over my mask.

I was dazed.

I couldn't inhale.

But I did have the gun in my right hand.

It was between us and I couldn't cock the hammer. He was so strong. I was sure this was it.

Then he realized biting wasn't working and he reared up to hit me. For just that second, I had room. I cocked and squeezed. The gun went off, tearing through the middle of him.

He still hit me, but not as hard as I think he would have.

I think that would have killed me.

Instead it just cracked my left eye plate and made me see stars.

He grabbed his stomach and rolled off me, sitting Indian style and breathing hard, not looking at me. His eyes were tearing up from the gas, or from the injury, I don't know.

Thank Christ I looked to my right.

The black one was stealing close to me, but quickly, like a border collie stalking sheep.

I don't know how to communicate just how terrifying these things are up close. It's hypnotic. You want to piss and shit yourself. You want your mom. It was big and fast and quiet and it was coming.

Then it sneezed. A great rope of snot came out of its muzzle.

It kept coming, but the spell was broken now.

I shot it.

It yelped, and broke and ran.

Crookedly, though.

It was hurt.

Maybe dying.

I managed to inhale.

I had a cracked rib.

I sat up.

Mustache was on his side now, looking small and white, bleeding uncontrollably through his fingers. I noticed the puckered white scars where his arm was burned from the fight with Martin.

I shot him again.

Jesus, Jesus, Jesus, this was a mess. Granny was nowhere to be seen. I got up and went to Karl Eicher.

He was all untucked.

His legs spasmed rhythmically like he was trying to run.

But he was gone.

His blue eyes were still open under his mask.

His cruel, schoolyard bully eyes.

His joking, pool-shooting eyes.

I took his mask off and shut his eyes.

I LOOKED BACK at the first one we shot, and I saw why he looked familiar. I also saw why I hadn't placed him.

It was one-armed Mike.

With two arms.

SOMEONE WAS COMING out of the entrance to the cave.

He was clutching a dirty cloth, maybe a towel, around him.

Freckled and homely and redheaded. I recognized him. He had played softball with us that first day. Pete. His name was Pete. He stumbled out into the cold rain with his free hand up, coughing, his eyes shut but tearing, his nose running freely.

"Please don't shoot me," he said, and sneezed horribly.

I didn't know what to do. He was so full of gas he was bound to die.

"I'm sorry," I said, and pointed the gun.

He couldn't see me, but he knew what I was doing.

"PLEASE!" he screamed.

"You're full of mustard gas," I said, shouting so he could under-stand me through the mask. "It's all over you."

"I know it's somethin bad. I just want to wash it off. I just want to stand in the rain and wash it off."

I felt myself unraveling.

"You can't," I said.

"Why?!" he yelled.

"It won't work."

"I'll go to the river then. I didn't hurt anybody. I promise. I just want to go to the river and wash."

I didn't say anything.

It occurred to me that he didn't know who I was.

"I'm gonna go now. Please don't shoot me."

"Okay," I said.

And I let him go.

Feeling his way past the trees.

Blind and poisoned and naked.

It wasn't mercy.

I would have finished it if I were merciful.

I let him go because I'm weak.

THAT'S ALSO WHY I didn't go to La Boudeuse to shoot the others, as I had imagined I would.

I didn't care anymore.

I was done with this place.

I took my shovel and buried Karl Eicher. I took my time and buried him deep. I put the rifle and helmet over his grave as markers.

I went back to the car and found Granny there, looking numb. I stripped out of my gear and left it by the side of the road, along with my weapons.

The car ride back to Chicago was long and silent, and I knew there'd be no more Christmas cards. As far as Granny could see, he had been fooled by two lunatics into committing some horrible crime. After all, he only saw us shoot and gas people. Naked people in a cave in the middle of the woods, yes. But people. He had been gone before the big bad wolf came.

All he said about what happened was, "I won't go to the police."

I said, "Thanks."

He kept his word.

And I kept mine.

ONCE I HAD taken Granny back to Chicago, I drove to the docks at Gary, Indiana, where the day laborers stood around a fire in a garbage can, trying to keep warm. It was early in the morning, and they were all still hopeful. They all came up to me at once, telling me what they could do. Painting, loading, carpentry.

I shook those offers off and tried to sound like a cop, saying, "Any of you guys know Karl Eicher?"

Several of them nodded.

"Any of you friends with him?"

Two guys said yes.

"He got family?"

They both shook their heads.

"Which of you knows him better?"

"I was in the merchant marine with him in '28–'29."

"Can you drive?"

"I can."

"I can, too," said the other guy.

"Merchant marine, come with me, I've got a job."

He got in the car.

I drove him to the bank near the train station, got a notary, and signed the car over to him. He looked at me suspiciously until I left him the keys and headed for the train.

"Why would you do this?" he said.

"Because I said I would."

He walked over and fingered the bullet hole in the body of the car, looking like Detroit's answer to Thomas the Apostle.

"Karl comin back?"

"No."

"You do something to him?"

"Yeah," I said, and I left.

He didn't follow me.

CODA

THE ONE WHO had been poisoned and shot went back to the burned-down plantation and became a man again. The woman had run off towards the river and he had let her go; they were just choosing where to die now. He pumped water from the well and washed his body and his mouth and nose, his eyes, but nothing helped. He couldn't stop sneezing, and every sneeze made his legs go numb, made him grind his teeth as the bullet moved agonizingly in his spine. Only the fact that it was silver and too hard to mushroom had prolonged his life; the hole in him was deep, but not wide. It was hard to know if the bullet or the wickedness Marse's great-grandchild had splashed on him would end his life, but it was ending.

The rain was cool, but not freezing.

He would like to die under a roof, but the only building left with a roof was the third slave shack, and he wasn't going to die there.

No.

Instead he dragged a crude chair from the ruins of the overseer's house and set it on the charred foundation where the library had been in the Big House. All that was left were the chimneys and the bricks of the columns, standing over the ruin like ribs. He got the foul, wet horse blanket and wrapped it around himself, and sat there wishing for a cigar.

He resolved not to get up again.

Not for water.

Not for food.

Not to change the position of his miserable back.

It rained harder.

He rested his chin against his chest.

He hoped the buzzards wouldn't knock him down when they fed.

He wanted the next white man on this land to see his bones upright in this chair, and to wonder why he had no crown.

AT LEAST, THAT'S how I imagine it.

My name is Frank Nichols, and I'm an old lush now.

Everything I told you about happened a long time ago and isn't important anymore, not to you. The war I fought in before I knew any better was dwarfed by another war, which was fought in some of the same places, against some of the same people. The town I lost my one true love in has ceased to exist. I looked for Whitbrow in a Rand-McNally

Atlas in 1948 and found that Megiddo Woods now extend past the river, almost to Morgan. Chalk Ridge is gone, too.

I never opened the boxes my aunt Dottie had in the cellar—I'll never know if they were full of her dead husband's clothes, old dolls and perfume bottles, Confederate dollars, gold bullion or, what I suspected and perhaps feared, letters from my mother.

I never wrote about the slave revolt, or about Savoyard.

I got one old friend killed and made another think I'm a murderer.

Things got less fantastical in Chicago, but I wouldn't say they improved.

Apparently I tried to sleep with my little brother's fiancée, but the fact that I don't remember doesn't make that any better. Then I went on a tour of Northern cities, losing jobs and going to the drunk tank until I had to come back here. My brother forgave me, I think, but he married that girl so there's no question of me staying there. I got pictures of the kids. But they're not kids now.

Somehow I turned into an old man. I got arthritis in my hips so now I go with a cane. Not a fancy walking stick; just a cheap, sad bastard cane with a rubber tip. I don't need it every day, but more and more of them, especially in the winter.

And, on top of everything else, I'm ugly now.

Not much hair on my head, but plenty in my ears.

Thick, boozy face and veiny nose.

Sloshy gut.

But she doesn't see that.

Eudora, I mean.

You see, she's in Chicago.

I was sitting in Wicker Park, off the wagon again, drinking my

*government check, eating free peanuts and smoking, trying to ignore a
fat younger guy telling Polack jokes. I was thinking about telling him I
was a Polack and asking him to step outside; he would have creamed
me, but he might have just shut up. There's no glory in fighting old
lushes in Wicker Park, unless you're one, too. Then maybe you can be
king of the old lushes.*

*Anyway, he was getting to the part where Kowalski holds his hand
in front of his face and dares his coworker to hit it with a shovel when
I looked across the street and saw her.*

My Dora.

My wife.

*Still in her twenties, by the look of it. Wearing a thin headscarf and
sunglasses like the girls wear now. Holding hands with that boy. That
damned mulatto boy. It was daytime. She took her sunglasses off and I
saw her eyes.*

I rushed out of there, but they were gone.

That was two weeks ago.

I thought I imagined it, but I've seen her twice more since then.

Once, on the el, in the next car, with her hand pressed to the glass.

*Once, when I was walking past the cemetery, across traffic from her.
Always when I can't get to her.*

But she's always looking right at me.

And she doesn't see an old man.

I can tell that.

She sees what I was.

What she can make me.

She's coming for me.

I saw the moon today and it was waxing, better than three-quarters

along, hanging there in the daytime like its own ghost. Jet contrails stretched a lazy A that just missed enclosing it.

It will be full by the weekend.

And Eudora will come.

I have this idea that she will ask me a question, and the question has to do with how many legs I wish to go on.

I had better figure out what I'm going to say.

THOSE ACROSS *the* RIVER